The TYCOON'S OBSESSION

AN AGE GAP AND SECOND CHANCE ROMANCE

D.A. LEMOYNE

D. A. LEMOYNE

dalemoynewriter@gmail.com
Copyright © 2024 by D. A. Lemoyne.
All rights reserved.
Published in the United States of America.
Title: The Tycoon's Obsession
Original Title: A Eleita do Grego
First published 2021
North Carolina – USA
Author: D. A. Lemoyne
Translated by W. Books
Copy Editor by Erin N.
Cover design by Angela H.
Cover Photography by M. Lancaster
Illustration by M. Ribeiro
Illustration by Linka
E-book and Paperback Formatting by MadHat Studios

All rights reserved. No part of this book may be reproduced or copied in any form or by electronic or mechanical means, including information storage and retrieval systems, without written permission from the author, except for brief quotations in book reviews or promotions.

The following book is a work of fiction. Names, characters, places, and incidents are either the product of the author's imagination or are used fictitiously. Resemblance to actual persons, living or dead, events, or locales is entirely coincidental.

The following story contains mature themes, strong language, and sexual situations.

It is intended for mature readers.

"I remember everything from that night. I wanted to forget, but I couldn't," she says.

"I won't let you forget. This time, I'm going to mark you so deeply that you won't be able to leave."

Christos and Zoe
(The Tycoon's Obsession)

Save Your Tears - The Weeknd ft. Ariana Grande

Take My Hand - 5 Seconds of Summer

Levitating - Dua Lipa ft. DaBaby

Afterglow - Ed Sheeran

Cardigan - Taylor Swift

Before You Go - Lewis Capaldi

Blurb

He is Greek, CEO, and almost twenty years older.
She is a young American on her first international trip.
He became her protector when she needed one.
She became the obsession he didn't plan for.

Christos
Until I met her, there was only room in my life for inhuman work hours and casual sex.

I never had addictions until I found **Zoe**, a waitress on one of the ships in a fleet I intended to buy.

My desire was instant, as well as my determination to bring her to my bed.

She gave me one night and then fled from me.

No, she *thought* she could escape from me, but there was no way I would let her escape while my desire for her remained unsatisfied.

Warning: may contain triggers

Warning: *The Tycoon's Obsession*, Book One of *Lykaios Family*, is standalone. Each book can be read separately, but it's likely that the next one will contain spoilers from the previous ones.

Zoe

Some people would say I'm too old to believe in fairy tales, but the truth is, no one is smart enough to resist a mad passion.

And not just any passion, but the kind that takes your breath away, makes your skin crawl just by hearing their voice, and sets your body on fire.

Christos

I don't believe in love at first sight, but being horny at first sight seems plausible.

When I met her, I knew I would make her mine; what I didn't count on was that she would disappear two days later without looking back.

An unexpected encounter.

An explosive attraction.

Neither is prepared for the overwhelming feeling until a secret changes everything and forces her to run away.

However, the billionaire CEO is willing to do anything to get Zoe back in his bed.

His desire for the only woman to ever leave him knows no bounds. Not even time is able to slow it down.

When, at last, fate gives them a second chance, he faces losing her again.

This time, forever.

*For everyone who loves passionate, sexy, and powerful Greeks.
North Carolina, 2024.*

Author's Note

The Tycoon's Obsession is the first book of **Lykaios Family** series. It tells the story of **Christos Lykaios**, the CEO of the fashion industry, and **Zoe Turner**, a rising top model.

Boarding a ship from a fleet he intended to buy, the arrogant Greek did not plan to become entirely fascinated by an American almost twenty years younger who is part of the cruise staff.

Despite being inexperienced, Zoe knows what she wants, and it is not to be used as a billionaire's playdate, but fate works to connect these two hearts in a way that not even time can diminish the feeling.

The Greek Tycoon's Obsession is an age gap story about second chances and unconditional love, which most of us dream about.

The story contains some triggers such as sexual harassment (not from the male protagonist and in a very brief situation), domestic violence (not from the male protagonist and in a very brief situation), the protagonist coming from foster homes, and detailed sex scenes.

The second book in the series, *About Love and Revenge*, featuring Christos's cousin Odin Lykaios, will be released soon.

Finally, my books **are always standalone stories**, but my literary world is interconnected, so you will eventually find characters from one series in another. However, I will always explain where they come from and leave a footnote directing you to the respective work.

I hope you fall in love with the universe I created as much as I loved making it.

XO,
D. A. Lemoyne

PROLOGUE

BOSTON

SHE TAKES MY HAND, squeezing it tight, and without her saying anything, I know she's just as sad as I am.

We talk a lot.

In fact, every day since I started living here almost a year ago. Pauline is the only person who can make me smile. My Mom died. She was the only one I had since Dad left for heaven long before her.

I tell stories to my friend because I learned how to read. My Mom used to do that, acting like the characters. It was so funny. I'm not good at that because I read slowly, and sometimes I even stutter, but she never laughs at me, unlike her mother, Aunt Ernestine, the owner of the house where I live now.

Pauline is much older than me. She's almost twelve now and says she's not a child but a teenager. Even though she's almost an adult, she can't get out of bed because her legs don't have the strength to walk. She had an accident when she was younger than I am now.

I wish I had the power to get her up and running so she can play with me, but as my teacher said the other day, *sometimes we can't understand God's will, Zoe.*

I don't know what that means, but it's not fair.

I found a way to make her happy: I do things in her place. When she wakes up and says she wants to go for a walk in the backyard, I run out of the house. Then I come back with my lungs burning and short of breath. But when I see her smile, I know it was worth it.

The first time I did that, she said I was crazy, but then she started to love the idea and now always asks me for things.

"Zoe, go outside and feel the rain for me."

"Zoe, tell me about the cutest boy in your school. He's going to be my secret boyfriend."

"Zoe, how does it feel to jump really high?"

I swing my feet, sitting on her bed. They don't touch the floor yet because her bed is high—it's a hospital bed, and it cost a fortune. Aunt Ernestine always says that, as if it's Pauline's fault it cost so much. We used to joke, trying to guess when I would finally be big enough to get my feet touching the floor.

Now, we'll never know because I'm leaving this house forever.

"Do you promise to come and get me when you're rich?"

I look at her and smile, which helps to soothe the pain I feel in my chest.

I've been secretly crying for a week. Ever since I found out I was going to live in an orphanage again. I'm very, very sad.

My so-called *aunt* reached out to the government man and said she was going *to give me back to the state* because the money she got to let me live here wasn't enough. She has other children here, too, so I don't understand why I'm the only one who's going to be sent back.

"How am I going to be rich, Pauline?" I ask. "My piggy bank only has two dollars from when I helped Mrs. Nole pick up the leaves in the yard."

"Remember our deal? You are me, so you do things for me? Well, I dream of becoming a famous *top model*. Gorgeous, *on the runway*, modeling, and with all the men in the world crazy about me. The thing is that will never happen because I can't walk."

"What is a *top model*?" I ask, trying the name on my tongue and finding it funny.

"They are very beautiful girls who walk on a ramp or are photographed. They get clothes for free and travel all over the world."

"It must be really cool."

"Yes, Zoe. It's the best job in the world! Promise me that you will do this for me and that wherever you go, in any country, you will remember that."

"I know your mother is sending me away, but does that mean I'll never see you again, Pauline?"

She looks at me weirdly, as if she knows a secret and doesn't want to tell me.

"I'm not sure, Zoe. Either way, when you feel sad and alone, look up at the sky and think of me. I will always think of you, too."

CHAPTER ONE

Eleven Years Later

BARCELONA

OH GOD, this is so uncomfortable!

Pauline, I must really love you, 'cause this idea of traveling the world is turning out to be more difficult than I imagined.

A cruise on the Mediterranean Sea might be the dream of every girl my age, but right now I'd give anything to get out of this sticky uniform and throw myself into the Boston snow. The thing is, even if I were in my homeland, that wouldn't be possible, of course, since it's summer there too.

I try to check the time on the clock inside the ship, but it's very difficult from where I stand. Because we're forbidden to check our phones during working hours, all I can do is hope I can get back to the air-conditioning very quickly.

I push those thoughts away, thinking how my best friend would give anything to be living this terrible experience during a humid summer day, trapped in a uniform that would leave anyone feeling uncomfortable. Like a banana, we're covered up all the way to the neck. I hate turtlenecks and would love to have a little chat with the stylist—*do they really have one?*—who designed this outfit for the employees.

"When will I be able to take a selfie with the handsome captain, honey?" a very pretty lady approaches me and asks.

"Good evening. Welcome to Dream Cruise!" I reply with what I had to memorize. "The captain will be available half an hour before the gala dinner today and will spare fifteen minutes to take pictures with the passengers."

"Only fifteen? I need at least an hour next to that hottie!"

I repress a laugh. She must be eighty or older, and the captain is fifty, but who said love sees age?

Well, I don't like him at all. The single time we were in the same room together, I concluded that he looked at women as if he were a gift from heaven to humankind.

I met a girl who was also hired to work on this week-long cruise but had previous experience. She told me he usually ends each trip with the female employees fighting for his attention. Also, most of them get to *visit* his cabin.

When the lady says goodbye, I take the opportunity to check if the photographer's material is all set up.

When I saw on the internet a few months ago that *Dolphin Cruises*, the largest cruise company in the world, was hiring young people with no previous experience needed to work on a trip across the Mediterranean Sea, I thought, *this is it.*

We went through two weeks of training, and since I had just graduated from high school, it was the perfect graduation gift to myself. I passed the training easily, and the company provided my passport.

My foster parents, a kind couple who finally took me out of the orphanage for good when I was eleven, could never provide me with anything like this. On the other hand, they gave me a lot of love, and even though they couldn't glue all the broken pieces of my heart back together, they made me feel wanted after so many temporary homes.

It was only about a year ago that I met my birth mother's distant cousin, but while I enjoyed meeting blood relatives, they never attempted to get close, really.

They have a lot of money, and when they invited me to family parties, I felt left out and looked down upon. Only one girl was kind to me: Madeline. She's my mother's cousin's daughter, terribly shy, and has dyslexia.

I tried very hard to get along with them, but I reached my limit when her mother asked me if I could help the maid serve the meal at dinner because one of the employees was absent. I agreed, but at the time, I didn't quite understand what that meant. When my adoptive parents welcomed people into their house, everyone helped set the table or washed the dishes afterwards, so I didn't think it was a big deal.

It wasn't until she handed me the uniform her employees were wearing that it hit me.

I gave her some excuse about how my mother needed me and never got in touch again.

Too late I realized that Aunt Adley saw me as an inconvenience, someone who wanted to enjoy the privileges of her wealth. It couldn't have been further from the truth. I just wanted to be part of a big family, as my adoptive parents have no other relatives.

I watch people start to walk around the ship in their fancy clothes. The women are all dressed up in long, shiny dresses, and the men are in tuxedos, like the ones we see in movies.

Sometimes, I daydream, thinking I want to live this life for at least one night, like Cinderella at the ball with the prince.

But it's basically impossible for that wish to come true, so I really need to stay focused and replace the water bottle that the photographer warned me from day one not to forget.

The good thing is that after I finish my shift, I'm free for the rest of the evening. I usually hang around the ship, but tomorrow morning is my day off, so I've decided to take a tour of Barcelona. Nothing too spectacular. Just a stroll around the city's streets and a visit to *La Sagrada Familia*, the most famous church in Spain. My mom never had the opportunity to leave the US, but she recommended I don't miss it, because it's one of the world's most famous buildings.

I pick up a box of paper napkins and place it near the water. The photographer sweats like a pig, and I always leave tissues or napkins close by. My mother used to say that a lady should never look sweaty in public. I think that goes for gentlemen as well.

It's funny that this is one of the few things I still remember about her.

I feel sad when I think about my mom nowadays; most of the time, it's not my biological mom but Ms. Macy, my adoptive mom. It's been ages since my biological parents passed away, and I've almost forgotten all the memories we shared. However, the time I spent in the orphanage and the pain I endured there, those memories are still crystal clear in my mind.

Of all the requests Pauline made the last time we saw each other; this is the first one I've tried to fulfill. Even though my body is perfect for modeling—at five feet ten inches—my shyness makes me want to hide from the world. I'm very outgoing inside my head. I talk to myself a lot, and I'm also very sarcastic, but when it's time to express myself publicly, things change.

"Zoe, are you willing to make a little extra money?" asks Tamara, a colleague who was hired along with me and who is also from Boston. We share a cabin in the staff wing.

"Always," I say, smiling. "I'm looking to buy some souvenirs for my parents, so any money that comes in will be welcomed."

"They need a waitress for the gala dinner at the captain's cabin. There will be only a few guests but some very powerful people."

"Look, that's quite an opportunity, but I really don't think it's a good idea. The chances of me spilling something on fancy guests' clothes are very high. I'm pretty clumsy."

"Don't be silly, the tips are awesome. I've worked a few times at events like these."

"But why me?"

"I gave your name; you should be called in. I know your situation."

I'm not offended by what she says because it's just the truth. "Are you sure about that? What if I do something silly and jeopardize your position?"

"Chill. Just relax and trust yourself a little more. It'll be alright."

Christos

CHAPTER TWO

BARCELONA

"WHAT DO YOU HAVE FOR ME?" I ask, desperate for him to give me an excuse to get up and leave.

"You're not being reasonable, Christos."

"I've never been accused of that. You have five more minutes."

"I thought our negotiation was on track."

"I did, too, until I found out you'd sugarcoated your profit this year. Do you have any idea what will happen if this gets to shareholders' ears?"

He paces, and once again, I regret having to deal with someone like him. If my analysts hadn't estimated that the profit would be fairly decent if we bought his company, I would have told him to go to hell.

Frank Morrison is everything I despise in a man: he has a weak, pliable personality and does what's expected of him. If you want to be an asshole, act like one. Embrace the persona and don't pretend to be afraid of anything or anyone. But if you change your character according to the situation, then you are nothing to me.

"What do you want me to do?"

"If—with emphasis on 'if'—we are going to negotiate, the company will have to do an audit on the last ten years. It only took my analysts an hour to find inconsistencies in the numbers you sent me."

Actually, I've already completed the auditing process and received the results via email. However, I want to play a little game with him and make him sweat. Moreover, I'm curious to find out if there are any hidden secrets or confidential information that my employees couldn't uncover, although I highly doubt it. Frank is far from being a financial expert; he's just a petty thief who attempted to deceive his own company and failed miserably.

He nods, but I can see he's paled. "What else?"

"If there's any indication of fraud, the deal is off."

"There isn't this was the first time..."

"Lucky for you, the fiscal year hasn't ended yet. According to my lawyers, there's still time to fix it." I cross my legs and face him. He looks like he's about to pass out. "Did you really think you'd deceive me? Did you believe I would invest in a nearly billion-dollar business without making sure of where I was standing?"

"No... I mean, you don't understand. I was... *I am* desperate."

"No, you're the one not understanding, Frank. Lie to me again, and you won't get another chance. I'll let the banks liquidate all your assets. Even that expensive watch you're wearing will have to be handed over as payment."

"It won't happen, Christos. You have my word."

I get up without replying because his words no longer mean anything to me. Once a liar, always a liar.

I despise white-collar criminals. They play with the lives of thousands of families.

"What's next?" he asks, sounding apprehensive.

"I want to see one of the ships. You told me there's one here in Barcelona. Let's go. Take me there."

"I won't be able to evacuate a ship with more than two thousand passengers."

"I didn't ask you to do that, but I want to speak to some of the employees—not the temps but the full-time ones."

"Why?"

"I would never go into a business like this without studying it first.

There are things that only these people will be able to tell me that no expert can attest to, just those who are there every day with the crew and passengers."

"May I ask for an example?"

"No."

As I cross the ship surrounded by my security guards, people turn their heads to me. There's nothing I hate more than that, but I went through an attempted robbery about a month ago, and since then, my bodyguard has been a little paranoid.

It's the price you pay for being rich. But not something that makes me regret the path I've taken to get here.

My father's story since we immigrated to the United States has marked me forever. My grandmother, his mother, died in Greece because she didn't have money to pay for healthcare. It made him leave his birth country and seek a better life.

I was still a kid, but I remember how late Dad would come home, how he never had a day off but was full of ideas and plans.

He learned to be a tailor and, in a short time, was in demand. The business grew to the point that he needed to hire employees and open branches.

To make a long story short, we were already rich by the time I turned eighteen. My dad's motto is "grow and multiply," and that has nothing to do with grandchildren—although I'm sure he wants them—but rather our bank account.

Today, I own the top ten *haute couture* and accessories brands around the world, with male and female segments, and I'm faithful to my father's motto. I've expanded my business and invested in several fields.

That's exactly why I'm attending this dinner party today.

My mother is thrilled with the idea that I'm going to buy a fleet of tourist ships. Anyone who saw her might even think I don't already own a gigantic yacht. The thing is, inside Danae Lykaios, there is still a humble girl from a small island in Greece.

No matter the amount of jewelry and fur coats she owns, she is a woman without an ounce of arrogance who loves talking to people—anyone. So being on a cruise—or several because, if I know her well, she'll board as many as she can if this deal becomes final—sounds like her idea of paradise.

"We'll have dinner with the captain in a room on the top floor, but you can visit the ship afterward if you want," Frank says.

I nod. "Isn't the gala tonight?" Based on what I know, the captain needs to attend this event.

He looks at me, surprised. "It is, but he won't dine with the guests. He rarely does. On our ships, only first class is admitted to the gala. Besides, the captain gets harassed a lot, especially by women. To avoid problems, he eats alone or . . . in special company."

"I won't take too long."

In fact, I don't even plan on having dinner. I have an actress waiting for me in a presidential suite at the Oviedo Tower. She's a casual date when I'm in Barcelona, and this will be the second time we see each other.

Despite owning an apartment in the city, I don't take girlfriends there. It could give the wrong impression. Like every Greek, family is important to me, and of course, I plan on getting married one day and having children, but I've never met anyone who made me think of them as anything more than a couple of nights of good sex.

"All right. As you wish."

⁙

Half an hour of conversation and I'm ready to go.

In fact, at thirty-five, I don't need more than a few minutes of conversation with someone to read them, and Captain Bentley Williams is nothing but a vain asshole. What I really want to do is walk around and talk to some of the staff members randomly.

I'm about to get up when I notice a delicious pair of legs in a miniskirt at the entrance of the room.

Yes, a *pair of legs* because she carries a tray twice her size. Unable to see her face, I follow her with my eyes.

She's tall, but she has delicate feet inside terrible pumps. Her hips are slim but mesmerizing, swaying sensually when she walks.

For a moment, I forget who's around me, too eager to see more of her.

Christos

CHAPTER THREE

I'M VAGUELY aware that someone is talking to me, but I'm too interested in finding out all about the goddess to pay any attention whatsoever.

Long legs and blonde hair are my weaknesses, and that's all I can see at the moment; I'm itching to find out to whom they belong. Thin, almost platinum hair and endless legs are enough to completely bewitch me.

The tray she's holding looks impossibly heavy for such a delicate frame, and my suspicions are confirmed when the glasses swing dangerously on it.

Another waitress shows up to help, and then, finally, I'm able to admire the whole picture—of her back. Like it's a game of hide-and-seek, she turns around before I can see her face.

And yet, the little I see is enough to make my pulse quicken.

I'm not the poetic type, but I swear to God, I feel like I'm seeing an angel.

My main business is fashion, so I have a keen eye for bodies, and the girl whose name I don't know would make an excellent runway model. With a body like that, she could show up dressed in garbage bags and would still be the only one seen by the audience.

I could imagine her hair being longer, flowing down in a delicate wavy waterfall, down her narrow shoulders.

I assume that without the high heels, she's about six inches shorter than my six-foot-four, but her body is all female.

I'm totally focused on her, and that's not normal for me. I love sex and women, but nothing takes my attention away from what's going on around me.

Even before she turns around, I grab my cell and send a text canceling my date. I don't sleep with more than one woman at a time, and there's no chance I'll spend the night with that actress when the mystery blonde awakens my body.

I type fast.

"Have fun in the suite. Order whatever you want. An unforeseen event arose. You will be compensated for it."

I make a mental note to ask my assistant to send her a piece of jewelry. I turn off my phone right away because I don't deal well with complaints or demands, and from my vast experience with women, I know that's what's to come.

"Christos, do you want a tour of the ship?" Frank asks beside me.

"What?" I'm finally aware that there are other people with me, but at that exact moment, the blonde turns, almost in slow motion.

Her beauty makes me dizzy.

She is stunning.

Her delicate nose, full-lipped mouth, and blue eyes with a hint of Asian descent, make an exotic contrast to the ensemble.

I see beauty every day, and to be honest, it gets tiring, even boring, after a while.

But the woman in front of me is perfect and unique. I have never seen a face with such striking features. She has translucent skin and the eyes of a Japanese woman.

Her breasts are small—as far as I can tell with the ugly front of her uniform obscuring them—but she's very sensual, as if her body was built for pleasure.

Look at me, I command, as if my thoughts have the strength to make her obey me.

"Christos?"

"Yes, I want to walk around the ship," I say, just to get him to stop talking.

What's her problem? Even when talking to the other employee, she doesn't look up from the floor or make eye contact with anyone, and I need her to see me.

The waitress who helped her starts serving us. Frustrated, I see the object of my interest walking away.

I stalled as much as I could during dinner to see if she would come back, but nothing happened. Minutes later, I announced that I was ready to see the ship.

I don't feel the slightest desire to spend more time with these people, each one despicable in their own way. But I don't go back on my word, even though I'm dying to leave. I barely listen to Frank's or the captain's explanations, even when I occasionally stop to speak to a crew member.

I'm about to call it a night, frustrated as fuck knowing I'll have to use other means to find out who the blonde is, when I notice a platinum cloud pouring out of a door and onto the deck.

I let the men know they must wait for a moment, and my tone makes it clear that I don't want intruders.

Like a mad stalker, I set off in pursuit of the person I imagine is the woman who awoke my libido. I believe that opportunities shouldn't be wasted, and if she's the one I'm looking for, I won't let her out of my sight again.

I walk slowly so I don't startle her.

She seems to be taking a picture of herself—a *selfie*—with the ship as background.

The temperature has dropped, and I realize she looks cold, still dressed in a waitress uniform. Even so, she doesn't give up on trying to get a good angle.

She also talks to herself from time to time, shaking her head like she's arguing, and that's when I find out there's a *voyeur* inside of me.

I'm not used to waiting for things to happen. This time, however, I'm keeping myself in the shadows, just watching her, my hands in the pockets of my suit pants.

At this hour, the deck is deserted because there's a party going on downstairs. In fact, from Frank's explanations, she shouldn't even be here; only authorized employees can use this floor.

As if sensing she's not alone, she looks back and, startled to see me, drops her phone on the floor. She bends down to pick it up and looks like she's about to run away.

"No. Stay," I command.

Zoe

CHAPTER FOUR

Minutes before

I CLIMB the stairs to the top floor on wobbly legs. I know I shouldn't do this. Coming to this floor breaks the rules I agreed to when I was hired, but the view from the top floor is the most beautiful. I need to take pictures like I promised Pauline.

I hold the little doll I always carry with me, the one that represents her so that we both appear in the picture. However, it's hard to find a good angle. I need a selfie stick.

The fact that my heart is beating like a drum doesn't help, either. If I get caught here, I'll get fired.

I tilt my arm a little, and it finally seems like we'll both look good in the photo. I'm ready to hit the button when through the camera I notice someone—a man—behind me.

I turn around to look at him, but due to the shock of being caught, I drop my phone.

Oh my God!

I duck down at lightning speed like a lunatic, ready to run—yeah, I'm not thinking straight. I should apologize for being in an unauthorized space and try to save the rest of the trip.

"No. Stay," the man orders, and I freeze in place as if I've been trained for this.

I'm staring at the floor, ashamed, but there's something in his tone that makes me want to obey him.

"You don't have to be afraid of me," he says, and I believe him, although I have no idea who he is.

"I'm so sorry. I shouldn't be here." I finally force myself to speak but still can't meet his eyes.

"What's your name?"

I see him through my eyelashes 'cause my damn shyness doesn't allow me to look in someone's eyes, even if I'm a little curious now. His voice is beautiful despite sounding harsh. I have no doubt it belongs to someone who is used to giving commands.

The first thing I notice is his broad shoulders, almost stick-straight. And when I say broad, that's the exact definition. His suit looks like it was painted on him, with not a single wrinkle in sight.

Curiosity overcomes my shyness, and I lift my chin to look at him directly. Maybe that's not very polite, but I stare at him.

He has a natural-looking smooth and tanned skin. He also gives the impression of having so much energy built up that I doubt he'd ever stay still, basking in the sun.

Must be over thirty.

Dark blond hair, cropped short, not a strand out of place—the opposite of mine, which is so thin that it is always flying around. Straight nose. A square jaw in need of a shave completes the picture. In a crazy way, I like it because it gives his aura of perfection a little humanity.

Move closer to me, a voice that comes from nowhere says in my head.

Closer? I don't think so. Going by his looks, he could be a royal. His posture is that of a true king.

I've never felt so affected by the presence of a man before, and I can't stop staring at him.

I meet his deep, blue eyes, which stare right back at me as if they're allowing me to examine him.

He still holds me in place without saying a thing.

"Name," he repeats, and this time, his tone is sharp, raising the hair on my arms.

"Zoe Turner."

He takes a step closer, but I'm not afraid—quite the opposite, I'm eager. Before either of us can speak again, though, I see the door behind him opening, and I run, afraid that superior staff could be coming to catch me.

I can't believe I'm here! It's like being in a movie. I finally get to see a sight I looked up so many times on tourist sites on the internet.

From Boston to the world, Pauline.

When I was hired to work on the cruise, I made a list with Mom of the places we would dock so that we could explore the cities' best tourist attractions.

We didn't have money to buy tickets in advance for all the museums I wanted to visit, but from what we researched, I would at least need the one for *La Sagrada Familia* because they are limited and sell out quickly.

When I arrived, there was a huge line of tourists outside waiting to get in, and I thanked God I was forewarned.

I read the pamphlet in my hand.

"La Sagrada Familia is a large unfinished basilica in Barcelona, Spain. Designed by Spanish architect Antoni Gaudí, it is part of the UNESCO World Heritage Site.

The construction of the Sagrada Familia began on 19th March 1882, under the supervision of the architect Francisco de Paula del Villar. In 1883, when Villar resigned, Gaudí took over as chief architect, transforming the project with his architectural and engineering style, combining Gothic and curvilinear Art Nouveau. Gaudí dedicated the rest of his life to the project and is buried in the crypt. By the time of his death in 1926, less than a quarter of the project had been completed.

Relying only on private donations, the construction of the Sagrada Familia progressed slowly and was interrupted by the Spanish Civil War.

In July of 1936, revolutionaries set fire to the crypt and stormed the workshop, destroying part of Gaudí's original blueprints, drawings, and plaster models. It took 16 years to piece together the master model's fragments. Construction resumed with intermittent progress in the 1950s.

Advances in technology allowed for faster progress, and construction passed the midpoint in 2010. However, some of the project's biggest challenges remain, including the construction of over ten towers, each symbolizing an important biblical figure in the New Testament..."

As I walk through the nave of the church, I see people photographing the walls. I'd rather look first and later buy a book with pictures because if I stop to take photos, I'll miss the real thrill of being here.

When I get out, though, I'm going to take my picture with Pauline. She's in my bag. So far on the trip, we have taken almost thirty photos together, and we are going to upgrade our album.

Before the cruise, I only had pictures of her inside Boston: at the Science Museum, at the Quincy Market—which I love to visit, even though I don't have the money to buy anything—and at Boston Harbor, my favorite place of all when it's not summer. That's when tourists fill the streets, and you can barely reach the port.

"No selfies today?"

My heart races when I hear the question because I know perfectly well whose voice is behind me.

It belongs to the beautiful man I ran from yesterday.

Zoe

CHAPTER FIVE

I TURN TO FACE HIM, hand on my chest. Not from being startled but in an attempt to calm the fast pounding of my heart.

What is it about this man that makes me feel this way? I'm inexperienced, but I live a normal life. I even had a boyfriend in high school, although there was never any intimacy between us.

It's not like I live on an isolated island and have never seen a handsome man, especially after I started working on the cruise. Not only the guests but the staff are charming and interesting as well. But there's something about this man that makes my legs weak.

Last night, after I ran away from him and the fear of being caught by my superiors doing something against the rules wore off, I couldn't sleep for a long time and just kept staring at the ceiling of the stuffy cabin I share with Tamara.

His face never left my mind, nor did the tingling all over my body.

I'm pretty sure he doesn't work with us—he doesn't seem to work for anyone but himself—and he's also not one of the regular guests, because I already know all the VIPs aboard and there aren't as many first-class members as there are economy-class guests.

I doubt that the man standing in front of me needs to save up for anything. He gives off such a vibe of power it's intimidating, although when it comes to me, it's not that hard to make me feel shy.

"You're not much of a talker, are you?" The voice sounds irritated, which ends up waking my anger as well.

"Not with strangers," I say, lifting my chin. "What are you doing here?"

"I ordered someone to follow you."

I open and close my mouth but can't make a sound, baffled by the confession.

"Don't have anything to say?"

"I don't know what to say."

"*Nice to meet you* would be a good start, Zoe Turner."

"I. . . *huh*. . .I don't even know your name."

"Xander Megalos," he says, extending his hand in greeting.

I stare at him. He's huge, and I suddenly desire to touch his skin. I hesitate before offering my hand. However, as soon as I do, he takes it, holding it tight.

A delicious shock ripples through my body, making me gasp.

His thumb caresses the back of my hand, and just like that, my pulse quickens.

It lasts only a few seconds because I force myself back to reality and let go of him before taking a step back.

The man is a stranger, and I'm usually pretty skittish in situations like this—I mean, not exactly like this one because I've never had anyone so handsome on my tail until now, but I've had some very embarrassing episodes when people mistook my kindness for something else.

"Why did you follow me, Mr. Megalos?"

"Why does a man follow a woman?"

"There's a name for that behavior in America," I say, rather than answering the question directly. I'm not sure of him, and I'm a bit afraid of embarrassing myself. I try to look more confident than I am because, if I'm being honest, I'm flattered that someone like him would bother pursuing me.

"Am I imposing myself on you, Zoe?"

I meet his eyes, tempted to say *yes*, but I'm not a liar. "No, but I'd like to understand why you ordered them to follow me, then."

"Because I want to get to know you better."

My heart is pounding inside my chest right now. "I don't understand. How could you want to know me *better*? We don't know each other at all, except for when I went upstairs, and you found me."

"You were serving dinner to the captain, and I saw you, but since you didn't look up from the floor, you mustn't have realized I was watching you."

My God in heaven, what a straightforward man!

Why do I feel like there's a butterfly revolution in my stomach instead of being freaked out by what he's saying?

"There's nothing wrong with being shy," I argue and risk a glance.

One corner of his mouth lifts with the shadow of a smile. "I didn't say there was, Zoe."

I feel my cheeks heating up. I've been acting impolitely since yesterday. My mom would give me a hell of a scolding if she found out. I started by going to the upper floor without authorization and broke several rules.

"I don't usually run away from people, and I'm sorry I left like that yesterday. I was rude, but I was scared. I wasn't supposed to be there," I say before he can stop me. "But I couldn't miss the opportunity to take a picture in that place."

"Do you often seize opportunities, Zoe?"

Is it crazy that I love the way he says my name? It sounds like caramel coming out of his mouth. He stretches out the syllables as if savoring each letter.

"I've never had that many to seize. Are you a guest? I'm pretty sure you're not, but I want to clarify that because, if you are, we shouldn't be talking at all." I look down at his hands and see no wedding band, but when I refocus on his face, I know I've been caught red-handed.

"No for both questions."

The heat in my face increases. "I don't understand," I say to try to cover up my embarrassment.

"I'm not a guest. I was on the ship because I was thinking of buying the fleet. And I'm not married."

I don't even try to save my dignity because I don't think he would fall for it anyway. "I can't talk to guests, only if I serve them," I explain.

"We're not on the ship."

"It's not just that. Most of the men there are married, and it wouldn't be right to talk to you, sir."

"I'm no *sir*," he warns.

"All right. It wouldn't be right to talk to *you* if that were the case."

"But I'm not. And I'm not a guest either, so we can skip that part."

"I don't understand."

"Have lunch with me."

"It's still morning. I came to visit the church. I'm not done yet. I don't know when I'll have another opportunity like this," I explain. "But if you want, you can keep me company."

I can't believe I said that, but the truth is, I'm very attracted to him.

Christos

CHAPTER SIX

I CAN HARDLY BELIEVE what I just heard.

Does she want my company while touring the church?

Zoe Turner definitely doesn't belong in my world. Not even close. I don't usually trouble myself approaching the women I'm interested in. It only takes a look to get everything done, and now, as I walk with her inside *La Sagrada Familia*, I wonder what the fuck I'm doing here.

In the daylight, the woman looks even younger than I first thought, and for a moment, I consider backing off because it's obvious she's inexperienced. The thing is, Zoe has been on my mind since the moment she ran out yesterday.

No, she had my full attention the second I saw her perfect, long legs balancing on an ugly pair of shoes.

"Is this your first time in Spain?"

"My first time out of Boston," she replies, turning to look at me.

And in that second, I understand why there's no way I'm going to back down. She's so beautiful.

"Is the name Xander Megalos Greek? Don't laugh if I'm talking nonsense, but it sounds Greek."

"Yes, it is," I reply without elaborating further.

When I introduced myself, I purposely gave her my middle name and mother's last name because I'm well-known around the world. As I wasn't sure if this could turn into something more, I chose to remain anonymous.

But after five minutes, I think it was a silly move. Zoe probably knows nothing about high society, which only makes her more attractive to me.

"Was I out of line for asking that?"

"What?"

"I'm not very sociable, so I'm not really sure how to start a conversation."

"Is that what we're doing? Being sociable?"

She shrugs. "You were willing to visit the church with me, so I thought..."

"I've already visited this church. I'm here because I want you. It's the same reason I sent someone to find out if you were getting off the ship today."

I see her throat move as she swallows hard. "That's a little scary."

"Probably."

"But flattering, too. Thanks."

Is she thanking me for wanting her? Zoe doesn't have a mirror at home?

"Let's have brunch. Today is Sunday, the day you Americans do it."

Again, she evades my question. "How did you get a ticket to get in here? I bought mine a while ago; it's not that easy to get one."

"Everything has a price. Money, contacts—it's all about knowing what the other wants and you can get anything."

"That sounds a bit cold."

"Straightforward, I would say. I always prefer honesty. Cards on the table." We're almost at the exit now, and I have a feeling we haven't made any progress. "What time do you have to go back to work?"

"The ship is not leaving until five, so I must be there at three. But I need to go; I have to buy some souvenirs for my mother."

"Come with me to my yacht."

"Thanks for the invitation, but I don't know you. Then again, I would be delighted if you joined me for a cup of espresso."

I look at her to see if she's playing with me, but her innocent expression tells me she's serious. "I have a counterproposal."

"Is this a negotiation?" she asks with flushed cheeks, and finally, I see that she's just as interested in this as I am, but maybe she doesn't know how to show it.

"Everything in my life is a negotiation, Zoe."

"What would be your proposal?"

"Coffee to start. Lunch in a little while. I want to get to know you better."

"But I'm leaving today."

Maybe you don't want to go.

But instead of scaring her off with my usual arrogance, I skirt around her doubts. "One thing at a time, Zoe. Coffee, then we decide the rest."

We leave the church, and after weaving through the crowd with my bodyguards, I spot my car just a few steps behind us.

But Zoe stops. "I thought we were going to walk."

"Not to where I'm taking you."

"I..."

"Are you an adult, Zoe?"

"Yes."

"Then you will have to make a decision. I want to get to know you better, but I won't force you. I'm inviting you for coffee, but not in a place where we'll have to yell at each other to talk. It's up to you to come with me or not."

"I don't know anything about you."

"You know my name." I motion to her hand, asking for the phone she holds as if it were a treasure. "Unlock it."

She hesitates but eventually obeys.

I open her contacts and save my name and phone number. Then I call myself.

"And now you also have my phone number. Share it with whomever you want if it means you're coming with me."

"I'm not a child," she says with a frown, and even that doesn't interfere with her beauty. "I might as well go get some *coffee*"—she emphasizes the word as if to make it clear to me that it will be nothing more than that—"without needing permission from anyone."

"Rebel much?"

"Not even close, but I don't like to be challenged, Mr. Megalos."

I'm sure she's only calling me that to tease me, but it only turns me on more.

I don't like pointless arguments, so I place my hand on the small of her back and direct her to the car.

I can't remember the last time I felt so aroused by a woman. When you've been in the seduction game as long as I have, there comes a time when everything gets boring and predictable. With Zoe, however, I don't know what will happen. Despite her shy nature, she makes it clear that she has a strong personality, and it's making my blood boil.

The driver waits for us with the car door open.

Zoe turns around and tells me, "I need to get back here before I go to the ship. I didn't buy my mother's souvenir."

"I can work that out." As she settles into the backseat, I turn to one of the bodyguards. "Go to one of those souvenir places and buy one of each from everything you can find labeled Barcelona and *La Sagrada Familia*."

"Yes, sir."

I get in the car, seeing she is fastening her seat belt.

"I'm going for a coffee," she says. "Nothing else."

"I don't remember asking for anything different, Zoe," I say, hiding a smile.

Zoe

CHAPTER SEVEN

"YOU'RE MAKING ME TALK, but you haven't said much about yourself."

In fact, he's watching me as if he wants to see inside my soul. If I wasn't so attracted to him, it might scare me, but being the subject of his attention feels delicious.

We're on the restaurant's terrace with only a waiter, no other patrons, or staff. He invited me to lunch after coffee, but here we are in a lunch-appropriate place, and he hasn't asked me if I want a full meal. I think it's because he has plans for me.

Of course, nervous as I am now, I couldn't eat anyway.

"Maybe I'm a better listener."

"You are?"

"Not usually, but I like your voice. In fact, I like everything I've seen of you so far."

I keep my eyes trained on the cup of espresso in front of me. "You are pretty straightforward."

"Life is short, Zoe. I don't waste time; I'm not that kind of man. When I want something, I go after it."

"And I am what you want."

"Yes," he replies, and an uneasy feeling spreads through me. It has nothing to do with his straightforwardness but with the casual way he says it.

It doesn't take a genius to understand that this isn't the first time he's after a woman he wants.

With that thought, my bubble just bursts. My dream of being Cinderella and feeling special to him has magically disappeared, and the reality behind the painting I created is not pretty.

Xander wants sex.

Somehow, for some reason, he found me attractive and decided to come after me.

To disguise how much, I feel like an idiot, I check the time on my phone. When I look back at him, I know he immediately realizes that our date is over.

"A long lunch on my yacht is out of the question, I suppose."

I nod my head up and down. "I have to go," I say, already reaching for my bag. "I have to go back and get my mother's souvenirs. Besides, it's not just lunch you have in mind."

He doesn't deny it, and like the needy fool that I am, I feel my heart sink.

Before I leave, he goes behind my chair and helps me up. It isn't enough that he's handsome and smells good; he has to be polite too.

He doesn't pull away, and the heat of his body against my back makes me shiver. I don't move, but I look back.

Sweet Lord Jesus, the man is such a handsome temptation. If I wasn't so starry-eyed, hoping to find Prince Charming one day, would I have willingly accepted his invitation . . . to be his mistress? Yeah, I think that's what men like him have.

I look into his eyes, saying goodbye in my head to the sexiest man I've ever met.

The problem is, I may not know anything about life, but I know myself. When it's all over—and by that, I mean this afternoon, since I have to get back to the ship—I'm going to feel alone and rejected again.

All the love I received from my birth mother is getting further and further away in my head. And as much as my adoptive parents, my incarnate angels, helped heal many wounds, the years of being adopted and returned to the state again and again left me with a legitimate fear of being abandoned.

I would have to be pretty crazy or stupid to just accept something like this at face value.

He lowers his head and whispers in my ear. "My gut says it would be delicious, Zoe."

His mouth is so close that the temptation to kiss him is difficult to resist.

I stare at him, feeling more confident because I've already decided to leave. "Mine too. But believe me, despite all that, neither of us is what the other is looking for right now."

When we get back to the car, at least three bags are inside containing dozens of souvenirs. I'm so embarrassed when he tells me he sent his employee to buy them for my mother.

I say I can't accept them, but he doesn't reply, so the only way out is to say, "thank you," get in the vehicle, and enjoy the ride back to the dock.

To my disappointment, he doesn't ride with me; he just directs the driver where to drop me off.

With the door still open, he looks at me so intensely that I want to take my chances and do something I never thought I would. I unbuckle my seat belt and get out of the car; my body almost pressed against his because he's still standing by the door.

He doesn't move, watching me like a predator.

I feel beautiful and wanted, and I carry out my plan. Feeling reckless, I wrap my arms around his neck and press our lips together.

I don't even know how to kiss a man like him, but I don't think about it. The only thing that crosses my mind is that this is the last chance I'll have to know how his mouth tastes.

It was meant to be a light kiss, but as soon as our lips touch, he wraps his hand around my waist and pulls me against his body. His fingers tangle in my hair with just enough force to make my head tip back without hurting me.

"I don't do anything softly, Zoe. Do you want to kiss me? Let's make it delicious."

And then, all those movie descriptions of starry skies, bells ringing, and a stomach full of butterflies happen at the same time as he takes control of the kiss.

Fulfilling his promise, his lips devour me, sucking, biting, his tongue asking for passage, the intensity of the grip on my hair increasing.

I melt against his body; my skin is on fire. My breasts ache, tender against his solid chest. My hands come to life, getting lost in his hair, nails scratching his neck lightly.

I'm so far gone that I forget everything around me. He apparently doesn't because he pulls away without losing grip on my waist, perhaps sensing that I'm not able to stay on my feet by myself.

He gives me a second, then takes a step back. "Did you change your mind?"

"I can't. I really want it, but I've had my share of rejection in life."

I get back in the car quickly before I lose my nerve because I know there's a good chance, I'll regret missing this opportunity to make this dream come true.

I lean my head against the seat, eyes closed, before I hear the door slamming.

This afternoon will be forever in my mind.

One can't meet a man like him and forget about him later.

Everyone will be ruined if compared to his beauty and masculinity.

I've always been attracted to older men but never to someone with as much of an aura of power as Xander.

Now, thinking about it, I remember what he said about being interested in buying the cruise fleet. This is another small sample of the wide gap that exists between us.

It's not just age or experience that separates us but wealth as well.

The car rolls through the streets of Barcelona, and that would normally excite me—people smiling and chatting freely, a different setting from my dull life in Boston—but right now, all I think about is our kiss and his gaze on me.

Zoe

CHAPTER EIGHT

I WALK the ramp to get back to the ship, feeling like I'm leaving a dream behind. Yes, I know it's crazy and that there's also a big chance this feeling is the result of my neediness, but what if it's more? What if, out of fear, I kept myself from living something incredible?

The crew greets me as I walk in. There are about three hours left before the ship leaves, so instead of heading straight to the tiny cabin to drop off the bags of souvenirs, I head out to the deck to watch the sea.

Some people talk to me, and I recognize a guest here and there, but I avoid eye contact because I'm not used to initiating conversation and I want to be alone and think about today.

I lean on my elbows against the railing and watch the sea.

I'm an adult now, but I haven't experienced anything yet. Would it be stupid to engage in something purely physical with that gorgeous Greek?

God, his kiss swept me off the floor. The force of his lips against mine, the urgency, and the way his body, without forcing or saying anything, made me surrender to the desire.

What would it be like to have someone like that as a boyfriend?

The problem is, he doesn't want a girlfriend. As far as I could gather, he was looking for an afternoon of sex, and that just doesn't fit in my life.

"Are you going to the crew party tonight?"

I turn to see who spoke to me. It's one of the first-class waiters who's never greeted me before. In fact, I've only seen him twice so far. "Hey. What party?"

"Yeah, this is the last port before we head home. You're American, too, right?"

"Yes, I am."

"This is my tenth trip, and before we reach the last port, there's always a fun party just for the crew."

It takes me no time to realize two things: I don't like the way he says that, much less the way he looks at me like I'm a piece of meat. In fact, I don't think I like him at all. The whole thing.

"I didn't know about any parties," I deflect, partly because it's true and partly because I don't want to be in the same place as this guy.

"It will be a lot more fun if you go, Zoe. There'll be some recreational substances there to make everything colorful."

Am I crazy, or did he just insinuate that there are drugs on the ship?

"Huh. . . okay. I'll think about that," I lie. "Now, if you'll excuse me." I start to walk away, but he grabs my arm.

"Nothing to think about, girl. Don't be silly. Our parties are unmatched."

I free myself with a tug and take two steps back. "You already said what you wanted, and I understand. Don't touch me again, or I'll report you to the captain."

To my surprise, the threat makes him laugh. "Good luck with that," he says cryptically.

I walk away from the insufferable man, pissed as hell that he ruined the rest of my afternoon.

I head straight for the cabin, thinking I'll shower and get some rest. When I arrive, the first thing I see is that the place is a mess. Tamara's clothes are scattered everywhere.

I leave my bags on the bed and head to the tiny bathroom with my phone in hand. Ten minutes later, I hear voices coming from the bedroom.

Did Tamara bring someone to our cabin? I know she's dated some guys from the crew, and I don't judge her, but we agreed that she wouldn't do that where we sleep.

I thank God I brought the dress and panties I'm going to wear. I usually do this because she's a little flighty. One time, she arrived when I was getting dressed and just left the door wide open for a few minutes, which allowed someone who was passing by to see me almost naked. Since then, I haven't changed clothes in the bedroom.

I dress quickly, but when I'm ready to step out, I hear what sounds like groans.

I hesitate, unable to believe this is happening. There's no way she's having sex in our dorm, but the sounds don't leave much to the imagination.

God, what do I do now?

I'm not a baby, but I don't want to witness live porn either.

I take a deep breath and try to think of an escape plan. Then I open the door and start to leave the room as quickly as I can.

But when I do, I get sick from what I see.

My bag is on the bed, so there is no way they didn't know I was there. Did they do it on purpose?

Tamara is kneeling and performing oral sex on the captain, who, as far as I can tell, has barely unzipped his pants. It doesn't look like an act between two people in love but rather something vile and sickening to my stomach.

Without looking at them again, I head for the exit, forgetting my bag and thinking about disappearing as quickly as I can. When I turn the knob, however, the door doesn't open.

I turn the latch and manage to unlock it, but it doesn't take me long to realize that there's someone outside preventing me from getting out.

My hands are sweaty from fear, and when I look back, they're both watching me, smiling.

"Party time," the disgusting man says. "Get rid of that chaste look, girl. I know you were on the ship's upper deck without authorization, so guess what? A diamond necklace from one of the guests disappeared that same night. You have two options: kneel down and satisfy me with that beautiful mouth of yours or be accused of stealing in a foreign country."

I'm terrified, but I'd rather be arrested than obey him. They would have to kill me first.

I run to the bathroom and lock the door, thinking about the only person who could help me.

Xander Megalos.

I look for his name on my contacts list, feeling my heart pounding in my ear.

I almost faint when he answers on the second ring.

"Xander?"

"Who's *this?*"

"It's me, Zoe."

"*Zoe?*"

"Yes. I need help. I'm locked inside the bathroom of my cabin . . . The captain and my roommate . . . won't let me out."

Christos

CHAPTER NINE

FROM THE MOMENT Zoe calls me, about an hour after we parted ways, to the moment I step on the ship takes no more than twenty-five minutes.

On the way there, I get in touch with Frank to authorize my entrance, so I won't have to go through check-in since I'm not a passenger. Desperate to close the deal as he is, he doesn't question why I want to come and just informs me an employee will be waiting.

The guy is surprised when I tell him to take me to the cabin Zoe is assigned. He tries to explain to me that it's the crew's wing.

Patience is not my strong suit, let alone giving explanations, but at this moment, her safety is at stake.

I still don't quite understand what the hell is going on because the story sounded so absurd that it was hard to believe.

How could she be stuck in the bathroom? If it's for the reason I'm thinking, my encounter with the captain won't be pretty. If he touched her, he can kiss his career goodbye.

As we talked on the phone, I tried to get her to explain what happened, but she sounded too nervous and didn't make sense at all. Something about a necklace missing and that they were blackmailing her.

However, everything starts to make sense when I arrive with my security guards in front of the cabin that the crewman pointed out as hers. I see a young man leaning on the door, arms crossed, as if he's guarding the hallway.

"Out." My voice comes out as loud as thunder.

"If you're a guest, this is the staff's wing."

I grab his collar. "Get out of my way."

This time, he seems to understand, and looking scared, he walks away.

"Open the door," I say to the employee who brought me in.

"I don't know if I can do that."

I pick up the phone and quickly make a call. "Frank, I want to get into one of the staff cabins. This will influence my decision to close the deal. Will that be a problem?"

"I don't understand, Christos . . ."

"Just 'yes' or 'no', Frank."

"Yes, of course."

"I'll let you authorize it with your employee."

Before they can even speak, however, the door opens, and the motherfucking captain comes out, tucking his shirt into his pants.

I go ballistic. Several possible scenarios run through my head.

It doesn't matter how much money I have now. I'm still the little boy from a Greek island, raised to deal with confrontation physically and to defend beliefs with his fists.

"Where is she?" I demand, pressing him against the wall, my fingers clawing at his throat.

"Are you mad? Let me go! Who are you talking about?" The man is turning purple, and the cynical smile he had on when he opened the door disappears.

"Zoe Turner."

The recognition on his face tells me she was telling the truth over the phone.

"Don't let him move," I warn my bodyguards, already walking into the bedroom.

"You can't keep me locked up. I am the highest authority on this ship."

"And from now on, I'm your new employer," I say, making the decision. "But you can call me God, too."

I enter the cabin as I watch my men position themselves to stop him from escaping.

There's a half-naked woman there, lying on the bed, but no sign of Zoe. When the woman sees me, she tries to cover herself.

"Zoe, it's me," I say at the bathroom door.

"Xander?"

Maybe this is the right time to correct the misunderstanding and tell her that everyone knows me as Christos and no one calls me by my second name, but somehow, I suppress the information. Even with the madness of the present situation, I like the idea that she doesn't know who I am yet.

"Yes, it's me. Open the door. You are safe now."

Seconds later, I hear the latch being released, but I don't know what will happen next.

Zoe, face puffed from crying, throws herself into my arms as if I'm her safe haven, and some totally unknown feeling spreads through me.

Oblivious to everyone around us, I hug her, touching her soft hair. "Let's get out of here."

"The ship is leaving soon."

"No, it won't because I'll call the police. It doesn't matter. The journey will go on. If you want to go home, fine. But come with me first. There's no way I'm leaving you unprotected here."

She pulls back a little to look at me, and I wait for her decision.

Seconds later comes the answer I wanted:

"Okay."

She is resting in my apartment suite. After I had a doctor come to examine her and make sure my housekeeper would take care of what she needed, I contacted my lawyers to make legal arrangements.

I've decided to keep the fleet—which is what I wanted anyway—but

I'll rewrite all the rules about relationships between crew members. From what the lawyers explained to me, this kind of harassment from senior officers is not unheard of.

I wanted to be present when they interrogated Tamara, and from what she told me, she had a consensual relationship with the captain. That wasn't my problem, but what she revealed next was.

She said that Bentley Williams had been planning to seduce Zoe since dinner yesterday when I first saw her. So, she'd been called in to assist as a waitress in his cabin. But when I showed up and asked to see the ship, the bastard had no chance of keeping her there any longer.

He and Tamara chose to have sex in the bedroom, knowing that Zoe was already there. They had the intention of coaxing her into a *little party*, but when she opened the door and found them, Zoe was so shocked she locked herself in the bathroom.

Tamara also revealed that the captain tried to blackmail Zoe about a supposedly stolen necklace, which was a lie—there was no jewelry missing. He was counting on Zoe's inexperience and being in a foreign country. He thought that if she felt threatened, she would eventually give in.

When that didn't work, he considered opening the bathroom door by force, but in a brief moment of conscience, Tamara convinced him otherwise, promising to reward him for her friend's absence.

Friend? What a *fucking* friend! Friends do not conspire or betray.

According to her statement, it wasn't the first time that the man had used more aggressive methods to convince someone on the crew to have sex with him. When verbal threats were not enough, he resorted to physical embarrassment or, at least on one occasion, he roofied them.

The lawyers said that those were serious allegations but because we didn't have evidence before what happened today, they were nothing more than hearsay.

It took my whole body's restraint not to kill the son of a bitch. I don't like to think about what might have happened if the situation had been different and only, he and Zoe had been in the room.

I asked my lawyers to dig into the ex-captain's life and punish him as best they could. I'll also make sure he never finds work as a captain again. Or in any other position.

I'm finally going to my apartment after almost four hours at the police station. After closing the door, I turn around and face the woman. From someone I was insanely attracted to, Zoe has become the one I need to protect.

I've never walked that path, so instead of planning, as I do with everything in my universe, I decide to let life show me the next step.

Christos

CHAPTER TEN

FOR THE FIRST time in my life, I don't know what to do.

At first, I was so mesmerized by her beauty, her perfect body, and her angelic face that I didn't even consider our age gap. But now, as I see her dressed in a robe too big for her delicate body, her hair wet from the shower, and no makeup on her face, I realize that Zoe is a very young woman.

I don't have to think too long and too hard, though. Without any indication of what might happen next, in the same way she did on the ship, Zoe comes to me.

There is no hesitation. She wraps her arms around my neck, pressing our bodies together.

This woman has the power to unleash a side of me that has never come out with anyone I was sexually involved with before—a protective instinct.

"Thank you."

I don't want to talk. Not yet. I'd rather smell her freshly bathed body, feel her feminine form molding to mine and the way her fingers trace the back of my neck.

I tense with desire because she wakes up a savage urge in me, but I know that's not what she needs right now. "Did you sleep?"

She steps back, seeming to finally realize what she's done. "Yes, and I'm sorry I jumped on you. I'm not used to this, but—"

I place my fingers over her lips. "It's been a hell of a day, and I'm the only familiar face you have."

"It's not that, but if I explain myself, you'll think I'm immature."

Despite all the shit we've been through today, I smile. "Try."

"I like hugs and being alone. When I saw you, I did it on impulse."

"Hug me?"

"Yes," she says, eyes on the floor.

There's a submission about her that excites the hell out of me, and I know it's part of her temperament. At the same time, she knows how to stand up for herself when she has to, hence her refusal earlier today.

"Are you hungry?" I ask, trying very hard to focus on something neutral.

"Yes."

"Want to go out to dinner?"

"First, tell me what happened at the police station."

I explain quickly without hiding the worst details, including Tamara's report that the captain even drugged a crew member.

When I finish talking, she's so pale I think she might pass out. "Sit down."

She looks around, seeming lost.

I pick her up and put her on the couch. When I look down, her robe is open a little, part of her thigh sticking out. I pull away so I don't give in to the temptation to touch her. I'm not a teenager. If everything goes my way, I'll have plenty of time to get to know every inch of her delicious body.

"I can't believe they planned something like this for me. How could Tamara betray me like that?"

God, she's too innocent for this world.

"Was I naive?" she asks as if she is reading my thoughts.

"No. I think anyone in your shoes would be shocked. I'm an experienced guy, and I never imagined a situation like that."

"I need to tell my mother. May I use your phone? Oh my God! What about my suitcase?"

"I already asked them to bring it here. You were probably asleep when they arrived."

"I don't even know what to do. I mean, I need to buy a plane ticket home, but I haven't received my week's paycheck yet. I need to figure out how to get it."

Her cheeks are red like fire, and I quickly understand that she has no way of returning to the United States unless she is paid.

"That won't be a problem."

"How so? Oh Jesus, I need to talk to my mom."

"You may use the phone if you like. I can also arrange your return to the United States. First, I have a proposition for you."

"Proposition?" she asks, looking suddenly alert.

I know I'll probably spend a few good years in hell for what I'm about to say, but she's irresistible. "Yes. Spend time with me in Europe. I won't be returning to New York until the end of the summer, so let's get to know each other better."

I've never gone this far with a woman. What I'm proposing to Zoe is to be tied up for more than a month with one another.

She opens her mouth and closes it again as if deciding, then finally speaks. "We don't know anything about each other."

"We'll have time for that. For now, no promises or demands."

"Is that what I did earlier today? Did I demand anything?"

"No. Actually, you argued with me, and I respect you for that."

"What you really wanted from me when you asked me out to lunch this morning wasn't to get to know me better," she states.

"No. I wanted you, and that was all."

Again, her beautiful mouth opens in an expression of astonishment. "You are brutally honest."

"Yes. Does that scare you?"

"I'm not sure, but I think I prefer honesty. What does it imply if I say I'll stay with you?"

"Whatever we both want."

Zoe may be young, but she's not that naive and understands perfectly what I *don't* say.

She stares at the floor. "If I say yes, I need to let my mother know anyway and give her your address, too."

"That won't be a problem, but I intend to leave the city in my boat. I don't want to stay here."

"Why not?"

"A lot of people know me. I want privacy with you."

"First, I will accept your invitation to dinner. Then I'll decide on your proposal. I need to think, but anyway," she says, getting up, coming over to the armchair where I'm sitting and reaching for my hand, "I want to say thank you again."

I separate my thighs and bring her between them.

She keeps her grip on my hand, and I play with the bow of her robe with my free hand. She follows the movement, exhaling heavily, but she doesn't pull away.

"I want you. To taste every bit of you, Zoe. But the decision to stay with me is in your hands. If you want to go home, all you must do is tell me."

"I've never done anything like this."

"I figured."

"And you still want me?"

I stand up and cup her face with both hands, my thumbs caressing her cheeks as I bend down to speak in her ear, my lips touching her lobe. "I don't tend to repeat myself, but maybe you need a sample."

I nibble, letting my tongue run over the soft flesh of her neck, and she trembles against me, but I don't go too far. She needs the courage to make up her mind, so I force myself to take a step back.

"Go change. We'll leave in half an hour."

Zoe

CHAPTER ELEVEN

"YOU EVER EAT with other people around?" I ask.

We are once again in the private wing of a restaurant—although, as I walked in, passing by the tables, I saw several heads turning to watch us.

I know it wasn't because of me, so it could only be because of him. Who is the man I'm with? I know his name and that he's very rich, but I'm starting to think he's famous too.

It may sound crazy, but I feel safe with Xander even without knowing much about him besides his name. He exudes honesty and strong character.

Self-confidence and arrogance, too, of course. But mainly something essential for me: he makes me feel wanted—or rather, desired, I correct myself.

Before we left for dinner, I called my mother. I didn't tell her in detail what had happened on the cruise, only that I couldn't go on because I didn't feel right. I also said that I would stay in Europe for another week, even though I still hadn't decided on Xander's proposal. It took me a good fifteen minutes to convince her not to worry, even if I didn't tell her I was with a man.

How could I when I still don't know exactly what we are?

"In public places, if I can help it, no," he finally answers.

"Because. . .?"

"I don't like noise nor having to yell just so I can have a conversation."

"Even more so with me, right? I mean, everyone says my voice is just a whisper."

He leans back in the restaurant chair as if he needs a little more space to watch me. "Out of shyness?" he asks without denying it.

"I think so. Or maybe because, like you, I don't like shouting either. I've had a lot of it in my life."

I see his brow furrowing in confusion and immediately regret saying too much. Telling him about my past is certainly not a good way to start our conversation.

"Why was there screaming in your past?"

"Not a pleasant conversation to have over dinner."

"Life isn't always pleasant, Zoe, but I can handle it."

"I'm adopted. I lost my parents when I was little. I was welcomed and rejected . . . several times. Most homes were not those of people who really wanted a child, but rather people who liked the idea of having a child, of being parents. Kids are hard work, and I think after a while, they decided I wasn't worth it."

For a change, I can't face him when I tell him that.

"How many times did you go back?"

I play with the linen napkin. "After a while, I lost count, but that's in the past," I lie because God only knows how much it hurt me every time; I saw the pity on the social worker's face when they brought me back. "I was adopted for real when I was eleven, and I got wonderful parents."

When I look back at him, his face is serious, and his jaw is set. "What happened to your birth parents?"

"They both died within a few years of each other. I don't even remember my father anymore, to be honest. My mom, yes, but it gets harder and harder to remember our time together."

"How old are you?"

For the first time since the conversation started, I breathe a sigh of relief. "Eighteen and a half. Too young?"

One of his fingers plays with his lower lip, and it mesmerizes me a little. "Yup. I thought you were at least twenty."

"What about you?"

"Thirty-five. Too old?" He plays with my last question.

"No. How you made me feel when you kissed me is far more important than our age gap."

After that, his expression changes. I don't know much about men, but I think it's desire. His gaze makes me shiver.

Until now, he only seemed to be studying me, giving me no clue what he thought about me, but in this moment, I feel in every fiber of my being that he wants me.

Yes, I know he said as much before, but the thing is, I don't really believe in words or promises. I've heard a lot of them before, and they were all broken.

Now, however, I feel it, and it makes me eager to have more of whatever he has to teach me.

"Are you done?"

"Yes. Are we going home?"

"Not yet. I thought of doing something different. Do you like to dance?"

"I love it. Why?"

"There's a friend's nightclub just a few minutes away."

"I thought you didn't like crowds."

"This one has an exclusive floor. We will have privacy."

"Are you doing this for me?"

"Yeah. After what happened today, you deserve some fun."

"You weren't kidding when you said you liked to dance," he says, whispering in my ear as he moves very close to me.

We're in a lounge that looks like the *VIP* wing of a nightclub. This is only my second club; the first one I went to was with friends from high school.

I couldn't compare this to my first experience even if I wanted to. It's all very fancy. Even the mirrors and armchairs look luxurious.

There is no one around, and I notice that, even here, Xander's bodyguards are lurking, preventing people from getting too close.

"I usually dance alone at home. Music takes me places."

His hands are on my hips, and my pulse is racing. He is not only drop-dead gorgeous but very sexy as well. The way he looks at me makes me want to grasp his body and be bold, but would my shyness even allow that?

As if sensing my desire, he pulls me closer. "And what else takes you places, beautiful Zoe?"

I lift my face to his. "I don't know yet, but I want to learn. Can you teach me?"

Before I take a breath, our mouths meet, at first in a kiss that seems more like a mutual exploration. Lips touching, tongues, teeth.

Before long, however, I feel the hardness of his muscular body taking over me entirely, making me want to be naked, and I melt in his arms.

Wanting more, I move my hips, swaying against his body, inviting him.

"I want to teach you everything, but not here. Shall we go?"

I know he's not just talking about us going home, and if I had a perfectly functioning brain cell, I'd probably say "no", but I'm not sure how much time we'll spend together. Despite my fear of suffering, I want him too much to resist.

"Yes. I'm ready."

Christos

CHAPTER TWELVE

THAT WAS NOT what I had planned—I intended a slow conquest.

Even though my life's motto is not to waste time, I know that Zoe is special. Very young too, which, for the first time, made me consider an alternative route and not go straight for sex.

I wanted to keep her with me for a while so we could get to know each other. Also, because she makes me want her more than I've ever wanted anyone else, even before we've had sex, and that's also a new experience for me.

They were good plans and intentions; the problem is that the flaming chemistry between us dictates its own rules.

Still inside the car as we are taken through the streets of Barcelona, our mouths don't part. Hands reaching out, eager to touch everywhere, jolting electricity, violent and uncontrollable.

Zoe's curiosity, her raw desire, sent my plans to hell. I feel like a teenager, dying to taste my first girlfriend in the back seat when I'm actually an experienced man with a sexual past very close to debauchery.

I barely realize when we arrive home, and when I get out of the private elevator, I already have her in my arms. Like a neanderthal, I walk into the bedroom without even thinking about slowing down, taking it easy.

The number of women who have graced my bed would make an average man blush. I like sex, and while I've never met anyone to this day who's aroused me with such intensity, I'm more than used to carnal attraction.

There is something about Zoe, however, that goes beyond the physical need. The primal desire to have her naked beneath me, an urgency bordering on madness.

I set her down after we're in the bedroom and open the outside door, bringing her to the penthouse porch.

Her breath is short as she watches me in the gloom.

I don't touch her. I put distance between us instead, but inside my heart is racing, the desire impossible to contain. Hungry and horny, full of desire to lose myself in that beautiful body.

I take a step closer.

"I never. . ."

"I know that beautiful Zoe." I run my finger along the strap of her dress, playing with it.

"Every time you touch me, my whole body tingles."

"Physical attraction," I say, trying to convince both of us.

She doesn't answer, just staring at me with those eyes like gemstones.

I turn on the central sound system on my phone, and a slow song starts playing.

"Let's dance?" She smiles, full of shyness.

"Why not?" I offer my hand, and she comes close.

Before taking her in my arms, I take off my blazer and set it on a chair.

When I finally have her next to me, she looks impatient and hugs me.

"Is it normal to feel so safe and intimate with someone I barely know?"

"Explain. I want to hear it. Tell me what you're thinking right now," I whisper in her ear.

"Being near you makes me shivery and shaky. I don't know the script in a situation like this, but I want it all."

I bite her ear lightly, and she moans. I reach for the zipper behind her and unzip the simple, short, blue dress, the color of her eyes.

"I don't feel so shy around you, and that's weird."

"Maybe our bodies recognize each other."

"Do you believe in that? Destiny?"

She's just in lingerie and heels now. I pull away to look at her.

She tries to cover her breasts and the front of her panties, looking very embarrassed.

"No, I want to see it all."

She pulls her hands apart and looks at me. The innocence on her face stirs something deep inside me.

"You're beautiful, Zoe Turner. And to answer your question, I don't know if I believe in destiny, but I do believe the universe lines up for things to happen. A minute more or less"—I get closer and place my hands on her slim waist—"and we would never have met, but here we are."

Everything in me pulses, throbs, and burns for her like a fire that cannot be put out.

Desire for Zoe is like a raging storm in full strength.

I tell myself there's no reason to rush—she's here right now; she's mine—but a feverish lust grips my body and mind.

She seems to sense my need, and her fingers play with the buttons on my shirt.

"Open them," I command.

One by one, she frees the buttons, focused on the task at hand.

When she's done, I release the cuffs of my shirt, and she slides it off my shoulders. Her actions show me that she's caught in the same web of desire as I am, because she doesn't seem like the type to make the first move.

She looks at my bare chest and licks her lips, embarrassed but also greedy.

The combination of shyness and boldness ignites me, turning my blood into lava.

"You're going to look at me the whole time, Zoe. I've never wanted a woman the way I want you, but I won't do anything without making sure you're with me all the way."

"Where? Where are we going?'

"Inside each other."

She now stares at me openly, lust overcoming her naturally docile temper.

I move my hand between us and touch her lingerie-covered breast. Zoe shudders, and her reaction only tells me what I already knew: she is sensitive, and when we have sex, it will be delicious.

Any barriers between us are unacceptable, so I reach behind her back and unclasp her bra.

I feel it before I see it, the hard nipples touching me. She moves, perhaps unconsciously, and moans as her nipples rub against my chest.

I kiss her mouth and neck in a downward trail to her thighs. I lift my head to look at her as I let my tongue touch the hard mound. She gasps, and her legs buckle.

I pick her up because moonlight seduction for a virgin might be more than she can handle.

In the bedroom, I try to lay her on the bed, but she sits up.

"Are you going to be naked, too?" Surprisingly, she doesn't seem shy anymore, just curious.

"Is that what you want?" I ask, my hand on my belt buckle.

A nod is her response.

Christos

CHAPTER THIRTEEN

I GET RID of my pants but not the boxers. I walk over to where she is and grasp both of her thighs, feeling them with my fingers. She instinctively widens them, leaning back on the bed, propped up on her elbows.

I replace my hand with my lips, and Zoe howls softly.

Damn, she's hot.

"I'll leave you naked for me."

I pull down her panties, and she follows my every move. When I first see her trimmed blonde pussy, my mouth waters.

I tease her nipples, caressing them with my thumb and pinching them with my index and middle fingers.

She whimpers, sitting on the bed.

"Learn to touch yourself. Have you done this?"

"No."

I take her hand and suck on her fingertips, then place it over her right breast. "Move it around and find out what you like."

When she does as I've ordered, I growl, mad with desire, and grab her left breast, sucking it hard. Hungry, I wrap my hands around the mounds, sucking them both at the same time.

She grabs my hair, pulling me closer. Zoe melts with pleasure in my mouth, and I've barely started.

My fingers follow the trail to the apex of her thighs.

I nibble on her nipple at the exact moment my thumb brushes her clit, and she almost stands up from the bed.

The strength of my desire makes me want to take her all at once, hard, and deeply, but even though I don't understand much about virgins, as my partners were always experienced, I know this first time will be important for her.

I take turns suckling and biting her breasts, storing her moans in my brain.

She's watching me, her eyes clouded with passion but also vulnerability, and that combo stirs the hell out of my emotions.

Zoe is a unique blend of devastating beauty, almost indecent sexuality, and an innocence that baffles me.

I spread her thighs, letting my hand cup her pussy and explore the soft heat.

She wiggles on my fingers, intuitively chasing her pleasure.

When she moans and closes her eyes, a frightening feeling hits me, along with an echoing voice: *mine*.

I shut this voice out, pushing it away, forcing myself to stick only to sexual pleasure.

I observe the outline of her mouth, swollen from my kisses. Skin hot with arousal, breathing heavy.

She watches me intently, but when I part her pussy lips and suck her clit, she loses it.

I lick her sex, my tongue tasting her for the first time. I revel in her body, not missing a curve, forbidding myself to stop until every part of her is tasted. When she comes, filling my mouth, I drink it all, sucking, swallowing, and it's not enough.

We have completely surrendered to the purest desire. Trapped in each other, oblivious to the outside world.

Right now, I just want to be inside her. There is nothing else I need.

Here, with me, Zoe is air and food.

I stand up, and she looks confused.

Without stopping to stare at her, I take off my boxers.

Her eyes widen. My cock is hard, thick, heavy, and I masturbate slowly, spreading some of the precum from my head.

I reach over and put my thumb in front of her lips. "Suck. Taste me."

She opens her mouth a little, and I rub the liquid on her bottom lip. Her tongue roams, and she closes her eyes, tasting.

"I'll teach you how to take me whole in your mouth, but not now."

When she looks back at me, there's no fear, only need.

I position myself over her body, our mouths coming together in an almost violent collision. The kiss isn't gentle but as hard and impetuous as my desire.

I cup her left breast, biting it lightly, and she screams, whimpering that she wants more.

I let a finger penetrate her halfway, massaging her inside, preparing her for me.

I watch in fascination as the shy girl transforms into a wild, demanding cat.

I can't wait any longer.

I get up to reach for a condom and put it on in record time.

I position myself over her body again and make light contact, testing, moving only a few centimeters.

"Will it hurt?"

"A little bit, I guess, but don't think about that, only about the pleasure I'll give you later."

She bites her lip. "I shouldn't, but I trust you."

I push into her just enough for her to feel my cock, and she grinds like she knows what I need. Damn, she's naturally sensual, even if she doesn't know anything about sex.

I move my hips, thrusting a little more into her. I lick her nipple, and she grips my shoulders tightly. The intensity of her desire shatters any remaining hold, and I push into her.

"Ahhhh... it hurts."

"Just a little, beautiful. Don't move, baby." I kiss her mouth and rotate my hips, so she feels me, but it also makes her more relaxed for me. "You're so tight, Zoe."

She moans and bites my chest. "I like it when you say naughty things. Keep doing it."

She tries to move, and I start a soft back and forth, preparing her for what's to come.

"Oh, God!" She pulses around my erection, and the restraint not to fuck her hard is killing me. When one of her legs lifts up, wrapping around my waist, I lose myself.

I push in a few more times without changing positions, and when she starts to moan loudly, scratching me, I alternate, sinking in harder in long strokes.

Her hips lift as if she can't wait to get more.

"Still feeling pain?"

"Still hurts, but I need all of you in me."

I rest on my elbows on the bed, thrusting with a steady rhythm before bringing a hand down to her clit. I rub the pleasure button until her breath tells me she's going to come. I don't stop until her last spasm subsides, and only then do I kneel on the bed, bringing both of her thighs to my shoulders.

Her eyes sparkle, glazed over with desire.

I get out almost all the way and thrust back in slowly so she can get used to it. Like this, she'll feel me very deeply.

"Show me everything," she asks. "I want you."

I penetrate her completely, our pubic hair brushing against each other. She feels like a tight glove around me, her inner walls convulsing.

I don't want to hurt her, but when she moves, moaning, I give her what she asks.

She's almost bent in half, her knees touching her chest, and the position leaves me on the edge of the cliff, very close to coming.

Mouths devour each other as I speed up, wetting our bodies with sweat.

It's like being hit by an electric shock. Every time I move in and out of her body, I reach nirvana.

I keep hammering nonstop, and she asks for more and warns me that she's going to come.

The pounding inside her is deep, and I know I'm close to my own orgasm, too.

I bite her nipples, but when I touch her clit for her to come with me, she delivers another orgasm in an endless moan, back arched, pussy squeezing me even tighter.

I silence her cries of passion, filling her completely.

For a long time, the dance of our bodies dominates the stillness of dawn; the sound of our bodies shocking fills the air like an erotic song.

I suck on her breasts, determined to make her come again, and as her hips begin to move in circles, trying to reach her own climax, I pinch her clit.

"Now, Zoe."

It's like flipping a switch. She becomes even wilder, locking her legs around me, and we reach heaven almost at the same time.

Her eyes are still closed, riding on the lust of our act, but I can't stop watching her.

Beautiful, naked, surrendered.

I make a decision.

Zoe will be mine indefinitely.

Zoe

CHAPTER FOURTEEN

I WAKE UP, but I don't want to open my eyes.

I used to dream, but today's reality is better.

The heat and scent of his body are still in me, permeating my skin and senses, and I love the feeling.

He's awake but not in bed.

I move around a lot during the night, and I'm spread out on the bed. There's no way he could be here without me feeling it.

God, I can't believe I did this. I lost my virginity to a stranger, a man whose name is all I know.

No, I quickly correct myself. I know a lot more about him than just his name. Xander saved me and helped me when I needed it. Despite what he's done, choosing to stay with him—and yes, I'm already determined to stay until the end of the summer—has nothing to do with the fact that he was my hero yesterday but because he makes me feel complete.

How crazy is that? Even though we don't know each other well, I feel more whole with him than I have ever felt in my life.

Despite the attraction he awakened in me, I didn't know what to expect, but it certainly wasn't what happened all night. To be honest, I was a little afraid of sex. Not the act itself but getting naked in front of someone or allowing my body to be intimately touched. However, ever since that kiss by the door of his car, when I thought we'd never see each other again, it felt like we'd been doing this forever.

Sighing, I surrender to the fact that I need to get up and reach for my phone to check the time.

I find it odd that I can't find my clothes on the floor, but then I see they're on top of an armchair, folded. He must be a neat person, which is the exact opposite of me.

When I go to the bathroom, I notice a note on top of my dress.

Sleep as long as you want. My housekeeper will serve you breakfast as soon as you wake up. Had to leave.

The words feel like a cold shower and make my stomach churn.

Casual, dry, straightforward.

Without calling me by my name or signing his.

In his world, what happened between us is normal, but not in mine. Of course, I wasn't expecting a marriage proposal, but he should at least have been here when I woke up.

God, what have I gotten myself into?

How should I act? Is this note some sort of sign, meaning that now that he's gotten what he wanted from me, I should go? What changed his mind?

I shake my head. I need a shower and a cup of coffee. I can't think clearly yet.

Half an hour later, showered, I feel more lost than ever, and it doesn't get any better when, as I enter the kitchen, a woman looks me up and down as if I shouldn't be here.

Normally, much of this feeling comes from my natural insecurity, but people usually smile when they first meet someone, even if it's out of politeness. Instead, she just asks me to sit down so she can serve me breakfast.

I barely eat, nervous and crazy to get away because that's who I am.

After a few sips of coffee, my confidence goes down rapidly. I'm on my feet, thinking about getting out of here really quickly, when she intercepts my path and hands me an envelope.

The handwriting is the same as the note, so I guess it must be from Xander, but just to confirm, I ask her.

"Mr. Christos, you mean."

"No. Xander Megalos, your boss, right?"

"No one calls him that, only by his full name: Christos Xander Megalos Lykaios. The whole world only knows him as Christos Lykaios," she says, frowning and looking at me with even more contempt, probably because I don't even know the name of the man I slept with.

But I'm no longer worried about what she thinks of me; I'm worried about what I've discovered.

"Christos Lykaios. Christos Lykaios. Christos Lykaios . . ." I repeat over and over as I leave the kitchen.

It can't be! Oh my God! Life wouldn't be so cruel.

I walk into the bedroom, too horrified to believe it's true. To distract myself from my despair, I open the envelope. Inside, there's money and another note.

I thought you might need it.

I start to shake. Is he paying me for our night of sex?

This just confirms that what I discovered is true. I slept with the same despicable human who destroyed Pauline's life.

Stunned, I google his name.

Yes, it's him: Christos Lykaios, Massachusetts College graduate, the same place where the accident took place. He's the one who ruined my best friend's future.

A man cruel enough to offer me payment for a night of sex, even though he knew I was a virgin before we slept together.

I put my things in my suitcase and leave the apartment without even bothering to say goodbye to the maid. Instead, I leave a note on the bed, not because I think he deserves it but to make sure I don't ever see him again.

Few words but easy to understand.

Don't look for me. What happened between us was a mistake I will regret for the rest of my days.

Just like him, I don't say goodbye.

He doesn't deserve that. He doesn't deserve anything.

I'm in line waiting to get on the plane when I see a woman staring at me intensely.

Even though I'm shy, I have a gentle nature, and if people try to talk to me, I politely answer them. Today, however, I just want to be alone.

I haven't cried yet, but my heart is broken. The guilt eats at me like acid.

So, when she takes a few steps closer, I seriously consider dodging, but I'm not rude.

"Hi, how are you?" she greets, and my first thought is that she must be confusing me with someone.

"Hi," I say, forcing myself to be polite.

"Are you a model?"

"What?" Of all the things I expected her to say, that wasn't one of them.

"I'm asking if you've ever worked as a model," she says, smiling, but then she shakes her head. "Excuse me, I'm being rude. My name is Bia Ramos; I'm a scout at an agency, and out of habit, I'm always looking for new faces. You're perfect."

"Forgive my bluntness, but this seems crazy."

"I know it wasn't the best approach, but I realized that you're about to board, and I didn't want to miss the opportunity. What's your name?"

"Zoe Turner."

She holds out her hand, and I hesitate but eventually take it. "Nice to meet you, Zoe. Here's the thing: I'll leave you my card, and you can google me to make sure I'm not a serial killer." She's smiling when she says that, and I relax a little.

I take the card she offers me. "What do you expect from me?"

"A screen test, although I have no doubt, I'll hire you."

"Look, I'm flattered by what you're saying, but I'm having the worst day of my life. Believe me when I say this is a big deal because I've been through a lot of them. So, I'll take your card and we can talk later, but today . . . I just really want to be alone."

"It's okay, Zoe. Just promise you'll call me."

"You have my word."

Christos

CHAPTER FIFTEEN

THE LAST THING I wanted was to be out of the house before she woke up, but my plans went off the rails the moment my phone vibrated early in the morning with a message from my lawyers.

We needed to decide which public statement to release about the ship issue. If everything came to the surface, the fleet acquisition would be a mistake and stocks would plummet.

I ordered that a rigorous investigation be carried out and the culprits brought to light. In this case, I think transparency would be the best solution, although I'm not too keen on involving Zoe's name in a scandal. In addition to being very young, if what I intend to do becomes a reality—staying with her without an end date—the press won't leave her alone.

My intention was to have breakfast together and clear up the confusion about my name. After yesterday, there is no reason not to open up.

I think about the blonde goddess tangled up in my sheets as I get up. She was passed out, exhausted, and I wondered if I wasn't too rough for our first night together. But then I remember that the second and third times, she was the one who came to me while I was trying to keep myself under control, fearing that I would hurt her.

Zoe, even inexperienced, is a sexual hurricane. It won't take too long for her to know her body well. I want to be the one to teach her to discover herself.

I've never made plans beyond a weekend with my past girlfriends, but I wonder if there would be room for her in my life when we get back to the States, my main residence. In our conversation at the restaurant, she told me that she lives in Boston, but her dream is to live on a rural estate—which doesn't seem to match the stunning woman she is.

The kind of life she craves couldn't be further from mine. I don't have any connection with the countryside; I'm a man of the world, not so much by choice but because of my business.

Anyway, I would like to explore this intense sexual attraction further. It's only been a little over three hours since I left her, and I'm already looking forward to getting back to the apartment and losing myself in her sexy body.

Before leaving, I left a note letting her know that my housekeeper would be at her disposal to serve breakfast. Shy as she is, I had no doubt that she would let herself stay hungry until I returned, and I had no idea what time I would be back.

I also left an envelope with my maid containing more than twice the amount she would normally receive from the ship. I don't want her to feel financially reliant on me, although the amount that represents her salary, for me, is equivalent to the value of a cup of coffee.

"Are you sure you want to close the deal?" my analyst asks, referring to the ships.

"Yes, I don't back down on my word. How long will this meeting last?"

"Half an hour."

I run a hand through my hair irritably, my thoughts totally focused on the beautiful woman waiting for me.

I slept next to her, which was new to me because I never spend the whole night with a girlfriend. Sharing a bed with someone can create unrealistic expectations, and my life is always black and white; any other colors are excluded. But when Zoe lay on top of me and I felt her body heat, her soft breathing, and her hands in my hair, any thought of getting up and leaving her was gone.

The need for her is a kind of addiction, a compulsion that only increases the longer I stay by her side.

And then there's the fact that she went through so much shit yesterday. I'm not normally a sensitive guy, but Zoe is in a foreign country and I'm the only person she knows.

"Not a minute more," I warn the men seated across from me. "Time is already running out. Make it worth it."

I can't say when I last felt this anxious to see a woman again. Never would be a great guess.

However, as I take the elevator to my penthouse, electricity spreads through my entire body.

I plan to take her to the yacht later today, but right now, the only thing I want is to be inside her again.

I enter the code to unlock the door, and before I can open it, someone inside does, but it's not Zoe; it's my housekeeper.

Weird. She should have left by now.

"Doctor Lykaios, I waited for you to arrive to warn you personally."

Her words trigger my concern right away. Something could have happened to Zoe.

Fuck, I shouldn't have left her alone.

I enter the apartment without looking at my employee, walking straight to the bedroom.

"Doctor Lykaios," calls the woman, so I stop at the top of the stairs.

"Not now. I need to speak with my . . . guest."

"But that's exactly what I'm trying to tell you. She's gone. About three hours ago, she left without saying goodbye."

"What do you mean, *left*?"

"She ate very little for breakfast, so I handed her the envelope as you ordered. About fifteen minutes later, I heard the front door slam. When I checked the security camera, she was already in the lobby."

"Are you sure she left with her suitcase?" Maybe she needed to buy something.

"Yes, with the suitcase," she says. She is an employee who is sent to my residences in Europe whenever I spend a longer period somewhere, although her fixed location is in my apartment in London. She doesn't sleep in any of my properties while I am in them, though. She is an excellent employee, but I sometimes have the feeling that she intrudes beyond her duties.

"You can go now."

"Do you need anything else, Doctor Lykaios?"

"I told you. You can go."

She turns her back.

"Just one more thing. Why didn't you call me to let me know that Zoe was gone?"

"I didn't think it was important."

"Let's get something straight: I'm the one who judges what's important in my life. Your job is to report anything unusual that happens on my property. Am I clear?"

"Yes, sir."

I turn my back and head for the bedroom, still believing it could all be a misunderstanding.

Of course, I hardly know her, but from what she's shown, Zoe doesn't seem like the kind of frivolous girl who'd run away without talking.

When I get there, the first thing I see is a sheet of paper on top of the bed.

I don't hesitate about anything, but I find myself slowing down before I reach it.

Annoyed with myself for acting like this, I grab the piece of paper.

Don't look for me. What happened between us was a mistake I will regret for the rest of my days.

I read it three times before I'm sure my eyes aren't deceiving me.

A mistake?

Did she call last night *a mistake*?

Who are you really, Zoe Turner? You are not the same beautiful girl who fascinated me. She wouldn't be so cold in a farewell.

I replay everything that's happened between us since the moment I first saw her.

Yes, I wasn't very subtle in my approach, but I didn't force it. I've never had to impose myself on a woman, and I even asked her yesterday if that's what I was doing.

The urge to pick up the phone and clear everything up is overwhelming, but I'll be dead before I let anyone crush my pride.

I'm Greek, and I don't bow my head to any man or woman.

As of that second, Zoe Turner is in the past.

Zoe

CHAPTER SIXTEEN

BOSTON

THE CEMETERY IS EMPTY, almost as empty as my heart.

Nothing went as I expected when I returned home. The guilt still consumes me, but it competes with how much I miss him, and I hate myself for it.

How could I be so stupid?

Besides being who he is, he treated me like a prostitute when he allowed that woman to give me money like she did.

God, I'm so ashamed!

Is she used to this? To dismissing his dates?

I push those thoughts away. It doesn't matter. It's none of my business.

"Hi, bestie. I didn't do very well on our first trip. The ship was fun, even though I didn't meet that many people. I'm still the same: shy and antisocial."

I sit on the floor by the headstone and gather some dry leaves.

"Anyway, I took a bunch of pictures with you, and they look amazing, but I haven't had the heart to develop them yet. I don't feel like doing anything lately; I think I'm depressed. I didn't tell Mom what happened at my first job or later in Barcelona. Her health isn't doing great, and Dad is afraid the cancer is back, but I'm so sad, Pauline."

I wipe a tear that runs down my cheek.

"I've been back a week now and should have come to visit you, but I was . . . I'm still dying of embarrassment. I did a very bad thing, and first of all, I need your forgiveness. I read somewhere that friends forgive each other no matter what. Would you be able to do that for me?"

Someone walks by holding a girl by the hand, and I get distracted for a moment.

Has the little girl, like me at her age, lost a family member?

A bird sings in the distance as if forcing me to focus on what I came here to do.

"I know you are with me all the time, following my steps from heaven, Pauline, but even so, I feel obliged to ask for your forgiveness personally, even if I have already done it in my prayers. He introduced himself as Xander Megalos, and I have no idea why. It wasn't until later . . ."

I take a breath because I'm choking.

"After we slept together, I found out he's the same man who hurt you in that accident. I was so angry with myself back in Barcelona, but thoughts are a crazy thing. When I landed in Boston, I wished it was all a mistake, bestie, because I fell in love with him. The night we . . . No, you don't need to hear that. I'm getting lost in what I really need to say. I just want you to forgive me."

I can almost hear her voice, as if she were still alive, saying that, yes, she forgives me, because Pauline was the best person who ever lived. I didn't get to see her again until shortly before she passed away. When Mom Macy adopted me, it was my first request: to take me to visit my friend. But by then, it was too late.

"I looked for your mother the day before yesterday. I couldn't eat or sleep properly because I needed confirmation. I wish it weren't true, but she showed me a photograph, and even though it happened many years ago, Xander's . . . *Christos's* face is unmistakable."

I take tissues out of my bag to dry my eyes.

"I wish I could tell you that I hate him, Pauline, but I can't. I can assure you that I hate myself for not being able to hate him. I'll make a confession and a promise: you asked me, as a child, to become a model and travel the world as if I were you; I only agreed because I wanted to see you happy. I loved to see your smile, but I never wanted that for myself. Modeling in front of people and traveling everywhere . . . isn't my dream. I want a house in the country. Someone who loves me and who I'm in love with . . ." And even now, in front of my friend's grave, it's his face that comes to mind when I say that. ". . . and lots of kids. A home no one can send me away from."

I blow away some flower petals that insist on staying on her tombstone.

"But I'll agree to one thing: first, I'll make your dreams come true, then mine. I met a woman, as you may already know, on my way back from Barcelona. She's something of a model scout, Pauline, and she invited me to audition. I called her yesterday, and she's going to send me a ticket so I can go to New York to do this test on camera. I can't guarantee that it will work or that they will hire me, but at least I'm trying to make your dream come true."

I get up, ready to say goodbye. It's already getting dark.

"I love you, Pauline. We haven't talked much since I grew up, but you, your plans, and the desire to carry them out to make you happy are what kept me from giving up whenever I was rejected by my adoptive parents. I couldn't give up because we made a pact. And I say, as sad as I feel now, I'm not going to throw in the towel because I'm doubling down on my promise. I will do what I can to be famous and travel the world with you."

BOSTON HOSPITAL

Fourteen Months Later

"Are you sure you really want to stay here, Zoe? I can book a hotel near the hospital. I don't mean to be insensitive, but there's a fashion show in a few days, and you can't afford to show up with dark circles under your eyes."

I take a deep breath, trying to calm down. I know she didn't mean it in a bad way; it's just her job.

After the test I took in New York, and I was accepted, Bia Ramos, whom I later discovered is Brazilian, became a good friend. No matter where in the world I am, if I need to talk, she always answers with comforting words.

Like now, after my mother had a serious relapse, she came from Oceania to give me some support.

"I'll be fine. I just want to be close to her for a little longer. As soon as she falls asleep, I'll get a hotel. I can't leave my father alone."

"Okay, baby, but will you call me if you need to?"

"Yes. There's also a son of my mother's childhood friend, a professor at Massachusetts College whose come to visit her, and Dad asked me to meet him."

"You're unbelievable, Zoe Turner," she says, running the back of her hand across my cheek. "Currently, one of the most recognizable faces in the world, the one any man would cut off an arm to take to dinner, is also the sweet girl who greets a family friend at the hospital like any ordinary person."

I look at the floor. "I'm simple, Bia. Don't fool yourself. All the glamor they surround me with or the clothes they dress me in have nothing to do with the real Zoe."

"So why all this?"

"Because I made a promise to someone very special. Now I thank God for getting into this world because it's what allows me to pay for my mother's hospital expenses."

"And if it's up to me, you'll earn a lot more."

"What do you mean?"

Bia and Miguel, her right-hand man, became my agents. She doesn't provide this service to any other model, but as soon as I got in, a rogue agent scammed me, pocketing far more than he should have on my payments.

"Now is not the time to talk about this, but we have a seven-figure contract on the way. They want exclusivity."

"I won't model for any other brand?"

"No, not even photograph, but believe me, you won't need to. For now, enjoy your time with the lovely Macy and your daddy. Then we'll talk. You know, if they want to buy your pretty face, I'll try to squeeze every last penny from them. Now I need to go."

I'm sitting in the hospital hallway, checking my work messages, when a shadow falls over me.

I look up and see a very handsome man watching me.

I don't want to sound cocky, but that's not unusual; my face is well-known these days.

"Good evening, you must be Zoe."

I turn my head to the side, wondering how he knows my name, but then I remember the visitor Dad was expecting. "Yes, it's me. And you are Mr. Mike Howard?"

"Just Mike, please. It's bad enough that my students call me that."

"I didn't mean to offend you," I say.

"I wasn't offended, Zoe. I just don't want to look so old."

"You're not," I say sincerely. "Oh my God. I think I'm making it worse. I'm really bad at socializing."

"Don't apologize. With me, you can always act like yourself."

I smile, believing it. I also believed many of the lies he told me until it was too late.

Christos

CHAPTER SEVENTEEN

Seven Months Later

NEW YORK

"BEAUTIFUL, ISN'T SHE?" Yuri, my assistant for nearly a decade, asks from behind my chair at my office headquarters.

I'm not a man who usually gives away what he thinks, but I'm so overwhelmed by the sight of her that I can't fake it. Yuri must see from the look on my face that I can't ignore the perfection in female form in the portfolio photos in front of me.

"Very," I say as if I don't know her, as if the woman hasn't been tattooed on every cell of my body for nearly two years, as if I haven't fought the desire for her with military discipline.

I followed her career and, of course, her rise. From the first time I saw her, I had no doubt that Zoe Turner would be perfect for catwalks and cameras.

Several times, I've been tempted to force a date so I could look into her eyes and understand what the hell went wrong that night, but I've never humbled myself for anyone, and I don't intend to now. So instead, I stayed backstage, watching her from afar, wanting her in silence.

I've spent a long time deciding what to do because I was sure neither of us would get any closure. I planned the logical path: lock her into a contract with one of my brands and keep her close until my obsession wears off.

I had already made the offer when she got married about six months ago, surprising the whole world.

I was a covert stalker but attentive enough to be sure she wasn't even dating, so when I saw on the news that it was an all-of-a-sudden secret notary marriage, I was shocked.

I feel as if I have a ball of iron lodged in my stomach when I remember that she's now committed to another man, because one word has been hammering nonstop in my brain since that night in Barcelona.

Mine.

Mike Howard, that's the asshole's name. A teacher twenty years older than her.

"I can't believe we finally managed to sign her. Zoe Turner has been hunted by several brands, and getting her to be exclusive to our group will take us even higher. It's an excellent deal for both parties."

I know what he's talking about. Yuri has as much knowledge about the fashion world as I do. In a short time, Zoe became a phenomenon. Now, she is one of the best-paid models in the world because she's signed a million-dollar contract with me.

No, she has no idea that my companies are behind it because I made one of my smallest brands, which most people are not aware belongs to me, appear as the contracting party. I've saved the surprise—and the shock, I'd say—of seeing her again for now that she's already signed.

There is even a meeting scheduled in a few days.

"And you know what's more incredible?" Yuri asks, having no idea where my thoughts are headed. "Despite her success, she's as sweet as a pot of honey. Kind, polite, shy. Incredibly, she hasn't been tainted by the arrogance that people with her type of beauty usually have."

I think about what he's saying, and I can't disagree. Despite the way she left me without an eye-to-eye conversation, Zoe has traits that made her admired in the fashion world: she doesn't have fits of stardom, and according to what is being said, she's very easy to work with.

The only thing no one suspects is that there is a block of ice where her heart is supposed to be.

"Can I ask you something?" says Yuri.

"No, but I know you will anyway."

"Why did you offer her so much? I mean, I'm not saying she doesn't deserve it, but . . ."

"I wanted her. I never bet to lose." I know I'm not being rational; I let myself be completely carried away by desire—whether for her or for revenge—but the fact is that I want her within reach.

He is silent, and reluctantly, I look away from the photographs to face him.

I'm not the most patient man in the world.

"Huh . . . I don't know how to say what I'm thinking without being obtrusive."

"You were never known for being discreet to begin with."

"When you said you want her . . . is that figuratively, like as her employer, or *literally*?"

"As an employer," I say quickly, giving him no further space for questioning, but then I fuck it up as the words escape my mouth. "What matters is that from now on, she is mine."

"Yours," he echoes but doesn't elaborate, although I suppose he understands what I didn't say.

It's the result of years of working together, I think. He knows me well. I never interfere when hiring a model, but with Zoe, I followed the process step-by-step, even offering more when her agent asked and agreeing to the no-nudity clause—which I would have left out anyway.

The truth is, as much as I tried to fight it, I knew my story with Zoe was just waiting to happen. What happened in Spain was an appetizer. We didn't have closure, and I don't leave any loose ends in my life. But from the moment I found out she was married, I changed my plans.

I don't go after another man's wife, so I kept watching her, and I have to confess that it gives me a petty satisfaction to see that Zoe isn't happy.

The goddess hardly ever smiles, which makes it pretty clear she is not living her fairy tale.

We almost met at events twice, but I avoided her. I didn't know if I could control my desire.

I also looked up the husband and didn't like what I found. He is a boastful, conceited little man who considers himself the quintessence of wisdom. I met many professors like him when I studied at the same university where he works as an assistant professor, individuals who need to diminish young people to feel better.

In addition, there are rumors of his involvement with students—current and former—including after they got married.

What kind of motherfucker would cheat on his wife just a few months after getting married?

That's none of your business, my mind warns, but that never applies to her.

"From your interest in her, I assume you'll be attending the meeting next week?"

"Yes. Why?"

"No big deal, I was just thinking about some rumors I heard."

"I don't like gossip."

"It's not gossip, but maybe it's something that piques your interest."

"Speak, Yuri."

"There's a story going around that her marriage has ended."

"What?"

"Yes, it seems that just six months after getting married, the dream is over. Soon, Zoe Turner will be single."

After dumping that on me, he leaves.

I get up and go to the window, trying to pretend the information is irrelevant to me.

But the only conclusion to which I come is that since Zoe Turner came into my life, I've become an expert at lying to myself.

Zoe

CHAPTER EIGHTEEN

BOSTON

I LOOK at the people sitting at the table, trying hard not to let my emotions show, but all I can think about is running out of here. The desire is so strong it makes me nauseous.

I'm in a cold sweat, and my forehead and palms are damp—I even thought I had caught the flu that has spread across the planet at an alarming rate. Several people have died, but no one knows for sure what the main form of contagion is.

I try to inhale, but the air doesn't come.

It's not the first time I've felt this way. It's been happening ever since I married Mike six months ago.

Yes, I was stupid and needy enough to believe that someone like him, handsome, kind, older, someone my family knew, would make me forget about Christos Xander, when in fact, I always knew that, at least for me, there would never be another man. I thought that maybe I could have a fresh start, as my love life had been on pause since I left Barcelona.

Dreaming for the rest of my days about someone who, even if he wanted me, I wouldn't allow myself to be with, was a journey down the road to madness.

I was so sick for the first few months that my mother went looking for a *pro bono* psychiatrist, who diagnosed me with depression.

Talking with him helped me get back on my feet and forgive myself. Also, based on his advice, I did more research on the accident involving Christos and Pauline but found almost nothing other than some vague reports. They didn't even explain who was to blame for the accident.

Her mother told me the Lykaios family was very wealthy and demanded a closed, confidential agreement. With no other option, she accepted it. The money, however, wasn't enough to pay for a decent life for Pauline, but the alternative was to fight against the powerful Greek family in court for years, at the risk of them pulling strings and the lawsuit backfiring.

I researched his name more deeply only once: a Greek billionaire who migrated to the United States with his family as a child, always surrounded by beautiful women, and who, as far as I read, has never had a lasting relationship.

To my surprise, I also learned that his main business is focused on the fashion world, and I was astonished to see that his group owns the most famous brands on the planet.

Still, in all the fashion shows and events I've attended, we've never met, so I think he must have several people managing his wealth, as I remember well when he said he would buy the cruise ship fleet in which I worked at the time.

God, that seems to have happened in another life!

I've changed so much since then. If the situation had been today, I would never have locked myself in the ship's bathroom in fear of the captain and the traitor Tamara, but I would have made such a fuss that even first class would hear. I'm still shy, but I never let people step on me. Now, I play by the rules of *tit-for-tat*.

People at the table keep talking loudly and laughing.

My head is pounding because I'm exhausted. I just want to go home and settle my story with Mike once and for all.

The day after tomorrow, I need to go to New York and introduce myself to my new employer.

A few months ago, Bia came to me with a proposal for a multi-million-dollar contract, an offer so unbelievable that it was impossible to refuse. I signed without a second thought because Mom's health care expenses are very high. She didn't have health insurance before she got sick, and when I tried to get her one, they claimed a pre-existing illness, which was true. The fact is, no matter how hard I worked, my bank account was always practically empty. All I have left of my savings are a few stocks I invested in on the advice of Bia and Miguel.

So, it's not like I can afford to say "no" to such a significant amount.

I'm going to New York just to work out the details, but it's all legally agreed, and that's one of the main reasons I want to file for a divorce today. Starting a new cycle without feeling like I'm in a constant war inside my own house will already be an advantage. I rarely stay in Boston for long, but when I do, I want peace, and I haven't known the meaning of that word since I got married.

I'm nervous as hell about the meeting with the new employer—yes, *employer*, because they paid to have my face and body in their campaigns for the next five years.

I'm not as fragile as I used to be, and I credit that to therapy, but I haven't gone from being a wild animal to the bravest person in the world, either. Premieres and interactions with strangers scare me, too, and there will be a bit of each in New York.

I hear Mike laugh and get even more irritated.

God, it was all wrong from the start.

The way I gave in to what I now see as cheap, well-rehearsed charm. I tried to make my mother happy because she liked the idea of me being in a relationship, but mostly I believed that a prince could rescue me from loneliness.

I only managed to add more disappointment to the many I've had in my past.

The one time we went to my parents' house for dinner, on one of my mom's good days, Mike was arrogant and belittled my family. We'd been married a month, but I'd been thinking about leaving him since our wedding night.

When I told my father of my intentions, he talked to me and asked me to wait a little longer.

"*Marriage and the coexistence that comes with it can be very difficult,*" he had said.

Difficult how? I'm twenty years old and feel more mature than Mike at forty, who behaves as if the world should pay him homage the way his students do.

"Have you read the book we're talking about, Zoe?" a very beautiful brunette asks me. I know she is one of my husband's students.

I hardly ever stay in the States because of business trips, but I've had two or three dinners with Mike's friends. All of them looked at me as if, just because I am a model, I had a pea instead of a brain.

Just one more day, Zoe, I promise myself.

I've waited and tried just like my father asked me to, but I can't even bear to hear my husband's voice. I'm getting sick again because he makes me feel like I have to thank him on my knees for marrying me when, in fact, he's a toxic, immoral human being.

"Zoe?" I hear his voice, but I don't turn to look at him, focused on the brunette. "I don't think it's my young wife's idea of fun to read something so complex," he says before I can open my mouth. I feel my face warming up as everyone starts laughing.

My psychiatrist told me the other day that Mike is unleashing anxiety triggers for me, but right now, it's really a *hate* trigger.

I look at his friends. People who've despised me since the first time we met. Teachers with spouses half their age, just like Mike and me, with the difference being that their women are respected, while I'm always the butt of teasing.

After facing them one by one, I turn to my husband, trying to strip him of the colors I painted him with before we were married so he would suit my dreams.

Tonight, the only thing I can see is a small, petty man who has to humiliate his wife to make himself feel better.

I get up from the table and grab my bag. "You are right. My atrophied model brain can't fraternize with such brilliant minds. So, I'll leave you to it with your average citizen's wages while I head home to review the seven-figure contract I just signed."

Zoe

CHAPTER NINETEEN

MY LEGS ARE wobbly as I leave the restaurant. I don't want to go back to our apartment, but my bags are there, and I don't see any alternative.

Jesus, I've never openly faced a single person in my entire life, and today, I did it with six at once.

I'm not rude; in fact, I'm rather patient. However, my glass overflowed when I saw that cynical smile on his face.

Who does he think he is to judge me? I read a lot, but even if I didn't, that doesn't make me stupid. As my mother says, not all geniuses have diplomas.

I order a cab from the valet, and just as I get in, I see Mike coming out of the restaurant. He calls out to me, but I ignore him because, as angry as I am, I'm capable of making a scene, and I don't doubt that someone will photograph it and print it in the newspapers.

I want to end my marriage exactly as it started: discreetly.

I have no doubt he'll follow me because even though we've never gotten as far as we have today, our lives have been hell since our wedding night and the recurring fights.

It was as if, by putting a ring on my finger, he thought he had a free pass to do whatever he wanted with me.

Not anymore.

I'm just finishing up packing my suitcase when I hear the sound of the apartment's alarm going off.

"What the hell has gotten into you today?" he asks as soon as he enters the room.

I don't turn to face him, and I know he shuts up because he sees me closing my suitcase.

I just got back from a trip, and in theory, I should stay in Boston until the day after tomorrow before heading to New York for the meeting with my new employer. I won't be leaving town today, but there's no way I'll stay with him for another minute.

"Zoe, I asked you a question."

I turn to him. "There is no longer any point in answering it. It doesn't matter anymore, Mike. You know perfectly well what I'm doing: leaving," I say, keeping my voice steady and silently thanking therapy, which has taught me to love and respect myself.

I was rejected in my orphanage years, but I don't have to keep allowing people to do that to me as an adult.

From the look in his eyes, I think he understands that I'm not just talking about the next trip; I mean forever.

Still, he pretends we're having another one of the many fights we've had in our short marriage. "You were very rude to my friends."

"More than they were to me?" I start, but I regret it. There's no point in prolonging this discussion when, inside my head, the decision is already made. "It's over, Mike. We both know that."

His face transmutes into pure hate. It's not the first time, but it still scares me. All the veneer of a fine man, an intellectual, disappears. "Because you didn't do anything to improve it. You never did anything for our marriage, Zoe."

"If by doing something about our marriage, you mean diving into your kinks, yes, then I didn't do anything for our marriage. I thought I was bonding with someone normal, not a man who needed . . . I don't even have the heart to put it into words . . . someone with *your preferences* to get turned on."

He's approaching so fast I barely see the hard slap coming before it smacks my face and I fall over, hitting my head against the bedside table.

Even dizzy and terrified by that violent action, I reach for my phone on the bed and run to the bathroom. It feels like a replay of that day on the ship, but this time, I'm going to call the only man I trust in the world.

"Zoe?"

"Dad, I need you to come get me at home. Mike just hit me. I want to leave, but he's outside the room."

"Zoe, my God! Do you want me to call the police?"

"No, please. That will cause a scandal. Once I'm at your place, I'll calmly consider what to do, but for now, I just want to get out of here."

"I'm coming, honey."

"Zoe, it's Daddy. You can leave now."

I look at myself in the mirror before opening the door. I haven't had the courage to do so until now. My whole face hurt, so I knew it must be ugly. The area where he assaulted me is sore, and I was afraid that upon seeing the evidence of his final disrespect towards me, I would lose it.

Now, however, I see that my imagination has lost its way to reality.

The entire left side is swollen, and my eye, which is naturally slanted in the area where he slapped me, is even smaller.

My God, there's no way I'm going to make it out of here without calling attention to my face. The last thing I want is for the end of my marriage to make the headlines in celebrity magazines.

"Zoe?"

"I'll be right there." I unlock the door, and as soon as he looks at me, his face flushes like a red pepper.

Instead of hugging me, he leaves the room, and I follow him because I can already imagine what will happen.

As I thought, my Dad has Mike up against a wall, and his face is already turning a little purple.

"Dad, don't do this; I just want to get out of here."

"Never touch my daughter again, you bastard, or I'll kill you."

He lets go of Mike, opens the apartment door, and waits for him to get out, but Mike still tries to get close to me. My father gets in the way.

"Zoe, forgive me. I lost my mind."

I look at him, thinking I should have walked away on our wedding night when he waited until we were married to tell me what he wanted from me.

"No. It's over. My lawyers will come to you with the divorce papers. The only thing I want now is for you to leave me alone."

He tries once more to get closer, but my father stops him.

"I wasn't kidding, asshole. Touch my daughter again, and I'll kill you."

This time, Dad doesn't wait for him to make up his mind but pushes him out of the apartment and closes the door.

Then he opens his arms for me. "Forgive me," he says.

"It wasn't your fault."

"Yes, it was. Right at the beginning, when you came to tell me that the marriage wasn't going well, I should have listened to you, but I was stuck on the fact that you were very young and maybe weren't used to a shared life. I had no idea he was abusive, kid."

"This was the first time he physically attacked me if that's what you're talking about. But there are other forms of abuse than physical abuse. He was drying me out, Dad, sucking my energy. Our marriage was a mistake."

"What do you mean by that?"

I think about what happened on our wedding night when he finally revealed himself. I didn't spend the morning resting in the arms of the man with whom I had hoped to have a family but crying alone in the next room.

"Nothing. It doesn't matter anymore," I say because I don't have the heart to tell my father about it. My therapist and Bia are the only people who know.

"Okay, but at least tell me what led him to assault you today."

"What makes a man attack a woman? Cowardice, knowing that she's someone with less physical strength? Because he sees her as an object that he can treat as he pleases? I think it's a combination of all that, but mostly the lack of respect, Dad. We haven't been okay since the first day of marriage. He played a character until he was sure we were bound by the law."

"And now, what are you going to do?"

"I'm going to ask Bia tomorrow, not a second later, to contact a divorce lawyer."

"You can also go to a police station. He should pay for what he did to you."

"I know, but we can't afford to have my name in the headlines. With that contract I told you about, I'll be able to pay off the mortgage on your house in full and give Mom more comfort, too. But if my name comes up in a scandal, they might terminate it."

"And will you travel a little less, too? You always seem to be going back and forth, honey."

"I don't know. In this new contract, they will have exclusivity over me."

"All right, darling. The last thing you need today is pressure. I just want you to know that I love you, Zoe. We both love you very much, and bringing you into our family was the best thing we ever did."

He's crying, and it makes me finally fall apart.

"Me too, Dad. I'm not good with words and even less with showing feelings, but I love you two so much."

"We need to put ice on your face. How did that bastard have the courage?"

"It's over, Dad. That's what matters. I was already determined to put an end to it, and there were even some rumors about it in the press. That's why I don't want to go to the police station. I'm going to ask Bia to hire a lawyer. When she finds out what Mike did, I'm sure she'll be able to keep him away from me."

"You're very strong, Zoe. Anyone who sees you from the outside as beautiful and delicate is wrong. You are made of steel, child."

"Not yet, but I'm learning."

Christos

CHAPTER TWENTY

"WHAT THE HELL are you talking about, Yuri?"

"To be honest, I didn't quite understand, Christos. All I know is that her agent, Bia Ramos, asked for as few people as possible at the meeting. And that it also happens in a discreet place."

"That part I've already heard; what I'm asking is 'why'."

"Looks like... *huh*... Zoe had an accident."

"What? When? And if that was the case, why didn't they report it?"

"I don't think it was that kind of accident, but rather a domestic one."

"A fall?"

"I really have no idea. Her agent shields her from the world as a mother would, but we'll find out soon enough. I took the liberty of arranging our meeting on the thirteenth floor because it's empty. Is that okay?"

"Of course. I just want to find out what kind of accident she had. Keep this in mind: from the moment Zoe signed the contract, she belongs to me, her whole life. I want to be informed of everything, even if she hasn't had a good morning."

He looks at me strangely, but I don't give a damn. The control freak inside of me wants to know what's going on and won't stop until he finds out.

I imagined our reunion many times in my head because I knew sooner or later it would happen.

Almost two years without seeing her in person.

There was a time when I tried to convince myself that Zoe Turner wasn't as much as my memory would have me believe. That her skin wasn't as smooth or that her moans and cries of pleasure each time I entered her body were like those of any other woman I'd ever been with. But now, just a few minutes before we meet again, I can barely contain my desire.

You know the saying: be careful what you wish for because you might get it? That is very true; only now do I realize that interacting, even if only professionally, with Zoe will be a hell of a lot.

Anyway, as long as she's married, she's off-limits to me.

Married, I repeat as a warning to my brain.

I'm not a liar; I want her, but I would never play the role of being a third wheel in a relationship. Betrayal is a word that doesn't exist in my vocabulary.

Impermissible. Unforgivable.

Don't invade another man's territory, even one as pathetic as Mike Howard.

I twirl the pen in my hand as a sort of exercise to slow myself down.

The secretary we assigned to this floor just announced that Zoe and her agent are coming up, and I'm trying to convince myself that what's making my blood pump so hard inside my body isn't my anxiousness to see her again but bitterness over the way she left. What we experienced was the best night of my life as far as sex is concerned.

I've been on my feet since the moment I arrived because I feel so much energy inside my body that I could run a marathon.

When the door opens and a petite woman enters, I tense up in anticipation.

And then the platinum curtain appears. We are finally face to face.

I drink in every inch of her, starting with her feet, like the first time, but now they are shod in fancy pumps, not the cheap ones from the cruise. She wears a pair of jeans fitted to her perfect body, and they don't leave much to the imagination. A white, sleeveless shirt completes the simple yet elegant outfit.

It's like taking a drive down a road you've been wanting to take for a long time, but in my case, I've already memorized every turn.

And then I finally get to the beautiful face.

One second.

This is the exact time it takes me to realize what happened.

I was in a lot of street fights when I was a kid in Greece.

Zoe was assaulted. That's the reason she asked for a discreet place.

I don't even think. None of my brain cells are working right now. I'm in front of her before I realize my feet are moving.

"Who did this?" I ask, standing still.

She hadn't looked at me yet, distractedly greeting Yuri, who formed a kind of barrier between us. But now her beautiful face rises, partially shielded by huge sunglasses. The mouth I kissed and taught to take me is open in an expression of surprise.

"You?"

"All of you, out," I command because she's the one I want to talk to.

In my peripheral vision, I see someone I believe to be her agent protesting. Yuri says something to her, but even so, she still asks Zoe if she wants to be alone with me.

"It's okay, Bia," she says, staring at me.

It's the first change I notice. In the past, she would have looked at the floor, embarrassed.

I don't move, even when I hear the door slam.

"I must assume, Mr. Lykaios, that you are my new employer." The voice is still soft, but filled with assurance. "If you're worried about how much money you'll lose because of the damage to my face, don't worry. I've been to a surgeon, and nothing has been broken. Only my skin is . . ."

"Who did this, Zoe?" I take a step forward, but before I do anything crazy, I put my hands in my pockets. She is a married woman.

What the hell is happening to me?

"I don't think it's a contractual clause to divulge every detail of my life."

Unable to control myself, I move closer to the point where I can almost feel the heat of her breath. But it's not desire that dominates me now; it's anger from seeing her hurt.

Mad with myself and with her because nothing I planned has gone as expected, I attack.

"Do you really believe that? You should take a closer look at the contract then because, for the next five years, you belong to me, Zoe Turner."

Zoe

CHAPTER TWENTY-ONE

I HOPE I'm being a good actress. It's hard to pretend that his nearness isn't shaking me when, in fact, my heart is beating almost painfully.

It's not about the reasons we shouldn't be together nor even about how he dumped me back then—by having that woman hand me an envelope of money—that comes back to me now, but everything we experienced in our one night together.

His kisses and the way his body moved over mine. Thick thighs asking for passage between mine. Demanding, powerful muscles against my softness.

The dark blue gaze looking for me in the gloom of the night we shared.

"I didn't sell myself to you when I signed the contract." I force myself to speak and realize he's focused on my mouth. "If I'd known you were behind it, I wouldn't have accepted."

"I doubt it. No one would simply give up such a large sum."

Damn you. He knows I'm bluffing. Even if I did know he would be my employer, I couldn't walk away from it. My parents' house has already been mortgaged twice, and the amount of money I spend on the hospital room and the nurses to stay with her 24/7 is obscene.

I'm not complaining. No sacrifice is too big for her and Dad, but it means that, from the start of a negotiation, I had to accept basically any and every job that came my way and traveled non-stop.

He's staring at me, and I don't back down, but admiring his beauty makes me aware of what I must look like. As if he can read my thoughts, he asks, "What happened to your face, Zoe?"

"Domestic accident." No way am I going to tell him that it was the result of my marriage breaking up. No one needs to know the level of disrespect my ex-husband reached.

Just yesterday, I went to a divorce specialist. After hearing the whole story of my short relationship, he advised me to try an amicable solution if I really want to avoid scandal, despite what happened two days before. This means I still have to meet with Mike to work out the details.

I'm staying in Boston for a few more days, so with my Dad and Bia present—plus the lawyer, of course—we'll have what I hope will be our last conversation before we sign the papers. My lawyer, Robin, tried to arrange a meeting in his office, but Mike claimed he couldn't make it because of work.

Mom is also home and under home care for the month. Whenever her health improves, the doctor allows her to go home temporarily to help her feel she's living as normal a life as possible.

"Does your domestic accident have a name?"

I notice his lips forming a thin line as if he's been struggling to contain his anger.

"Is my personal life of your concern, Mr. Lykaios? Or should I call you Xander Megalos?"

He looks bewildered for a moment. "They're my middle names."

"I know now. Considering that quick dismissal the next day, it makes perfect sense you wouldn't want to give me your full name."

I regret it immediately after it slips from my lips. Damn, the last thing I need is to show vulnerability in front of him. Because if I'm being honest, as soon as I found out his true identity that day, I would have left anyway.

"It doesn't matter; it's in the past. Now I think we should let our people in."

"Take off your glasses, Zoe."

I should send him and his sense of authority to hell. Instead, I find myself obeying. I do as he asks and look into his eyes. What happened wasn't my fault, and I won't be ashamed because I married a coward like Mike.

I know I don't look as bad as I did on the first day, but the bruise that formed still left purple and yellow traces, which no makeup could hide. The slap hit me so hard that it was a miracle I didn't break a bone, according to the surgeon.

"Did your husband do this to you?"

I could deny it, but I'm tired of this game. I just want to know the outcome of this meeting; then I can go back to Boston.

"Ex-husband. I started the divorce process." No, I don't know why I said that or even what he is thinking.

His expression goes back to neutral for a moment. "Answer me. Did he attack you?"

I nod, but I'm not facing him this time. "But like I said before, the surgeon assured me..."

He comes close, and my pulse goes wild. I can't find air for my lungs.

"You're single now?" he asks.

My back is almost pressed against the door, and I know I should stop him, but I can't. I don't want to.

"Yep."

Christos's strength and intensity are something primal and raw, meeting all my feminine needs.

How did I ever think I could replace this man? Regardless of what he's done and that we can never be together, I'm his.

"Do you consider yourself single right now, Zoe?" His voice sounds hoarse.

I move my head up and down slowly, and then my forbidden thoughts, the ones I don't allow myself to have when I'm daydreaming, come true.

His hand touches my waist like he's testing me, like I'm something precious. Reflexively, I flatten mine on his chest. His grip tightens, and there's no distance between us as his mouth takes mine without warning —the opposite way his hands started.

His tongue is demanding and enters my mouth without giving me a chance to retreat. I respond with the same need, taking everything from him as well.

I lose track of time and place. I just know I want more.

"Why did you leave when, with just one touch, you melt in my arms, Zoe? When your body still recognizes and responds to me even after so long?"

I moan against his mouth, hungry and delighted, pressing myself against him, but then he suddenly pulls away, making me feel lost and empty.

The way he stares at me is cold and brings me back to reality.

God, what did I do? How could I forget who he is?

"It doesn't matter anymore. You had a choice in the past and made a decision. Let's get down to business. That's what you're here for, Zoe."

Zoe

CHAPTER TWENTY-TWO

THE REST of the meeting is a blur to me.

I shouldn't be, but I'm focused on him the entire time, to the point that Bia has to call my name twice or thrice to get my attention.

The time apart led my mind to play with the image of a cruel, unscrupulous man who, even though he knew he had destroyed a girl's life due to his own negligence, ran away from his duty and simply offered a paltry sum to heal his own conscience.

When I found out, in Barcelona, who he was, I knew nothing about Christos Lykaios other than the insane desire he awakened in me. But now, when trying to analyze him from a distance, what Ernestine, Pauline's mother, told me, makes no sense.

Of course, people change. I'm not the same naive, fearful girl he met on the ship, but that's not what I'm talking about.

Character is something you can't change, and Christos doesn't show, I now realize, anything resembling someone who would run away from an obligation.

I look at his hard face, a shadow of a beard already growing. He doesn't seem to be aware of my presence. While I'm unable to get my neurons to function properly, Christos remains impassive, not even looking in my direction.

I hear the conversation, but I am totally oblivious. I know that some new clauses are added, and when Bia asks me if I agree, I nod. But as far as I know, I could be trading my kidney on the illegal market. I can't say what the clause contains, not even to save my own life.

"So, the first shoot will be in Greece, on Mr. Lykaios's private island."

Wait. What?

I look at Bia, confused, but she looks absolutely calm, so I repress it to freak out later.

That can't mean much. There are always many people around for photoshoots or for filming commercials. It's not like we're going to be alone—it doesn't even mean he'll be there.

"With that, I think we're done," says the other man, who I know is called Yuri, and only then do the eyes of the one who was my first *everything* turn to me again.

It lasts a few seconds.

Soon, he gets up. "Good afternoon, ladies. Our meeting is over," he says. He turns on his heel and walks out of the room, leaving me confused and lost.

He looked mad at me.

Why did you leave when, with just one touch, you melt in my arms, Zoe? When your body, even after so long, still recognizes and responds to me?

How could he ask me something like that after treating me like a nobody?

The pieces don't fit together, and not just for the two of us. The honor that Christos shows goes against everything Ernestine ever told me about him.

I rub my temples, feeling a headache coming but determined to investigate that story again.

"What happened in there, Zoe?"

"What do you mean?"

"I could start by saying that you seemed totally oblivious to reality throughout the entire meeting, but that's not even what I'm talking about. Before that, it was obvious to everyone that you already knew each other. The sexual tension between you could light up a country."

Bia is my best friend and confidant. She knows everything about my wedding, even the sordid details of the wedding night. She hates Mike with all her heart, and it was because of her advice, much more than therapy, that I decided to go through with the divorce.

Regardless of what happened after that brunette at the restaurant tried to humiliate me and Mike laughed at me, I already intended to end it.

But what Bia says now has nothing to do with my ex-husband. I never told her about my history with Christos; I think the time has come.

"Yes, we have a history. And I think I need you to help me understand it."

Christos's assistant comes back down the hall and says that the Greek's private plane will take us back to Boston. I automatically nod, still overwhelmed by our encounter.

An hour and a half later, inside the aircraft, Bia looks at me in shock. "I don't even know where to start, but I'll try to organize my thoughts. The first thing I must say is that I am now sure you being hired was no accident. He still wants you."

I've already come to that conclusion, too. It's not that he wants me, because despite his desire, there is a lot of pent-up anger, but my hiring wasn't fate's doing.

"Did you run away from him because of your friend? Look, I'm sorry, Zoe, but Christos Lykaios is a well-known figure not only in the fashion world but as a billionaire philanthropist. I've dealt with rich people for a long time, and I've never seen his name in the midst of rumors of illegal practices. I'm talking about drugs, mostly. Look at him. Sound like someone who takes drugs to escape reality, gets into a car, causes an accident, and evades accountability?"

"No. He doesn't."

"Quite the contrary, the man is a dominant. He looks like he wants to have control of the world in the palm of his hand."

"I know, and even when I was young, I did research to check that story. But as Ernestine said, the deal they made was behind closed doors. I'm so confused."

"You were too young. What you experienced was surreal, but I promise I'll dig deeper. Where did you say the accident happened?"

"In Boston. According to Ernestine, he was a college student and Pauline was very young."

"I have an ex-boyfriend who is a police detective and has contacts within the DA's office. I promise I will find out the truth. Now, let's get to the money in the envelope. Okay, it wasn't nice that you woke up and he wasn't there, but I blame your youth again for a lot of what you felt. Honestly, I'm going to play the devil's advocate here, but Lykaios doesn't have to offend a woman to get rid of her."

"Not even pay her?"

"With those looks? Baby, I bet even if he was a beggar, he'd have fans after him. With all due respect, the beauty of that man could turn the world around."

"You don't have to apologize to me; he's not mine."

"If you say so . . . The fact is, I have many more years on the road than you do, Zoe, and I can say, without fear, the man wants you. And judging by the state you were in, it's reciprocal."

"There's still Pauline's matter."

"Yes, there is, and I promised I'd investigate. But what if it was all just a lie from that woman? For God's sake, she gave you back to the orphanage when you were a little girl."

"She and several other families. It's more common than you might think, Bia. And I swear I'm not trying to defend her; I'm saying this because it's a fact. In her case, there was never any intention of adopting me; I just didn't expect to be returned so quickly because I loved Pauline. I still love her."

"The purest friendship in the world: between two children. Innocent hearts."

"She was beautiful and so happy. Pauline is my best childhood memory. Even after she was gone, I kept talking to her in my thoughts, celebrating each achievement with her. That's why I was so horrified when I found out who Christos was."

"I'll look into it, Zoe, but even if I don't have solid information, I can assure you that whatever happened wasn't what that Ernestine woman told you."

Christos

CHAPTER TWENTY-THREE

I PLAN EVERYTHING.

Aside from Zoe—the way we met and my spontaneous invitation for her to spend the summer with me—I'm not an impulsive man. My life is basically a file, with each folder labeled and in its proper place.

Attack the enemy at their weak point. Don't let anyone be prepared or anticipate my moves so the punishment is as painful as possible; that's who I am. Right now, though, I want to go after Mike Howard and wring his neck for beating her. Feel the pleasure of hearing him crack in my hands.

I pick up my phone and call the one person who won't judge me.

"What's up, friend?" he answers. "I know that when you look for me, it's because you don't see any other way out. You're the hero; I'm the villain."

"There's nothing heroic about me, and we both know it."

"But you're not quite the bad apple, either, like I am."

"I need you to find out everything you can about Mike Howard. He's a professor at *Massachusetts College*."

"Her husband," he says because the man just seems to know everything.

I've never discussed Zoe with him, but I don't doubt he knows all the details of our history and even my obsession with that woman.

Yeah, because what else can I call my feelings toward her? Even after she left me with nothing more than a note calling what happened between us a mistake two years ago, today was proof that nothing has changed. I keep craving her with every fiber of my being.

"Ex-husband. He assaulted her," I say.

"What happened?" His laid-back tone changes to a tenser one, and I know why. Abused women are his Achilles' heel. Having witnessed his adoptive father do the same to his mother many times in his childhood, Beau doesn't tolerate this type of cowardice.

"She didn't tell me the details, but her face is bruised."

"Son of a bitch. What do you need?"

"Whatever you can find out. I've already done some research by normal methods. I want to dig deeper, though."

"Give me two hours, and I'll even tell you when his first baby tooth fell out."

I look at the report in front of me.

I don't know how he managed it, but a little over two hours after I called him, my secretary came in saying there was a carrier with a folder that could only be delivered to me. I had no doubt it came from Beau.

However, before I can open it, my phone lights up with a message.

Zoe.

Yes, her number is still among my contacts. And apparently, she kept mine as well, considering none of our contract clauses mention personal contact.

> Zoe: I would like to ask you a question.

What power does this woman have over me that just reading a simple fucking message is enough to make my blood boil?

I press the call button. "And why should I answer it?"

"Forget it, Christos."

Shit! That would be my cue to end the call and keep everything between us on a professional level, but how can I do that when I can still taste her tongue in my mouth?

"What do you want to know?"

"Was the money you left in the envelope for me in Barcelona a dismissal? A coded message for me to leave your apartment?"

"What the hell are you talking about?"

"I thought it might be some kind of payment for—"

"Don't finish that sentence, Zoe. Don't offend us both like that."

"All right. It was just that. Thanks."

"There's no way you're going to hang up like that. We're not done yet."

"What do you want?"

You, naked, under me. Your silky thighs on my shoulders as I eat your pussy. Hearing you scream, asking me to go deeper into your tight body.

"Have dinner with me."

"The contract doesn't prohibit that?"

"Fuck the contract, Zoe. It was you who came to me, and now I won't stop. I'm coming to Boston."

"But I . . . we . . . Today is impossible. Besides, it's not a good idea for us to be seen together."

"You told me you're already in the process of getting a divorce."

"Yes, I am, but I haven't said anything to the press yet. It would be crazy to meet. We are both very well-known."

"I'll have someone pick you up tomorrow for lunch, then."

"That's not why I texted you. I wasn't planning on a date."

"You met me two years ago, Zoe Turner, and you know perfectly well that being subtle isn't my strong suit. If we're going to clear things up from the past, it won't be over text messages or even on a fucking phone call. Be ready by noon."

"Do you intend to come to Boston later today?"

"Right now. I'm heading for the elevator. Noon on the dot. Don't be late."

After I hang up, I text Yuri to see if my plane is ready to take me to Boston. It must have gotten back from there just a few hours ago.

I also bring the folder Beau sent, and I plan to read the report on Mike Howard on the plane.

Beau has contacts who are able to find out even the best-kept secrets, but although my opinion of her ex-husband was the worst possible, I didn't expect this.

It wasn't only the betrayals but the orgies with students, regardless of gender. It seems that he and a group of professors participated in these little parties where they swung partners or everyone was doing it at the same time.

I can't believe she ever got involved in this. So, the only conclusion which I can come to is that he cheated on her shamelessly, putting her health at risk.

Son of a bitch!

I've done a lot of crazy things when it comes to sexual satisfaction, but always with one partner at a time. And if there's one thing, I would bet my entire fortune on, it's the fact that Zoe didn't fit into his lifestyle.

I push those thoughts away because just thinking about another man touching her gives me homicidal feelings, let alone imagining her going from one to another.

I turn the page to a paragraph about recurring aggression against ex-girlfriends.

How is it possible that he got away with such allegations on paper? At least half a dozen women claim to have been beaten by the bastard.

As I read on, my hatred grows. As if it wasn't enough to hurt her, he stole her.

Zoe doesn't know it yet, but all her investments are gone.

Apparently, he's been stealing from her for months, but yesterday, there was a large transfer of what she had left, as well as the sale of her shares.

Right now, her checking account is insufficient to even pay for her mother's medicine. Now, more than ever, she'll need our contract to work.

I pick up my phone to solve the first issue: destroying the world as Mike Howard knows it. But that's not even close to what I have planned for him. He will agonize through life until I end his existence.

Ten minutes and a phone call. That's all it takes to make his universe crumble. Tomorrow, he will be dismissed from his post as an assistant professor because I demanded it.

As a former student and one of the university's most generous patrons, all I had to do was play the card that my contribution might be suspended if my request wasn't granted, and the bastard was out.

Welcome to the first day of your last days on this fucking planet, Mike.

I can't wait to meet you in person.

"Two phone calls in the same day. That means you've read the report."

"Yes, and I want you to appoint someone to take care of her. Watch her from afar just in case he tries to get close. I want men to secure her parents' house while Zoe is in town."

"It's okay. I can arrange that by tomorrow morning. But what about him? Will you put an end to the matter?"

"You know me. What do you think?"

"Something discreet?"

I know he's talking about the death of Captain Bentley Williams, which many believe to be a suicide, but we both know that is not what happened.

"Yeah," I reply, without elaborating further.

"Have you made up your mind, then? Is she yours from now on?"

She was always mine.

"Nothing has been established."

"But you want to protect her anyway," he says.

"Zoe just signed a contract with me. It's in my best interest to take care of her safety."

He doesn't say anything, and I understand because, even to my own ears, that sounds like a shitty excuse.

"You know how my men act in cases of danger, Christos."

"I know, and that's why I'm asking you. At the slightest sign of risk, there can be no hesitation."

"Don't worry, it will be done. Starting tomorrow, Zoe will have someone watching her twenty-four hours a day. Your . . . employee? Prefer that term? She will be protected."

Zoe

CHAPTER TWENTY-FOUR

BOSTON

"HOW ARE YOU FEELING, MOM?"

She looks excited today, and my heart always lightens when I see her smile. Seeing a loved one slowly losing their strength is not pretty; cancer is the worst disease of all.

There are moments of hope for the three of us, and also those days that border on despair.

I've been praying a lot for her to get better but not to suffer. Otherwise, I'd rather God's will take place. It's a drop of hope in an ocean of certainty.

The doctors don't have the answers I need. She gets better and worse. And that's why, more and more often, they allow her to come home.

Thank God I'm able to pay for her to have a room set up like in a hospital, along with a nurse. It doesn't matter to me how much time she has left; I want her to enjoy all the comfort I can give her.

"I'm fine, baby, but also very sad."

I look at my hands. I don't need to ask why. I know it's because of Mike's abuse.

"Don't think about it, Mom. This week, everything will be fixed."

"Your father told me that you asked him for help days after the wedding. I'm so embarrassed that he told you to stick it out a little longer."

"And I regret having listened to him. I thought there was something wrong with me, Mom. I always think there's something wrong with me because I don't have many people who love me."

"It's their loss. There's nothing wrong with you. You are a beautiful girl, inside and out."

"When do we know we love someone, Mom?"

"Are you talking about Mike?"

"No. Even before what he did, I could never have loved him. If I'm being honest, I didn't even like him. I think what happened is that I was too scared to lose you. You and my father are the only stable thing in my life. He showed up and looked like a shoulder I could cry on—older, affectionate, and understanding. I got mixed up in all that. I'm not saying I gave him a reason or apologizing for his behavior, because there's so much more that I'm not willing to share at the moment. I'm just saying that I was also wrong to marry someone I'd only known for a month."

"If it wasn't Mike you were referring to when you asked me about love, then who is it?"

"Someone from the past."

"The man from Barcelona?"

"Why are you asking me that?"

"Zoe, you came back from there half-dead. I didn't want to pry, and you didn't seem willing to talk, but I knew something serious had happened. Then there was the depression, and I focused on getting you better. Nothing else mattered."

"It's that man, yes. I found him again. And I think I love him. That I've always loved him, but . . ."

"But what?"

"He may have done something very bad in the past."

"Did you talk to him about it?"

"No. I only met him again today, for the first time since Barcelona. We'll have lunch together tomorrow."

"Aren't you rushing? I mean, you're barely out of the last relationship."

"What if I miss this chance? What if I lose him forever?"

"But what about what you said about him doing something bad?"

"I'm not sure, Mom. In my immaturity, I judged and condemned him without even giving him a chance to defend himself."

"Follow your intuition. You're a sensible girl, and you've never given me any trouble. As for this business lunch, I'd rather you didn't go to a restaurant. Doctors are talking on TV about the increase in cases of this new flu. They envision something worldwide. Your father even bought masks about two weeks ago. It looks like they already ran out in stores—hand sanitizer too."

I remain silent, looking at her sadly.

"What is it, honey?"

"I can't stop working. If this new flu thing is serious, I'm going to need to talk to you over video call only. The risk that I might get infected at some airport is huge, and I wouldn't forgive myself if I harmed you in any way."

She holds my hand, and my heart sinks when I realize how skinny she is. I bring her fingers to my lips and kiss them.

"Let's not suffer in advance. For now, just take care. I would like you to wear a mask if you need to go outside."

"That would be great. Especially looking like this."

"How can you joke about something like that?"

"I can't, Mom, but I can see you're blaming yourself for what Mike did, and that's not fair. No one can be held responsible for this cowardice but himself."

"Neither your father nor I had any idea he was like this, or we would never have allowed him to get anywhere near you. Mike was a good guy when he was younger; I don't know what happened."

A short time later, she begins to doze off.

I walk to the window, but I'm not paying attention to the night outside; I'm stuck inside the memories of my wedding.

A dream that turned into a nightmare.

Being the silly girl who dreamed of lifelong love, I was joined by a depraved man who knew how to hide his other side until it was too late.

I think about what my mother said about Mike being a good guy. I doubt it. He probably hid his true self from everyone, as he did from me. No one goes to sleep good and wakes up a perverted liar. I think it takes years of practice to learn to pretend so well.

God, if she only knew what I've been through. The only thing that kept me going for so long was that we barely saw each other. With my travels around the world, we've barely lived together for thirty days total in six months, probably less. And when we were together, it usually ended in a fight, as it did the night, he assaulted me.

What would my parents and friends say if I told them that the gold-star man, an assistant professor at one of the largest universities in the country, told me point-blank on my wedding night that he was only ever satisfied with group sex? That he could never be horny in a regular relationship? That he expected me to sleep with his friends so he could watch because he couldn't get aroused any other way with a woman?

Girls usually talk about their wedding nights with wonder. In mine, there was no sex, no affection, nothing. I was locked in the suite next to his, throwing up nervously and crying.

We weren't going on a honeymoon anyway because I had work commitments, so the next morning, I ran to ask my Dad for help.

That's when he told me that living together in marriage was difficult.

Even with no experience, I knew it had nothing to do with living together; it was a defect inside Mike that couldn't be corrected.

I spent the first month away, and when I came back, he was the kind man I knew again, but he never tried to touch me. I think he believed that I would be curious about sex and that I would eventually give in, which just proves he didn't know anything about me. I started feeling disgusted.

Our relationship was never based on physical attraction on my part but on friendship. So, him not giving any indication that he wanted to have sex with me, I'm not ashamed to admit, was a relief.

The three days I was in Boston, we talked like we used to, even though he slept in the next room. To be honest, I got used to the dynamic because it wasn't until after we were married that I realized I didn't want another man touching me.

The lull lasted until I got back home a month and a half later.

Again, after a disastrous dinner with his friends, he blamed me for our marriage not working out and brought up the whole group sex thing again.

I decided to leave the house and stay with my parents, determined to tell Bia everything the next day and ask her to help me with the divorce process.

That same night, Mom took a turn for the worse, and we thought we were going to lose her. The doctor suggested an alternative and very expensive chemotherapy, a new method. I had to focus on having money to pay the hospital bills because I would never forgive myself if she died because we couldn't afford to treat her.

Life was a merry-go-round of bad emotions during that time. I traveled, fearing I'd get a call from my father saying that she was gone. I was always tense, getting very little sleep and eating poorly.

Feeling suffocated, I told Bia everything, and she said she would support me a hundred percent to try to get a divorce discreetly. It was with that in mind that I returned home that week. Regardless of what had happened, I would have ended our union. His hitting me was the missing stone in the grave of our relationship.

What relationship, Lord? There was no relationship, just a mistake. We were never even friends. I see that now.

I remember the call from Christos.

Did I mess up sending that text? Should I have waited for Bia to clear everything up with her ex-boyfriend before talking to him?

I don't regret taking the initiative for the first time, accepting the fact that it could all have been a terrible misunderstanding.

God, he wanted to see me today, even! It must mean something that he was willing to drop everything to come find me, especially after how things ended up between us.

I knew that I hadn't forgotten him and would never forget him, but I didn't expect to feel him so strongly inside my heart after so much time had passed.

It was as if he had touched me only yesterday. As if I was still the insecure girl who gave herself to her dark hero that one night in Barcelona.

I need to hear his side of the story, if only to move on.

However, right now, still unsure of anything about Pauline's accident, I know that whatever the outcome is, there will never be another man for me.

Zoe

CHAPTER TWENTY-FIVE

"WHERE ARE YOU GOING?" Bia asks, almost scaring me to death as I walk down the hall.

"I was going to borrow your car. Mine is out of gas, and I want to buy ice cream."

"Too excited?"

I nod my head.

"You can take it, but first listen to what I have to say. I just spoke to my detective friend and . . ."

"I thought you said he was an ex-boyfriend."

"If I tell you what I really call him, you won't like it. I'm afraid you'll faint."

Despite all the craziness that's been going on these last few days, I start to laugh because Bia's mouth is as foul as a sailor's, even though she looks like a Victorian-era lady. "Speak. I think I've already given a lot of evidence that I'm a big girl. I can take a swearword or two."

"Fuck buddy."

"Oh Jesus!"

"I warned you."

"And what would that be?"

"The relationship is strong enough for me to consider him a friend but not strong enough for me to want him as a boyfriend. He is a good guy. I like men who break the rules."

"Is an outlaw your dream?"

"Who knows? I've never tried one. But I'm not going to lie and pretend it doesn't turn me on having wilder sex."

"Too much information, miss," I say, covering my ears. "Now tell me about what your friend said." I still haven't said anything to her about my meeting with Christos tomorrow. I'm going to need some courage before I make any confessions.

"He said that by tomorrow, he'll be able to access what we need and that it's common for very wealthy people to make a confidential agreement on the amount of the compensation when involved in civil lawsuits. But it doesn't make much sense to demand such a clause if the amount is insignificant, as Ernestine told you. Besides, he did a cursory search and found no criminal charges against Lykaios. Usually, in such cases, both run together."

"I don't know if I understand."

"Which part?"

"The one about the amount he paid."

"He explained that, usually, when confidentiality is required in a legal deal, the amount is astronomical."

"It's not possible, Bia. I was a kid, but I was well-aware that there were essential things missing in that house. When my birth mother was still alive, we weren't even close to rich, but there were fruit and cookies for me. At Ernestine's house, it was borderline poverty. She controlled every spoonful of rice we ate."

"What if she spent the money?"

"But you said it would have been an astronomical amount."

"Yes, but even high amounts, if mismanaged, can go away. There are many cases of people who win the lottery and then end up in poverty."

"That's true. I even watched a documentary once about the ex-rich."

"Well, it's all speculation for now, but we'll find out, Zoe. I promise."

I approach and hug her. "You are the best friend I could wish for."

"I'm more of a mother, aren't I? Because of my age."

"Well, I'm going to pray that I'll look as beautiful as you do at forty-five."

She smiles awkwardly. Like me, she doesn't know how to handle compliments very well. "Did you mention going for ice cream?" She suddenly changes the subject.

"Yes, I will allow myself that luxury. After everything that happened today, I can go off the diet."

I starve, literally, to keep myself within the measures of the contracts I sign, but every now and then I allow myself to cheat, even though I know that tomorrow I'll probably have to run ten kilometers to make up for it.

"Do you think you'll be able to stay in this life for a long time? I mean, currently, your modeling career is very promising, and you can model and photograph until you are almost my age. The fashion industry has finally understood that the modern woman has the money to pay her own bills by her thirties, not at the age of twelve."

"I don't think I can. It was never what I wanted for myself. I intended to stay for a couple of years, just to fulfill the promise I made to Pauline."

"And you did it right because, with the contract you've just signed with Lykaios, you've just become the fifth best-paid top model. Not to belittle you, but he didn't have to offer so much. It should take you at least another three years to reach that status. This man has feelings for you, Zoe."

"I want to be wrong so bad about Pauline, Bia. When I saw him today, it was like we had never been apart."

"I want you to be, too, but please take it easy. I'll always be cheering for your happiness, but this time, you could stand to slow down a little. Your *rendezvous* in the past, from what you told me, was explosive."

I look at her, not knowing how to answer. Of course, I think she's right, but slowing down is a fool's dream if you consider what happens when Christos and I are close.

"We'll get this story about your friend's accident straightened out. I have faith in God, but now tell me, what flavor of ice cream are you going to buy?"

"Don't you want to come with me?"

"Forgive me, but no. I'm tired, but I'd like an ice cream," she says, winking.

"Lazy. Lucky for you, I like you enough to share my goodies."

※

It takes me longer than I intended at the supermarket because apparently, everyone decided to go shopping at eleven o'clock at night.

If it were in another neighborhood, I wouldn't leave the house alone at this hour, but it's pretty quiet here. Besides, dressed as a boy, as Bia calls my sweatpants three sizes too big, baggy coat, and hair hidden by the hood and sneakers, no one would believe it was me.

Oh, and following my mother's recommendation, I decided to come wearing a mask. I felt ridiculous when I left the house. But to my surprise, when I arrived at the supermarket, the clerk was not only wearing one but also explaining to me that the governor would make it mandatory starting next Saturday. Then, as I went down the aisles, I saw several people were masked, too.

That's insane! I need to read more carefully about this virus. My life is so busy that I'm usually exhausted when I have time off. People think modeling is super easy, but no one has any idea what it's like to stand for ten or twelve hours to shoot a commercial in the freezing cold wearing a tiny bikini.

I pass a refrigerator and smile when I see my reflection in it.

In my profession, I can never neglect my appearance because paparazzi may appear at any time. But Bia told me that I was right to go undercover because it would help hide my bruised face.

So, as I scour the fridges for the flavor I want—strawberry with chocolate chips—I feel like a secret agent.

Of course, there's only one tub of my favorite flavor, and the lid is halfway open.

Ew.

Damn, I'll have to choose another one. God knows if some crazy person did something to the ice cream and made it filthy. There is no way I have the guts to eat something without it being sealed.

"May I help you?" an employee asks.

I don't look at him, afraid he'll recognize me, but then I start laughing behind the mask. How could he?

"I wanted the strawberry one with chocolate chips, but the only tub here is open."

"Oh, the kids around here! They've been coming here to do that lately. But if you're not in a hurry, I can go inside and check if I can find more."

"Would you do that for me?"

"Certainly. Strawberry with chocolate chips is the best flavor."

"Isn't it? And I've been wanting to eat it for over a month now."

"Wait a minute, sweetheart; I'll see if I can find any."

Mike

CHAPTER TWENTY-SIX

\\\\\\\\\\\\\

FINALLY, that nosy Bia Ramos has left. I was losing hope, thinking she was going to spend the night at the old bastard's house. But now that her car has left, I can put my plan into action.

Before getting out of the van, I look from side to side to make sure there's no one around. When I confirm the streets are empty, I grab my gear. From what I've researched on the internet, I'll only need ten minutes before it's all over.

And *over* is a good word because, when it ends, there won't be a single thing left standing.

I didn't intend to go back to her anyway. After seven months together, six of which were spent married, I was patient and loving, but I realized the ice princess would never give in and fit into my lifestyle.

Making Zoe my wife was no accident.

One morning, my mother was showing me a picture of a friend's adopted daughter in the newspapers, and I had to admit she was beautiful. However, that wasn't what caught my attention but rather what she told me about the girl.

A rising twenty-year-old model, she had a pocket full of money that, unfortunately, was being wasted on old Macy, who wouldn't be kind enough to just die already and get off her daughter's back.

For a long time, I looked for a stable partner who would go along with my sexual preferences. And what better person to groom than an orphan who was once a needy girl rejected by several families?

Yeah, I got my mom to tell me all about her. Getting adopted by Macy and her husband was sort of her last option. Zoe was already too old for other families to want her, so she was very lucky to be picked by them. Maybe that's why she's so grateful and keeps spending money on her two useless parents.

She was such an easy target that I didn't have to make that much of an effort. A friendly shoulder for a needy woman is irresistible.

I wasn't too worried when she didn't show eagerness to have sex, because going to bed with one woman just doesn't turn me on. I've even tried the famous little blue pills, but even with them, it feels like I had a meal without seasoning. That's why my secret relationship with a Mexican girl didn't work out. A few years ago, I went on vacation in Mexico, and I made the stupid decision of committing myself to her in front of a judge. It lasted a month. I abandoned her without warning, came back to the United States, and never thought about it again. As the marriage was never registered here, no one has any idea of the mistake I made.

I think of my current wife, the icy blonde—or would it be more accurate to say my "second wife"?

This idea of being married to two women, one not knowing about the other, excites me too much. I feel like a sultan.

I used all my charm so that, after our wedding, she would understand how things worked. But that's when the uptight little saint surprised me with a horrified look.

For God's sake, what century does she live in? Doesn't she understand how lucky she was that I chose her? Would an acclaimed professor who could fuck any student with a snap of his fingers lower himself to her level, that of an outcast?

She cried and locked herself in her room on our wedding night. Then she went to her parents' house, and only then did I realize that I had rushed things. Yes, I dreamed of Zoe naked, going from me to my other sex partners, but I also wanted the thousands of dollars in her bank account. Sooner or later, the old woman would die so I could enjoy what was rightfully mine.

I'll admit that her frivolities were already getting on my nerves, so as punishment for not giving in, I started playing games with my friends when we went out to dinner, usually coming up with topics she didn't know, to show her how stupid and inferior she was and that she should be happy and honored to be seen with me in public.

She never said a thing until that last day at the restaurant, when she looked like she was possessed and was rude to my friends by humiliating me in front of everyone.

But of course, I knew she'd just closed a million-dollar deal, and I couldn't just let her go. I went after her at our house, but I'm not very good at making amends. And all because of her, that bitch, I ended up hitting her hard.

That was it. That's all it took for the princess to call Daddy and start a war.

This week, we were supposed to meet and discuss the agreement of our divorce, but unfortunately for her, and fortunately for me, I'll probably attend my lovely wife's funeral.

I set up a three-million-dollar life insurance policy for her. With that amount, I'll have peace of mind forever and work just for fun. The money from the shares I sold and what I took from our joint account was only good for paying off my debts.

But now it's all over. I'll say goodbye to that life of sacrifice and middle-class paying job like that little bitch threw in my face that day.

Mike Howard is about to become a millionaire.

Zoe

CHAPTER TWENTY-SEVEN

HAPPINESS EXISTS and has a first and last name: strawberry ice cream.

The nice gentleman got not just one but two tubs. Now I'm fully committed to the fact that I'll eat one all by myself. Bia usually likes to share both the ice cream and the guilt for giving in to temptation, but today, I'm going to go crazy and eat the whole thing.

I also stayed a little longer there, buying some things for breakfast because, poor thing, Dad doesn't have time for anything else these days. He's been so tired I'm afraid he'll end up getting sick, too.

I take a turn to get to my parent's house, and a small animal, which I believe to be a skunk, chooses to cross the road at that exact moment, almost giving me a heart attack. I stomp on the brakes and watch it until I'm sure the bastard reaches the other side, taking its time as if it doesn't have any worries in life, while my soul, on the other hand, has just enough time to come back to my body.

I go back to driving and listen to the radio station talking about the flu. Jesus, I'm starting to freak out. I cannot think of myself alone but of those who are elderly.

With the amount of travel I do, I'm certain I'll end up getting it. And if that's the case, I won't even be able to see Mom. Her immune system is very fragile due to her cancer treatment, so she can't even think about exposing herself to something like that.

Bia went so far as to say she believes that, if the situation worsens, very soon they will order a country-wide lockdown and even close the borders.

It sounds like something out of a science fiction story, and I hope it's all just scaremongering. I can't afford to stop working. My family, especially my mother's health, depends on me.

There are only two more minutes before I get home. The night is dark; there's not a single star in the sky, so when I see a flash, I find it strange.

First, I think it's fireworks—but it doesn't make any sense; we're far from the Fourth of July.

The closer I get to it, the stronger the uneasiness that spreads through me. When I finally get closer, I scream in horror.

My parents' house is on fire.

I leave everything behind in the car, and as I run, I call 911. "My parents' house is on fire. My mother has cancer; please send someone!"

"Ma'am, what's your name?"

"Zoe Turner. Did you hear what I said? My parents' house is on fire!"

"Please calm down."

"The hell I'm going to calm down! The address is 1014 Peanut Drive."

I drop my phone on the floor and run to the door just as it opens, and my Dad comes out with Mom in his arms. The nurse comes screaming right behind him.

Thank God!

But then I remember Bia.

"Where is Bia, Dad?"

"I don't know if she managed to get out, baby."

"Oh my God, no!"

I run inside but can't get too close to the room Bia is staying in. The heat is unbearable, and I start to feel short of breath.

"Bia!"

"Zoe?"

"Come on, I'm here!"

"I won't make it, Zoe!"

"For God's sake, don't say that. Of course, you will!"

"Get out of the house, Zoe. Take cover!"

"No. I won't leave without you. No way I am leaving without you!"

"I locked him in, Zoe. I managed to lock the bastard inside the room."

"Who? Who are you talking about?"

"Mike. He was the one who set the house on fire. He thought I was you."

I hear the fire department sirens in the distance but don't know if they'll make it in time. I need to save my friend.

I grab a blanket from the only chair that isn't on fire yet, and like I saw in a movie once, I cross to where she is.

"You're crazy, Zoe! Go away! We'll both die! Save yourself!"

"Not without you."

I feel the heat of the fire on my legs but force myself to keep going until her hand takes mine.

We are both crying.

"You are crazy, Zoe! Why are you doing this?"

"I would never leave you."

We start to make our way to the exit, and even though I am dizzy, in pain, and out of breath, I can already see people outside and firemen coming in. But then, like in a nightmare, a heavy beam falls in front of us, and everything turns red. The world is a fireball.

Screams, crying, and sirens confirm I'm still alive. My eyelids flutter as I try to open my eyes, but it's like they're glued together. My legs burn.

Voices come and go. Somehow, I know I'm outside.

I never liked open spaces. It's not agoraphobia, but I prefer places where I feel protected.

They're moving me, and there's an oxygen mask over my face.

I try to recall what happened, but it's all very confusing.

"She's responding!" a voice announces next to me.

"Great! She's too pretty to die young."

"You're kidding, right? Pretty? The woman is beautiful! This is Zoe Turner, the top model!"

I feel a hand on my face, pushing back my hair.

"Jesus, it's really her! I didn't recognize her because of the smoke. She is very lucky that her face wasn't damaged. It would have been a crime if she hadn't managed to escape."

At the mention of the word *fire*, my memory starts to come back.

The fire, my parents. Bia telling me that Mike did it.

Where is my family? Nurse Ann? My friend?

I remember going into the house to try to save her and the beam falling down in front of us. Then, before my vision turned black, the terrified look on the face of the woman who has become one of my cornerstones.

If everyone leaves me, it will be my fault. And as punishment, I will be alone forever.

Christos

CHAPTER TWENTY-EIGHT

BOSTON

I GREW up listening to my mom say that phone calls in the middle of the night are never good news.

This concept of night, for me, is relative. I've always slept just enough. I need only a few hours of sleep to feel energized, so it's not a problem when the phone rings at almost one o'clock in the morning but rather who is calling.

Beau.

When he calls, no matter the time, he always brings with him an ominous vibe that something bad is about to happen. He is a man of few words and never engages in social interactions without a purpose. This is especially true because we spoke twice today, which is a record for both of us.

"What happened?"

"Your girl, Zoe. There was a fire. She is alive but has been hospitalized."

It takes me less than a second to stand, my heart hammering in my chest. "Send me all the information, which hospital, and anything else you can find out. I'm just going to change clothes and be on my way."

As I get dressed, I don't allow any other thoughts to enter my mind besides the fact that she's alive.

I'm used to repressing emotions. It was this self-imposed discipline that kept me from going after her when she left me in Barcelona. But right now, none of my fucking rules apply because nothing is stronger in me than sheer terror.

Minutes later, I leave the hotel room in Boston while texting Yuri about what has happened, and the name of the hospital Beau has just sent me.

I'm not a family member, so to reach her, I'll have to use my influence. From what Beau told me, Zoe's parents were also in the house, which means there's no one else responsible for her. As far as I know, they're all she has in terms of family.

For the first time in years, I have failed to follow any security protocol or plans; I just want to find her.

When I get to the elevator, my phone rings again.

"I have a driver outside your hotel," Beau says, and I don't even ask how he knows where I'm staying.

I'm not the type who usually depends on someone, but at this point, I'm relieved that he's stepped in and taken care of everything. "Tell me what happened."

"The house caught fire; they suspect arson. If that's the case, I already know who is responsible."

"I'll kill him."

"He disappeared; I already sent people to hunt him down. But that's not important now. What matters is that you know that everyone in the house survived."

"All of them? How many were there?"

"The parents and the agent, Bia Ramos."

"How did you find out about the fire?"

"Because I trust my gut. As we agreed, I was going to send protection over to her house starting tomorrow . . . well, today. But something told me to get there sooner. However, by the time my men arrived, the fire department was already there. They couldn't do much else, so they did what they were best at: investigating. They found a van parked outside the house, and before the police got there, they looked for fingerprints. It belongs to—or at least it was driven by—Mike Howard."

"Do you think he found out we did a background check, and that's why he sought revenge?"

"No. He hasn't been informed he's been laid off by the university yet. I believe he would try something, anyway. Most likely, he tried to kill her because he didn't want a divorce. But for now, it's all speculation, and I work with facts."

"How do you know he didn't die, too? You said the van was parked by her parents' house."

"Because one of my men has already consulted with someone from the fire department. It looks like Zoe repeatedly said her husband's name while being rescued. The paramedics thought she was calling him. But if you want my opinion, I think she was trying to inform us that he caused the fire. Anyway, after the fire was contained, they searched the scene, and there were no bodies. Even if he was there, he got away."

"I want him, Beau. Find him, but don't do anything. I will personally finish this matter."

"As for Zoe, you can't know her real condition until you talk to someone in person. From all we know so far, she didn't suffer any serious burns; they were all second-degree."

I close my eyes for a moment. Imagining her hurt is like having a razor opening up my chest, the exact feeling of something tearing me apart from the inside.

"It doesn't matter. She is alive. Everything else is secondary. The only thing I wouldn't be able to give her back is her life. As for all the medical care she needs, she will have it, even if I have to buy a hospital for that."

I hang up the phone and get into the car, which, as he said, was already waiting for me.

I barely get the door closed before my phone rings.

"Christos, it's me," my assistant says. "Your permission to enter the hospital is already cleared. Just say you're her boyfriend. But there's something you need to know. It's very serious. I have information from within the government. This new flu has been spreading worldwide, and people with symptoms have been admitted to the same hospital where Zoe is with her parents and agent."

"And the level of contamination of this virus is very high," I say because I've been reading and following the news. I think the world was not paying attention to the seriousness of the problem until now. But I'm always two steps ahead, and based on what the experts said, I already predicted it wouldn't be just any flu.

"Yes, very high. Deadly, actually, especially for people her parents' age. What I'm trying to say is that the government is going to institute a lockdown on shops and all businesses that are not essential. Zoe's parents will be discharged later today; they didn't suffer anything serious. They were the first to leave the house. But as you may know, her mother is a cancer patient. She will likely need to go back to get medical care soon. I thought about setting up a clinic with everything she needs, but outside of a hospital setting. If isolation is enforced and she's hospitalized, they won't let her husband get close."

I think of my parents, who have been together for over forty years. If Yuri's statement is true and they had to split up, I don't think they would survive. "Do whatever it takes. Hire doctors and nurses exclusively for her."

"What about Zoe?"

"I'm arriving at the hospital now."

"Her condition is not serious, although she has been sedated, but Bia Ramos is in a coma. Even if we arrange for Zoe to be moved to a safe location, her agent will likely have to stay in the hospital. No doctor will discharge her now."

"One thing at a time, Yuri. Provide everything for her parents. I'll take care of the rest."

Christos

CHAPTER TWENTY-NINE

GETTING into the hospital and getting her status is relatively easy. There's almost nothing that money or influence can't buy, and I have both to spare.

Her parents, along with the nurse, will be redirected to a clinic that has been set up especially for Zoe's mother's care.

When I arrive, I'm informed that I still can't see Zoe because she is receiving treatment, so I go to her parents and introduce myself as their daughter's new employer.

What more can I say? That I'm the man who's obsessed with their girl?

Macy and Scott are humble, friendly people. Her mother reminds me of my own mother, someone who can smile even when faced with the greatest of adversities.

She seems physically very fragile, which contradicts her personality. Lucid, she asks me questions about the details of the fire. I don't have all the answers at the moment, but I intend to find out everything.

In addition to trying to kill Zoe, that bastard set fire to the house with two elderly people inside. I hope that what Beau discovered is true and that Mike is still alive, because I personally want to rid the planet of that worm.

Neither of Zoe's parents, nor the nurse, are able to tell me what happened, only that they woke up to Bia's screams telling them to run out of the house. Mike Howard's name isn't mentioned, so I assume they have no idea he's involved.

Interestingly enough, when I explain the need to move them to a private clinic, Zoe's father doesn't look surprised; he only says it would be the best option. Like me, he truly believes in the lethality of the new virus more than the average citizen in the U.S.

People inside the hospital, mainly staff, are already wearing masks, which shows that many high-ranking people knew this virus was more contagious than originally reported. You can't take action that quickly unless a massive security protocol is already orchestrated behind the scenes.

I ask permission in writing to take care of Zoe, and then her mother asks me something that baffles me.

She asks if I am *the man from Barcelona*.

Her dad looks at us confused, so I guess that she only told her mom about us.

I say yes, even though I have no idea if that is a good thing.

Before saying goodbye to them, they ask to talk to the doctor who is treating their daughter. I stay with them.

The doctor explains to us, as Beau has already told me, that the agent, who apparently is also a friend—she was staying at Zoe's parents' house—is in a coma, while Zoe has been sedated only for pain relief.

Neither suffered unmanageable burns; they were second-degree but not deep within the skin, although painful, and the recovery time could be from one to three weeks. Even so, they may leave scars.

I'll have to talk to the doctor alone later. If Zoe's situation isn't as severe, I'll move her from the hospital as soon as possible, as I will with her parents. I won't risk her getting the virus.

Nothing can be done for the agent. I don't believe they would authorize me to move someone in her condition.

As I understand it, the main concern for the medical staff is that both inhaled smoke. In addition to that, Bia Ramos received a strong blow to the head, and that's the reason for her being in a coma.

I mentally file away the information, as I always do, committed to making the necessary arrangements for Bia to get the best possible care, but my thoughts are all on Zoe.

I've rarely ever felt so lost.

It's as if life is forcing me to rip off the pride bandage, I've been wearing, as if I'm receiving a call from above, an awakening.

For two years now, I've been going in circles, keeping my distance, stuck in a true abyss, when I knew all along that there was no chance of burying what had happened between us in the past.

I decide the game is over.

I could have lost her today. She is the one woman to ever mess up my world in a short period of time and make me feel and want more.

I don't know what will happen from now on, but I won't keep my distance anymore.

"Christos, I'd like to speak with you alone," her mother asks after the doctor and Zoe's Dad walk out into the hallway.

"Of course."

She motions to the armchair next to her bed. As soon as I arrived, I arranged for them to be transferred to a private room. "Please sit. I want to talk about Zoe."

"About me being *the man from Barcelona*?" I repeat the words she used.

"Also, that. For now, let me tell you about my girl. First of all, keep in mind that I'm very old, but I'm lucid. Yesterday, I talked with my daughter, and now that you're here, I just put two and two together."

"I don't know if I understand."

"I believe you want to see Zoe right now. So, do I. But from what the doctor said, she's still sedated; we have time. I'll start from the beginning: I've always wanted children, but who knows why God determined that I wouldn't have any of my own—at least, not biological ones. When my husband and I decided to adopt, we thought and evaluated a lot beforehand. We were never rich but rather regular working class, both with jobs from Monday through Friday and humble paychecks. However, we believed that we checked all the right boxes to be called father and mother: plenty of love to give."

"When we first met in Barcelona, Zoe told me she had been rejected from several homes," I tell her, and in fact, that memory serves me well.

I don't know if I have forgotten the details. More likely, I pushed them to the back of my mind in a sort of defensive instinct against the woman who, I now have the courage to admit, hurt not only my pride but also my feelings.

"Yes, we took her in during her preteens, and I swear on all the holiest of holies, I've never seen a sadder look on a child. She was always beautiful, but that wasn't what made me so sure I wanted her for myself; it was the hopelessness on her face. I'm not going to go back in time and recount every detail, because I don't feel emotionally strong enough to do so. It was a difficult time for the three of us until we managed to convince her that we would never give her up."

I give my full attention to the conversation. Hearing Macy's words is like watching a teen movie starring Zoe. She tells me how the girl was afraid to state her wishes, always afraid of not pleasing them and ending up back in the state's care.

"Why did people reject her?"

"Who knows? Probably because they didn't realize parenting someone was a 24/7 job. You can't switch off a child when you get tired of playing with them. You need to pay attention and give love. It requires dedication. But I am telling you this so that I can get to the time you two met in Barcelona. I don't know what happened there. She didn't tell me what happened on the ship nor that she had met anyone. But when she came back, she was deeply depressed. Even the prospect of a new career, which began shortly after she returned, didn't improve her condition. She traveled a lot but locked herself in her room and hardly spoke whenever she was home."

"Do you think I'm the cause?" I ask, confused as hell. "Zoe left me with just a note." It's uncomfortable to share details of our short relationship. I'm not one to confide in anyone, but since the cards are on the table, so be it.

I remember her asking me about whether the money in the envelope was some kind of payment.

Was that possibly the reason she left? Did she think I paid her for the night we had?

No, there had to be more to it. I may have been determined to win her no matter what, but I never treated her like a luxury escort.

"Keep in mind she was only eighteen. She was always mature for her age but still very young." There's no scolding behind her tone. "If you're here after all this time, it's because what happened between you two isn't over yet."

"Not for me."

She nods. "I can't say if the depression was linked to what she experienced in Spain, and I don't even want to get involved in your relationship, but I'm telling this whole story so I can beg you, Mr. Lykaios... if what you want with my daughter is just an adventure, please leave right now."

I open my mouth, but she holds a hand up, stopping me.

"Zoe is much stronger now than she was a few years ago, but she's already experienced too many losses. You are a rich man and also generous. I thank you with all my heart for what you're doing for me, but don't hurt my daughter, or I'll curse you all the days I have left on Earth."

Christos

CHAPTER THIRTY

IT'S three in the afternoon, and Zoe's parents have already been transferred to the clinic that was set up exclusively for them. I also asked Yuri to arrange a property to install them in if they wish to return to a *home*, and to help them get new documentation.

I transferred a large sum of money to Scott's account. They lost everything in the fire, including bank details and credit cards.

I have consulted with the medical team, and there is no change in Bia Ramos' clinical condition. Also, as I suspected, moving her to a private clinic is out of the question.

Now, I'm heading to Zoe's room. I'm finally allowed to see her, even though she's still sedated.

After the revealing conversation with Macy, my head is boiling with information, and I can't come to any conclusions.

Yes, she was . . . she *is* very young, but it couldn't have been just the mix-up over money that made her run away from me.

What, then?

The truth is it doesn't matter anymore. Everything is minor in the face of what has happened, the possibility that, at this moment, she could be dead.

I know that when I cross the threshold, there will be no more masks.

I reach for the bedroom doorknob, but before I can go inside, the doctor responsible for the team that takes care of Zoe and Bia approaches.

"Mr. Lykaios, we need to speak urgently."

"Now?"

"Yes. Three patients who passed away yesterday tested positive for the new virus. If you have the means, I advise you to get Miss Turner away from here as soon as possible."

"But she hasn't woken up yet."

"Yes, I know. But just as you arranged a private clinic for her parents, I think you can do that for Miss Turner as well. The burns she suffered aren't life-threatening—although, perhaps in the near future, she will need corrective surgery on her hand—but none of that is as important as getting her out of here. She can recover at home. I'm sure you can set up home care in record time."

"Will she remain sedated?"

"Only for another day or two, but you should take her out of here today."

I watch him walk away, thinking that, once again, all my plans with Zoe have gone awry. What matters now, however, is making sure she stays safe.

I leave to arrange her transfer to a house Yuri has rented.

There is a team in place now, and the doctor advised me to leave as soon as possible.

Again, I'm standing in front of Zoe's room. At any moment, the personnel who will assist with her transport will arrive, so I take advantage of a few minutes to check her without witnesses.

I open the door and watch her from afar before getting close. Knowing that she survived the fire and seeing her with my own eyes are two completely different things.

The burning in my chest becomes unbearable, making me feel like I'm suffocating.

Fear. I was afraid of losing her.

Some might question that feeling because up until a few days ago, Zoe was still married to someone else. But what the fuck is a piece of paper next to the certainty inside of me that she always belonged to me? Will she always belong to me?

She could have died—the voice repeats in my head—*and then all that would be left are the memories of that night.*

She's still asleep, so I have time to examine her at my leisure.

The bed is elevated at a thirty-degree angle, as the doctors informed me is standard procedure in case of smoke inhalation, even though they have already cleared her nasal passages. Her face doesn't even have a scratch on it; her right hand, resting on the linen sheet, is bandaged, as are her legs, but nothing can destroy her perfection in my eyes.

When I first met her, I thought it was her beauty that attracted me. Now, I realize that there is no way to define what she awakens in me. The feeling of being pulled by a magnet, the sense of souls connecting—things she herself pointed out the night we slept together. It's as if everything between us *should be*. No explanations, no rules. We simply must be.

The bed seems too big for her delicate body. Zoe shouldn't be in a hospital bed, injured, helpless.

A mad desire to wake her up, to prove to myself she's okay, takes hold of me.

Once again, I swear to myself that I will get revenge on Howard. There will be no mercy.

Beau is running an investigation parallel to the police. I'm sure it is much deeper and more efficient, and I'm sure we'll eventually catch him.

With the number of deaths around the world increasing, as well as the number of cases in our country, the new disease is already being treated as a pandemic, and newspapers and sites don't talk about anything else. This pushes what happened at Zoe's parents' house into the background.

Of course, I used my influence to hush up the incident as much as possible, but if the fire had happened at any other time, it would have been talked about in the newspapers for months. Even if they don't know Zoe's ex-husband's whereabouts, the police already suspect his involvement.

They interrogated her parents, and both reported that their daughter was in the process of getting a divorce. Along with that is the fact that the police were unable to locate Howard anywhere, which solidified their suspicions.

What the investigators don't know yet is that they'll never get their hands on the bastard. There is no way to judge and condemn a dead person. Because that's what Mike Howard already is.

Zoe coughs, her face turning a bright, reddish color, but then she's breathing normally again.

Even after she left, when I refused to admit my desire for her anymore, there wasn't a day when, not even for a brief moment, the blonde goddess didn't occupy my mind.

I caress her face with the back of my hand, and it feels like I'm getting fresh oxygen in my lungs. For the past two years, I have been in denial about how much I want her. I prefer to view that feeling as a grudge. I'm not used to losing anything, and Zoe's abrupt departure from Barcelona took me by surprise.

All the theories I'd created about her before were shattered when we met in my New York office. She wasn't frivolous, nor did she simply leave because she'd changed her mind.

What happened between us was neither a figment of my imagination nor a one-sided attraction. Every kiss and moan we shared that night was real and filled with desire.

And now, after almost losing her, I've decided that I'm no longer willing to deny myself anything regarding her.

I want everything, and it will be with her.

As if my wishes are heard, her eyes open and she stares at me. "Christos, what happened?"

Then realization dawns on her face, and she screams in pure terror.

Zoe

CHAPTER THIRTY-ONE

A Few Days Later

THEY SEDATED ME AGAIN. I know this because, through my sleep haze, I heard a man talking to Christos. I didn't spend the last few days completely unconscious, even though I couldn't make out what people were saying.

I was terrified when I saw him in the hospital. My confused mind believed that no one but me had survived the fire, but now I remember I saw my parents leaving, as did nurse Ann.

And what about Bia? Where is my friend?

I open my eyes and struggle to sit up. I try balancing myself by resting my hand on the bed, and I cry out in pain. The skin is tight and burns. It's not bandaged anymore, and when I finally see the back of it, I start to feel dizzy.

I pull back the sheets and look down at my legs. There are also no more bandages, just a few scars from the burning, but smaller than the one on my hand and painless.

Suddenly, something crosses my mind. I reach up to touch my face but stop and get out of bed to try to see myself in the mirror.

Jesus Christ, please don't tell me my face got burned. I need my image so I can pay my mother's medical bills.

My God!

When I stand up, however, my legs weaken and bend.

A nurse appears, and when she sees me on the floor, she rushes to help me back up. I immediately realize that, even though she is dressed in white, we are not in a hospital but in a house of sorts.

"Darling, I only left for a moment. I'm very sorry!"

"It wasn't your fault. I shouldn't have tried to get up." I struggle to speak, but my voice sounds like sand in my throat, and I cough.

The woman is very strong because she easily lifts me up. After helping me get back to bed, she asks how I'm feeling.

I don't know how to answer that. Instead, I ask where I am.

"We're at Mr. Lykaios's house. I don't know if it belongs to him, but he brought us here four days ago."

"Four days? And he . . . *um* . . . Mr. Lykaios stayed here, too?"

"Yes. In fact, for the last forty-eight hours, no one has been able to leave. It was officially decreed that the world is going through a pandemic, and the governor, in addition to setting a curfew for after five in the afternoon, asked people not to leave their homes, except those who work in essential services."

"What? Curfew? We can't leave the house? Where are my parents?" I feel restless again.

"Safe, in a clinic. Even before the lockdown was enacted, there were rumors of an absurd increase in the number of cases. It seems that Mr. Lykaios saw what was coming. That's why you're here, too. It was on the advice of the staff who attended you. No one should be going to the hospital except for serious emergencies, as the risk of contamination is very high. Now, please try to calm down. Are you in pain?"

"No," I say, looking at my hand again. "Did I hurt my face?"

"No, my love. I don't know exactly what happened to you. What I heard is that your house was on fire. You got very lucky. You were only left with this little scar on your hand, which a good surgeon will be able to fix."

"It's not about vanity or anything. I need my face to make a living. My family depends on me."

"Oh!" She looks startled. "I know who you are, of course, but I didn't know that you worked to help your family. Anyway, stay calm. Nothing worse than that happened."

I work up the courage to ask what I need to, but the fear of the answer makes me nauseous. "When I passed out during the fire, there was a woman with me. She is my agent and my best friend; her name is Bia Ramos. Do you know where she is?"

"I don't know the details. Just that she's still hospitalized."

"Can you please help me change my clothes? I need to find a phone and find out where my friend is."

"I don't know if I should. Better talk to the doctor first."

"Christos . . . is Mr. Lykaios here?"

"Yes, I believe he's in his office on the first floor."

"I need to talk to him, but maybe I need a shower first."

"We'll give you a bath, as best as we can, to protect your injuries. Believe me when I say that the feeling of water on them will be very painful."

It is very hard, but with the help of the nurse, I take a shower with my legs hanging out of the tub.

She washes my hair for me because of the burn; at least for now, my hand is useless.

It's the only physical pain I'm feeling. Actually, it's more of a burning sensation. But nothing compares to what's making my chest tighten.

Bia alone in the hospital? Why didn't he bring her here too?

"Want help getting down?"

"Yes, please. Take me to Mr. Lykaios."

My steps are uncertain because I feel weak. I'm also afraid of using my hand on the banister for support and hurting myself even more. The stairs are endless, and it takes us about five minutes to go down all the way.

When we finally arrive at the bottom, a very angry-faced Christos stares at me. "Zoe, what the hell do you think you're doing?"

Because of my natural shyness and being used to running away when confronted, I back up a step, which causes me to lose my balance. To prevent the fall, I use my injured hand to grab the banister and cry out in distress. The pain is so intense that tears well up in my eyes.

Seconds later, arms lift me. Without a word, he walks with me into a room and closes the door.

"Put me down," I beg, trying to save some dignity.

"No."

"I don't want to fight."

"I'm not fighting, just keeping you from dying."

Damn controlling man!

Knowing there's no chance I'll win this battle, I let myself be carried away in silence until he settles me on a comfortable couch. But he doesn't walk away. He sits on the edge of it—an almost impossible task since he's huge—and examines my injured hand.

I shudder at the touch.

He notices but doesn't let go. "Don't do that anymore," he says. "You could have fallen down the stairs."

"I needed to come talk to you." I don't look up at him because, even in pain, his closeness makes my body heat up. "Nurse Beth couldn't tell me what happened to Bia. I know my parents are fine, and I really appreciate what you did for them, but now I want to hear about everything else."

"Calm down."

"I can't. I need to know where Bia is, Christos. Please tell me the truth."

"Bia's in a coma."

Christos

CHAPTER THIRTY-TWO

SHIT! That's not how I planned to tell her, but I'm not known for sugarcoating things.

"Tell me everything."

I was expecting tears, so it surprises me when Zoe's face looks serene instead. This is definitely not the woman I was with in Spain, but it's fascinating all the same.

At our meeting and later at the hospital, I assumed she would need to be taken care of, perhaps based on what happened in the past. Now, it only takes me two seconds to understand that no, Zoe is sensitive and maybe has been through a lot more shit in her young life than most people, but she's not a fragile little flower.

I get up and sit on the chair opposite her because the desire to touch her is too much, but the timing is not right. "I'll tell you everything, but first, tell me how you're feeling."

"I have no pain, just the wound on the hand that bothers me a little."

"From what I've gathered from the doctors, you both passed out inside where the fire was burning. A beam fell and hit your agent in the head."

"So, it's serious?"

"I think any blow to the head calls for care."

Again, no tears, but the uninjured hand clenches into a fist. "It was Mike... my ex-husband."

I try not to show any surprise at the confirmation. Zoe has no idea, but I already know everything about him. "How sure are you?"

"Bia told me. I went out to buy something. My hair was hidden, and I was wearing baggy clothes and a mask because my mother asked me to."

"*Mask?*"

"Yes. The nurse told me that we are locked up here because of the virus. Mom told me that my Dad predicted this months ago. He's a Virgo with a Capricorn rising," she says as if that makes any sense to me, "so he's always prepared for the worst."

"You shouldn't have left the house alone so late."

"I don't usually do that, but I had a craving," she says, her cheeks flushing. "Maybe I shouldn't say this because you're my new employer, but the truth is, I was treating myself to a tub of ice cream."

"Because of the meeting? Did that make you anxious?"

"That too, but mostly because of what had happened that last week. As I told you, I filed for divorce. I'd already started the divorce process with a lawyer."

"I want to know about that later."

She doesn't respond, and I don't insist.

"So, tell me more about the night of the fire. You'll have to give a statement to the police, but I have spoken to my lawyers, and they will arrange it through a video call."

"Is the spread of this virus really that serious?"

"It was worse than anyone could've imagined. Many infected people didn't realize they had the virus, so it spread quickly. Research facilities around the world are in a race against time to manufacture a vaccine. Now, let's go back to the night of the fire."

"I went out for about half an hour. It took me longer than I intended because I couldn't find the flavor I wanted... God, that seems so futile now, next to what happened."

"Continue."

"I stayed there longer than I intended. When I got back, the glow in the sky told me right away that something was wrong. I called 911 and ran into my parents' house. They were already coming out onto the front porch, and Dad was struggling to carry my mother in his arms. Ann, the nurse, followed close behind, but there was no sign of Bia."

I try to swallow down the tension and hatred I've been holding back for days because I don't want her to know I have plans for that bastard Mike.

"I got into the house. It was very hot, and there was fire everywhere. Bia was screaming that it was Mike and that she had trapped him in the bedroom. As I understand it, he confused the two of us because I left the house in my friend's car, wearing oversized clothes. Now she's in a coma because of me."

"No, Zoe, you couldn't have foreseen that. How could you? Unless . . . wait. Had he threatened you before?"

"No. Not threatened," she says, looking uncomfortable.

"So no one could have suspected that he would go to that extreme. I found out he had been snooping around."

"He was?"

"Yes. There was a van near your parents' house. If he hadn't attacked then, he would have done it when you were all asleep." I feel my jaw tighten at the possibility. The anger that seizes me is immense.

"My God!" She covers her face with her hands, and the sight of the wound makes me angry. Lockdown or not, I'm going after the bastard.

"You shouldn't have entered the house, Zoe."

"Bia couldn't reach the exit from the hallway. How could I leave her there, alone? I did what I saw in a movie: I wrapped a blanket around my body and walked through the fire. I protected both of us and we were just about to leave when the beam fell, I think. But I didn't realize it had hit her head."

"You said your ex-husband didn't make threats before," I repeat, trying to understand what drove that jerk to go this far. But the word *ex-husband* scratches my throat like acid.

"Yes. What you saw on my face, the beating I took, was the first time it happened. That was the night I told him that our marriage was over."

Hearing her say that makes a lot of confused emotions escalate inside me.

She is single, or at least, she no longer considers herself married.

But she *was* married.

Somehow, what happened between us wasn't strong enough because she replaced me while I was stuck in time.

I get up and walk to the window, turning away from her. "It wasn't your fault. Neither the aggression nor the fire. It wasn't something that could have been predicted."

"But after he assaulted me, I should have stayed in a hotel. I ended up putting my family at risk."

"Rehashing the past doesn't change anything," I say, turning back to face her. That applies to both of us, of course. And I'm not just referring to the recent past.

I think she understands that because she opens her mouth, but before she says anything, I continue.

"As for your friend, her life is not at risk, but unfortunately, she cannot be moved from the hospital. The biggest concern now is the virus. But as soon as the doctors clear her, I'll arrange for you to meet."

"You mean bring her here?"

"Or I can arrange a residence for you two. I don't think it's a good idea for you to stay with your parents on account of Macy's health, but the final decision is yours."

"I thought no one could leave . . . I mean, I thought we'd stay here."

"I can't stop my life. You are not a prisoner, but you have no deadline to leave. I only ask that if you are to leave again, this time, let me know face-to-face."

Zoe

CHAPTER THIRTY-THREE

"MOM?"

"Zoe, my sweet baby, I can't believe you're awake! I've been calling every day."

"Ask Dad to connect to video call. I want to see you."

"I'm all disheveled. You're going to be scared."

Against all odds, I start to laugh. Macy has always been very vain. Even though cancer took away almost half of her weight, she makes a point of keeping her growing hair tidy. She also never forgets her lipstick.

After Christos left me, the nurse came to see me with a phone in a box. My previous line was transferred to the new device. The man simply thought of everything.

Being with him again is like riding a roller coaster—exciting and a little scary. His mood swings confuse me. When I saw him, he gave me a lecture and then seemed to want to stay by my side. A few minutes later, he said I could move if I wanted to.

The Zoe he knew would run off without a second thought, but that's no longer how I face my problems.

We have to talk, but now is not the best time. However, I don't intend to go anywhere. When Bia is released from the hospital because

God willing, it will be soon, I'll ask him to bring her here. As for me, I won't budge until we clear up everything about the past.

I'm tired of being afraid to live.

I left Barcelona because I thought he was involved in the incident with Pauline. But if I'm being honest, I would probably have run away when I got that money in the envelope, anyway.

Not anymore. I almost died and lost my family and friend because of that sick man I married. The time has come to face adversity like an adult.

Dad shows up behind Mom on camera, waving.

"I love you both. I can't express how much. Forgive me for what happened."

They are so old. So fragile.

"We only found out that it might have been Mike who set our house on fire when the policeman came to interrogate us at the hospital. You're not to blame for anything, sweetie. If Bia hadn't been so smart, the worst could have happened."

"I promise I'll work hard to give you another home, Mom."

The insurance is supposed to cover the damage caused by the fire, but as the house has already been mortgaged twice, it won't make any difference to my parents. My goal is to pay off their debts and buy them a new home.

"It doesn't matter, Zoe. Houses can be replaced, but lives cannot. I would like to hear news of Bia. I'm worried about leaving her alone in that hospital."

"Me too, Mom, mostly because she has no family but us. I plan to call Miguel later to confirm that, because if it's not so, we need to let whoever they are know."

"How are the burns?"

"They were superficial. The one on the hand might leave a mark, but I can correct it with surgery. And you?"

"We and Ann had nothing but a little smoke inhalation. Our only concern now is your and Bia's health."

"What about your . . . *um* . . .other pains?" I hate the word *cancer*.

"I think I've been through so much emotionally these past few days that God spared me everything else. I hardly needed the medication."

"That's great! What about Daddy?"

"I'm fine too, sweet pea," he says, showing his face again. "Now, you take care, okay? And let us know about Bia as soon as you hear anything."

I end the call and google the number of the hospital where Beth said my friend is.

They take a long time to answer, and when they do, it takes a good ten minutes before they tell me that her condition has not changed.

I need to call Miguel later. He's probably elsewhere in the world, but he'll want to hear about our friend.

I don't see Christos anymore. Yesterday, I had dinner alone in my room because the nurse told me that Mr. Lykaios was locked up in his office and didn't want to be disturbed.

I understood that as *keep your distance,* and like a good girl, I obeyed.

But today, I've decided that I won't stay in the suite anymore. If my presence bothers him, why did he bring me here? Maybe he doesn't want to talk, but I do.

I feel better this morning and no longer have a hard time with my burned hand. The problem is if I hit the back of it by accident. So yeah, then it burns like hell.

Along with the nurse, a doctor is staying on the first floor of the house. But he said yesterday that since I don't need any more close monitoring, Beth is enough for me. Apparently, hospitals need all the professional help they can get as the virus keeps spreading.

This morning, I called my mother again and asked about Mike's disappearance.

She didn't know anything about it either. When she tried contacting his mother, her old friend, no one answered. Or rather, she answered but said she didn't want to talk to anyone in our family.

The police must have looked for her, of course. It's the only reason she could be angry, as I've only met her once. She didn't even attend my wedding at the registry office.

It's only today that the memory of what happened that night of the fire comes to light.

Mike probably went mad. Does he hate me so much he's willing to destroy his own life just to get revenge because I left him?

I've never considered myself a violent person, but he shouldn't feel safe if he shows up and I have a gun in my hand.

I walk to the bedroom door, glad my legs are steadier now. I intend to walk around the huge garden of the house. I've put on one of the dresses that are in the closet, and it surprised me that it was exactly my size.

God, he's thought of everything.

Why take care of me if, now that we are together, he seems to want to stay as far away as possible?

I shake my head, confused. I have no idea what these mixed messages he sends me mean.

I've barely stepped out of the bedroom when my phone rings. I left it on the bedside table, so I return to get it.

"Hello?"

"Zoe Turner?"

"Yes. Who's speaking?"

"My name is Nick Irving. I'm a police detective and a friend of Bia Ramos."

Zoe

CHAPTER THIRTY-FOUR

OH, *the fuck buddy!*

I feel my cheeks heat up. "Yes, now I know who you are. If you're calling to find out about Bia—"

"No, I've already managed to see her. I'm with the Miami Police, but when I heard what happened, I flew to Boston."

"And they let you in?"

"I used persuasive methods," he says cryptically.

"I'm so worried about her, Mr. Irving."

"The worst is over, Miss . . ."

"You can call me Zoe."

"Okay. You can call me Nick. The doctors told me she's in an induced coma now, Zoe." I sit up in bed, thanking God in my thoughts. "There was no serious trauma. Her brain isn't even swollen anymore."

"Oh God!" I groan but regret it two seconds later. "I'm sorry, it's just that I'm very touchy about hospitalizations, especially when they involve loved ones. Bia is my best friend."

"She also speaks very highly of you."

"Thank you so much for calling me, Nick. I was in agony without news about her."

"It's good to know you feel calmer, but that's not why I called you."

"No?"

"Nope. Bia asked me to look into a financial settlement for an accident. Apparently, the indemnified party claimed that they didn't get enough for the victim's treatment, in this case, a little girl named Pauline Lambert. Does that make sense?"

"Yes."

"The deal was for a million dollars."

"What? That's not possible. They were always so poor. Ernestine... Pauline's mother still lives that way."

"Yes, I know. I'm a detective, Zoe—almost like a sniffer dog. The moment I feel something is not right, I don't stop until I know everything. I know how she and her daughter lived, and there's a reason for that. Your friend's mother handed all the money she got to a boyfriend so he could invest it, but the guy disappeared, leaving them with nothing."

"Jesus Christ! Why would she do something like that?"

"If you want my honest opinion, she never intended to use that money for her daughter's treatment. She thought the indemnity was a kind of lottery ticket. And there's more: the Lykaios family wasn't even obligated to provide any money. The accident wasn't their fault. It was Ernestine's boyfriend who was high and driving the vehicle with your friend in it. That was the cause of the accident. He died instantly. Even the person Bia asked me to investigate, Christos, was injured as well. He broke a leg and was hospitalized when they thought he had a concussion."

I feel my stomach turn. After I met him again, I already suspected that Christos wasn't the kind of person Ernestine had painted him to be. The story didn't happen as she had said, but I didn't imagine it to be something so sordid.

"I don't even know what to say. If her boyfriend died, who got away with the money, then?"

"Another one. Apparently, the woman has bad taste in men. I don't know what this man, Christos, means to you, dear, but if you have any doubts about his character, you can go and live your happiness in peace. He did much more for your friend than he needed to. Some say he had no obligation at all."

"If he wasn't to blame, why did he offer the deal?"

"My guess is, first of all, because both he and his parents are honorable people and have enough money saved to provide for several generations to come. Besides, even though they weren't at fault, it wouldn't be good for the Lykaioses to have their name linked with an accident. In any case, they did much more than they should have. If your friend spent her life after the accident in need of anything, the only person to blame for that was her mother."

"Thanks again, Nick. You have no idea how much you helped."

"You can return the favor by keeping me informed of Bia's condition. It's not often I can up and leave everything here in Florida, so I don't know when I'll be able to see her again."

"Don't worry about that. As soon as I know something, I will call you. Is this your number?"

"Yes. Well, I have to go. Take care, Zoe."

"You too."

"Just one more thing. When the cops find your . . . your ex-husband, eh?"

"Yes."

"When the cops find him, I intend to keep a close eye on everything and make sure he never sees the sunlight again."

After he hangs up, I can't get out of bed. There is so much information to process, especially regarding Pauline's suffering.

A million dollars!

More than enough money for my friend to enjoy her life comfortably.

There is something far more serious that I need to correct, however.

Christos.

I judged and condemned him without even giving him a chance to explain.

When I asked him if the money he left for me in Barcelona was a payment for our night together, he told me not to offend both of us by saying something like that. And now, with Nick's call, I realize that I wasted two years of our lives sad and blaming him for something he didn't do.

There is no guarantee we would still be together now, of course, but we would at least have enjoyed that summer.

I leave the bedroom, determined to clear up our story once and for all.

I want a second chance for both of us, and I'll do whatever I can to get it.

The office door is closed, as usual, but I can hear music inside.

A saxophone.

He mentioned once, at our only date in Spain, that he played the instrument—usually when he was stressed.

The soft melody takes over the house, calming the anxious beat of my heart. In a sort of trance, I walk towards the sound. It's almost like a calling.

The music gets louder as I approach. I don't know if he wants to see me, but we've spent too much time apart. I feel hungry for him after what I found out today, guilt-free.

I look down at my feet, working up the courage to touch the doorknob. I take a deep breath and slowly open the door.

I lift my head, and he's playing with his back to me, apparently lost in his own world. I feel like an intruder and turn to leave.

"Don't go."

In my head, it's like a replay of when we first met, as if life is allowing us a fresh start.

"I'm sorry for interrupting you," I say, watching him place the saxophone on top of an armchair. "No, it's a lie. I don't regret coming in. I've been away too long, Christos. I want you."

Christos

CHAPTER THIRTY-FIVE

I'VE WAITED a long time for this.

The time when I would make her mine again.

I know that despite what she said, she's nervous, but she's also turned on. Her eyes sparkle and her cheeks have a brighter shade of pink.

I get closer, overwhelmed by her beauty. "You're perfect."

Zoe shakes her head and raises her burnt hand. "Not anymore."

"You will always be perfect for me."

"I don't usually believe compliments. People seem to say what we want to hear, but I feel beautiful next to you."

We are close but not touching.

"You said you want me. Taste me."

"I don't know how to seduce anyone."

"Just breathe, Zoe. Just one breath from you makes me horny."

She glues our bodies together, then closes her eyes for a few seconds. "Just like last time."

"What?"

"The same tingle. The shivers. Being close to you is like being able to touch the sun, Christos."

I can't resist moving my mouth down the silky skin of her face. Soft and feminine. Her fragrance...

She places her hand on my chest and, like me, breathes in my scent. At that moment, we are two animals, male and female, recognizing their partner.

A healthy hand comes to my face.

"I remember everything from that night. I wanted to forget, but I couldn't," she says.

"I won't let you forget. This time, I'm going to mark you so deeply that you won't be able to leave."

I take her mouth in a needy kiss, even more urgent than the one we shared in my office.

Licking, sucking.

An erotic, wanton, immoral contact.

Soon, kisses are no longer enough; I want to feel her skin.

I want to see and touch her tits, her pussy, her ass. I want to taste her with my tongue and my teeth. Hear her groans and screams for more.

I pick her up and head upstairs to the room I'm staying in.

After I lay her down, I take a step back, my eyes devouring her sexy body, covered by a light dress.

She doesn't seem willing to wait, so she comes to me. She bites my chin and runs her finger along the collar of my shirt. She opens a button and kisses the patch of skin there, then bites once more.

My cock is hard as steel, and I find it difficult to let her explore.

"I missed you so much," she says.

Uninhibited now, she opens the rest of the buttons. But because she does it with one hand, it takes time, so I take the opportunity to watch her.

"Look at me, Zoe."

"I dreamed of touching you," she says. She finally gets rid of the shirt.

"I can't allow that today. I can't take it easy or wait. I'm dying to feel that tight pussy sheltering me."

I run a finger along the neckline of her dress and then run my tongue along the valley of her breasts.

"Oh..."

"Too much fabric." I pull the garment over her head, and she lifts her arms to help me.

She's only in her underwear, her pointed nipples begging for my tongue. I lean over and take one between my lips.

"Ahhhhhhhh..."

I suck harder, letting my teeth graze her, and she leans against me.

"Bed. I don't want to hurt you." I sit her on the edge, my legs out. I pull off her panties and breathe in her woman's scent.

She screams at the contact of my stubble on her sensitive clit, which emerges from between her luscious, horny lips.

"I want this honey running down my chin."

I part her thighs and lick her pussy.

I suck on her clit and prepare her for me, my middle finger playing in her wet heat.

She tries to back away, restless, and eager. I know she's close to coming. She's delicious and sensitive.

A little later, she lets me know she's coming, but even when her pleasure fills my mouth, I don't stop.

It's not a choice. I can't stop. Her taste is the best delicacy in the world.

I have to force myself to get up and take off the rest of my clothes. Zoe is still surrendering to her own climax, a little disconnected from the world.

Like the first time we had sex, a visceral desire drives me to possess her over and over again.

She opens her eyes, and her gaze on my naked body doesn't make it any easier for me to restrain my hard-on.

"I don't want to use a condom. I'm clean."

"Me too, but I don't take the pill. There was no reason to."

"I'll be careful, but I want to feel your wet flesh around my cock. I want you to feel every vein opening you up."

"You're going to kill me if you keep saying these things."

I move between her legs, spreading them wide. I lick her clit one more time because I can't resist, but I can't wait to be inside her either.

"I'm dying to feel you in me."

I brush my cock at her pleasure point, and she moans.

"Please."

I put just the head into her, and watching my erection part her pink flesh, I sink all the way into her.

We both scream. My body is tense as I slowly step forward to re-enter her narrow walls.

I push hard, and she lifts her hips, all female, hot, needy.

Zoe is on fire beneath me, feverish, begging, sucking on my nipples, ordering me to go harder.

She holds me inside her, not just physically.

It was like that from the start. I was in her; I've always been in her.

I focus on our bodies, as I can't name what we are or feel.

I push harder and feel her stretching to accommodate me. She's so hot, and her muscles pulsing around me are robbing me of my wits.

"I'm crazy about you, Zoe," I say, pushing harder. "I haven't been with anyone else since you left because no one else would satisfy me. It's just that pussy and your horny moans and that beautiful face that I want."

My words seem to trigger something in her. She goes wild, her legs closing around my waist, pulling me in for a harder fuck. I speed up my thrusts, and she asks for more.

The sensation of our luscious bodies coming together is erotic as fuck, driving me into an even greater state of madness.

I fuck her deep and fast, and she howls, coming in constant spasms.

She squeezes and releases my cock inside her body, and I'm hallucinating, out of control, licking everywhere my tongue reaches, needing every piece of her.

I pump into her a few more times without restraint. I wanted to prolong this delicious torture to infinity, but when my cock thickens even more, heavy, dying to pour itself into her, I know I've reached my limit.

I massage her clit, wanting to drag her with me. "Come," I whisper, nibbling at her earlobe, and she does, calling my name.

I pull out of her and kneel between her legs. I pump my hand around my cock, and then my orgasm hits with the force of a wild gallop.

I look at my cum, splattered on her breasts and abdomen.

I lower myself onto her body, leaning on my elbows.
She spreads her thighs farther to accommodate me.
"You're mine, Zoe."
"I never doubted that, Christos. From that first night, it has always been you. I love you."

Christos

CHAPTER THIRTY-SIX

"TELL ME ABOUT YOU. This thing between the two of us is crazy. I feel like I know you deeply, but at the same time, like I don't know anything. Back in Spain, you didn't give me much information about yourself."

"Why did you leave? I know that what happened between us was just as intense for you."

"How couldn't it be? You were my first." She looks away. "My *only one*."

"What?"

"I don't want to discuss this in detail right now, but Mike and I . . . We've never . . . Please, let's not ruin everything by bringing him into it. It's enough to say that my marriage was never consummated."

I want her to tell me more about it, but I let it go. However, I wouldn't be myself if I didn't investigate what I need to know. "I'll talk about myself. But if we're starting over, I need to understand why you left, Zoe. This is how my mind works: organizing one room before going into another."

"I need to get dressed. It's a serious subject, and I don't want to talk about it naked."

I reach out and turn on the lamp.

She holds the sheet against her body as she gets up. I stare at her without turning away. We both know that, after tonight, even better than before, I know every piece of her body, every curve, because I did a study on my goddess.

Looking embarrassed but paradoxically, with defiant eyes, she drops the fabric, allowing me to see her.

My dick reacts. "Are you teasing me?"

"No," she says, but I know she's lying because her nipples are hard.

"Want to talk or fuck?"

"You said you wanted to clarify . . ."

"The past can wait a little longer." I stand up, and her throat moves when she sees my arousal.

I move my hand on my dick, and she follows every move attentively.

"Kneel down, Zoe. I want to fuck your mouth."

Obediently, she does as I say. But I'm surprised when, after just licking the head of my cock, she takes me deep.

The feeling of her hot tongue, her soft, hungry mouth engulfing me, is so good that I'm afraid I can't stand it.

I never let others hold the reins during sex, but seeing her being brave enough to take the initiative is turning me on.

I thrust my hips forward, and she gasps, but soon enough, she gets the hang of it.

"Just like that. Take me whole, Zoe. You suck it really good."

I caress her face, seeing my naked woman swallowing my cock. I pinch her nipple, and she sucks me harder.

I reach my limit.

"I'm going to come. Relax your throat. I want to see you drinking me, love. Swallow it all."

I hold her face and go deeper. Once, twice, three times, before I pour myself into the warmth of her mouth.

I close my eyes for a second, the intensity of the orgasm knocking me out of orbit.

I bend down and pick her up, placing her in my lap. "You're not going anywhere anymore, my Zoe. You should never have gone anywhere."

It's already morning, and now I see we were pretty optimistic to think we could have any serious conversation in our first forty-eight hours together.

We didn't leave the room except to eat. I took the opportunity to dismiss the nurse because the doctor had already left.

Zoe left our room to say goodbye to her, and the shyness of realizing what Beth would think made me see how young she still is.

Now, with the house just for us, I make some pasta while she watches me from a stool by the kitchen island.

"Tell me why you left. The serious subject you said we would talk about."

"It wasn't because of the money you left in the envelope, although it crossed my mind... Anyway..."

"I would never offend a woman like that."

"I know that now, but I'd only known you for a very short time. To be honest, I still don't know you." She brushes a strand of hair out of her face. "What I'm trying to say is, yes, I was offended by the money, but I would have left anyway after what I found out."

"Let's clear up the money issue. I was going to buy that fleet anyway, which made me, in a way, your employer. You didn't get paid for the time you worked there. You were in a foreign country, after all the shit you'd been through, and penniless. I didn't want you to stay with me because you had to but because you chose to. That money, despite being more than stated in your contract, was a security for you."

"I ended up using it anyway," she says, cheeks red. "I wouldn't have been able to leave if I hadn't. But I'm not sure I understood what you said."

"You said you didn't know me well, Zoe. The opposite is also true. I figured that everything that happened between us was mutual but there could come a time when you would want to leave, and you were too shy to talk to me."

"Since you're clearing up a few points, let me do that too, Christos. I was very young..."

"You still are."

"Yes, but I knew what I wanted when I agreed to be with you. I would never let a man touch me against my will. It never crossed my mind that money was security for me. I've never had a serious boyfriend. And as I said before, that wasn't what made me leave but rather an error in judgment."

I drop the knife I'm using to cut the tomatoes and approach her. I'm not easily surprised. "You misjudged me?"

"You introduced yourself as Xander Megalos. That morning, when I called you Xander to your maid, she corrected me, saying that you went by Christos Lykaios. I had heard your name many times in one of the foster homes I lived in. I went through several, as I told you, but in one in particular, there was a little girl. She was quadriplegic after a serious car accident. Her name was Pauline Lambert."

Ice spreads across my chest. I know who she's talking about. How could I forget?

Tears run down her cheeks, and I want to comfort her, but I don't know if that's what she wants.

"Her mother, Ernestine, painted you as the devil himself. The man responsible for the accident was drugged..."

"What?"

"Let me finish, please. She repeated every day that, because of you, my best friend, my only friend at that time, couldn't walk or sit up, among other horrible things that I don't want to remember. At the time, I had recently lost my mother. It was already the third temporary home I'd stayed in, and Pauline and I built a very strong bond. I ran laps without wanting to, stayed in the rain for a little while, and jumped on one foot just because she couldn't do any of that. It was for her that I became a model. That was her dream, the last request she made when I left her house. Remember the day we met?"

"You were taking pictures."

"Yes, with a little doll in my hand, symbolizing her. I loved her with all my heart. In return, I hated you, the man who hurt my friend. But even when I found out your real name, I didn't want to believe it, so I went to Ernestine's house. She repeated the whole story she had told me when Pauline died."

"She died?"

"Yes, at a very young age. Right after Macy adopted me."

I run my hands over my face.

Holy crap. I would never have imagined such a thing.

I walk to the stove to turn it off. "If you're here with me, I assume you already know the whole truth."

"I know, and that's why I made a decision, Christos. When we first got together and I found out who you were, I thought fate was mocking me. Now, I think differently. I believe we met because that's how it's supposed to be. I'm not asking for anything because I'm not completely free yet, but I'm not leaving this time. If this thing between us ends, you'll be the one having to say goodbye to me."

Christos

CHAPTER THIRTY-SEVEN

HER WORDS KEEP HAMMERING in my head.

If this thing between us ends, you'll be the one having to say goodbye to me.

Destiny. Choices.

Leave everything in the hands of fate?

No, we are past that.

Decisions. That's the central point now.

We went our separate ways, then around the world. In the end we found ourselves where we were two years ago. This time, hopefully, with a different outcome.

"I'm Greek, as you already know." I begin by giving her what she asked. Zoe is right. When we first met, in my arrogance, I didn't share anything about myself because I thought we would have time for that later. So I continue, "I am an only child. My parents have been married for over forty years and moved to the United States when I was just three. I worked for a good part of my life between London, New York, and California."

"I love California."

"I thought your dream was to be a farmer."

She lifts her head from my chest. "You remember that?"

"I do remember."

She looks uncomfortable and changes the subject. "Where in California?"

"My house?"

"Yes."

"The main one is in Sausalito, near San Francisco, but I also have other places in the country. New York, Chicago . . . My job demands a lot of travel, and I don't like hotels." That's something Beau and I have in common. We both own properties across the country so we don't have to stay in hotels.

"I understand. They are so impersonal." She smiles. "I always miss my pillow."

"Your pillow?" It's only now that I realize I'm thirsty to know every little thing about her. No newspaper or research could have given me what is part of her secret world.

She smiles again and nods her head. "Yes. I have one in the shape of a boomerang, and I can't sleep well without it. What other fields do you work in besides fashion?"

"I'd have to get my notebook. Sometimes I even get lost. I have several companies, but most are linked to fashion."

"Did you add the exclusivity clause because you wanted me back?" she asks pointblank.

"I don't know how to forgive people, Zoe. To be blunt, I told myself I wanted you around but didn't give myself a real reason."

"To get revenge."

"Perhaps."

"When we first met two years ago, I didn't know what you wanted from me. I wanted you, but I thought it was impossible for a man like you to be with an inexperienced, unsophisticated girl like me. You charmed me, Christos, and I became very depressed when I thought you were the one who hurt my friend."

"I wasn't to blame for the accident, Zoe, but I'm also not a saint."

"What does that mean?"

"That I'll go to hell, but I'll find Mike Howard. And then, I will punish him for what he did to you."

"Punish in what way?"

"You don't want to know, baby. Just keep one thing in mind: I never forget or forgive."

"You forgave me."

"There was nothing for me to forgive. What happened was a misunderstanding. You were wrong to leave without asking me my side of the story first, but as your mother said when we spoke, you were too young. I don't have that excuse. I blame my Greek pride for never going after you."

"My marriage was a mistake."

"Because you didn't love him?"

"That too, but mostly because I never forgot about you. And I hated myself for it. Even though I thought you were to blame for Pauline's accident, I wanted you."

"Then why did you get married? I mean, dating, I get it, but marriage is a very definite step."

"I could blame my youth for that, too, but it happened less than a year ago, so it's not a good excuse. The truth is, I was vulnerable." She shakes her head from side to side. "If it were the other way around, it would break my heart."

"What?"

"Seeing you married to another woman."

"Why?"

"Because I knew I got married for all the wrong reasons, but not you. That's not part of who you are, Christos. The day you marry a woman, I think she will be yours forever."

"Yes, it's true." Like my parents, I know that when I decide on a woman, she will be the only one for me.

"Mike and I . . . we've never been intimate."

"Because he was promiscuous?"

"How do you know that?"

"I told you, Zoe. I'm not a saint. I investigated him a little when I found out you married him, but when I saw your face that day, the way the bastard had hurt you, I asked for a deeper investigation."

"He wasn't just promiscuous; he was much worse. Our relationship was never based on physical attraction. We exchanged no more than half a dozen kisses in the month leading up to the wedding, which was also the entire time we'd known each other. Anyway, I had barely signed my name at the registry office when I knew I had made a mistake, but I only understood the magnitude of that mistake when, on our wedding night, he told me that he would only be satisfied with group sex. I'm ashamed to tell you the rest. It's so perverted."

"It's not necessary. I know everything."

"I was very stupid to get involved with him, and my family almost paid the price for it. Bia could have died."

"Naive, hasty, yes. Not dumb. He was a friend of your family's."

"Yes, it's true."

"There is something I need to tell you. I told you I investigated Howard, but what I didn't say is that I ended his career at the university. That same day you left New York, right after finding out he'd assaulted you, I destroyed his professional life."

She looks surprised but not shocked. "Is that what you meant by punishing him?"

"No, that's what I did because he dared to hurt you. For trying to kill you, there's no forgiveness."

"If I said that this side of you didn't scare me, I'd be lying."

"But it's who I am, Zoe. For better or worse."

"And yet, as relentless as you were, you wanted me back."

"It's not something I can control."

"And would you do it if you could?"

"I don't know. This thing between us, I've never experienced anything like it before. I have never been jealous of a woman, never considered anyone as mine. But I was furious when I heard about your wedding. I wouldn't have hired you if I'd known you were married."

"Am I a horrible person if I say I'm glad you didn't find out until we closed the deal? Otherwise, I don't think we'd ever have gotten close again."

"I don't believe that. Life always finds a way to line up the pieces on the board. Our game wasn't over. We barely started, and you soon abandoned the match."

"And how much longer do you think it will take to get to the end?

Even this feeling, this madness that takes over my body when you touch me, that makes me forget my own name... will it end?"

"Perhaps never."

I hope never.

But she's not ready to hear that yet.

Christos

CHAPTER THIRTY-EIGHT

A Week Later

"MOM, you can't leave the house."

Jesus, I'm trying my best not to lose my temper, but I swear to God, she drives me crazy, not taking anything seriously. I've lost count of how many times she's told me over the last few days that she's not going to give up the few years she has left—which I think is an exaggeration, as the women in her family have lived to over a hundred years old—stuck indoors.

One would think they're in a tiny studio, not in a nine-bedroom mansion.

"Christos, I'm not saying I'm going to take a stroll through the city, but we don't know how long this situation will last. We have to find a way to see each other."

"The safest way to do that is if I drive there to see you."

"It's a seven-hour drive."

"Mom, even though I have a private jet, there are still flight attendants who are in contact with other people. I won't risk contaminating you."

I run a hand through my hair, frustrated. I'm very close to my parents. Although work doesn't allow us to get together regularly, we visit whenever possible, even back on my island in Greece.

"I want to see you. You never told me about your previous girlfriends, but you've mentioned Zoe five times in the last few minutes."

I did? I didn't even notice. "I'll talk to her, but I could introduce you through a video call."

"Nothing replaces a hug. I know you, son. You've lived longer than I'd like hopping from one woman to another, and if you're claiming this girl as your own, there's a lot more to it than simply taking care of a model who's just signed a contract with one of your companies and then had a horrible accident."

I haven't told her I met Zoe years ago, because the story isn't just mine to share. However, Mom is not naive. She knows that Zoe means something to me just because she's staying with me during a lockdown.

"You're right. That's not why I asked her to stay with me; it's because what we have is special." I simplify and change the subject. "We'll keep in touch and follow the news. I think the best solution would be for me to drive there."

"It will be a whole thing. With the number of bodyguards following you, the trip will look like a motorcade."

We chat for a few more minutes until she says my father is waiting for her to take a stroll with him around the property. They try to stay in shape, even with the lockdown, and that's the only exercise they've been doing.

Thank God the house I'm in has a gym. I have too much pent-up energy inside my body. Even with the sex marathons of the last few days, I still feel agitated a lot of the time.

I reflect on what my mother said about me never having a woman this close to me.

It's not that I had the idea of a perfect relationship in my mind; it's just that I'd never met anyone special before Zoe, and that made me want something more permanent.

My parents' relationship is based on compatibility, that kind of love that the world knows is forever. A love I never thought I'd have. But now Zoe and I have finally given up resisting each other, I wonder if I didn't find it two years ago.

I'm a skeptic by nature. I believe in lust, in physical attraction, and somehow, I've always separated it from love. From the outside, my parents seemed more like friends than lovers, but maybe I was just attacking the issue the wrong way.

When I imagined myself in the future, I thought I would end my days with someone who, more or less, followed the family model I witnessed growing up. Now, however, I'm beginning to understand that love doesn't have a mold into which a relationship must fit but that each couple's story is what shapes love, making it unique to them.

As if she can guess that she is in my current thoughts, Zoe knocks on the door and, without waiting for an answer, enters.

Zoe has changed. She's more confident about what she wants, and although shyness is an important part of her nature, she no longer bows her head to life.

"I don't know if you're working, and I didn't want to interrupt, but I just got a call from the hospital. Bia is awake."

"Great news," I say, holding out my hand to her. I've set up an office very similar to the ones I have in other countries.

She walks over to the table, hesitating. I don't think she's being shy. She can't be, not after what we've done in the last week. I can say with certainty that I have never known a woman's body as I know hers now.

Zoe is wild in bed. More and more, she shows me what she likes, and I'm committed to finding out all about her needs, learning what makes her moan for more or scream with lust.

My body reacts to the memories of what we've done in the last few days, and she notices when I pull her to sit on my lap.

She looks at me, and I know she's turned on, too. We can't stay dressed around each other for long, but as much as I want to sit her at my table and eat her for breakfast, I don't want her to think that all I want from her is sex.

I already made a fucking mess in our first round together back in Barcelona. This time, I intend to change the script.

"Did they say when she will be discharged?" I ask, brushing the hair away from her neck and kissing the exact spot where a vein throbs.

"I can't concentrate with you doing that," she confesses, squirming in my lap. "It's very nice."

"Sorry," I say, not at all sorry.

She turns and straddles me. "For a CEO, you are a terrible liar, Mr. Lykaios."

"You already knew that. Accused me of being brutally honest once."

"I prefer it that way. I hate liars."

I know she's talking about her ex-husband, but I don't want to walk down that road right now. What I had to say to her about the bastard, I've already said. Now, the problem is between me and Mike Howard.

"I want to talk to Bia on the phone. You think they'll let me?"

"If she woke up from her coma, they must have moved her to a private room as I ordered. There's definitely a phone there."

"I'm dying to hear her voice, but I also want to tell her what happened because she must be so confused. I need to let her know that you've provided documentation for all of us."

I lean back a little in my chair to watch her. "Doesn't it bother you that I always take the lead in everything?"

"You're helping me, not trying to dominate me. If that was the case, I would have already asked you to *move over*."

Fuck, why does everything that comes out of my sorceress's mouth have to be so exciting?

I clear my throat because it took me less than three minutes to forget that I must restrain myself from laying her on my desk and taking her from behind. Zoe makes me hungry and horny just by standing close to me. No matter how many times we have sex, my desire just doesn't fade.

"My mother wants to meet you."

She stares at me.

"What?"

"Do you want me to meet her?"

I don't need to think about it. "Yes, I do."

"I won't lie."

"About what?"

"About being in the process of getting a divorce. I think she won't like to hear that."

"My mom isn't like that, Zoe. She's Greek and can be pretty conservative, but above all, she believes in happiness."

"Well, I think we have the right ingredients, then, Mr. Lykaios. Or should I call you *doctor*, as the help do?"

I smack her on the ass. "Sassy."

"Only with you," she smiles.

"Why do we have the right ingredients, Zoe?"

"Huh?"

"When I said my mother believes in happiness, you said that our relationship has the right ingredients."

"I can only speak for myself. You make me happy, Christos. If that's what's important, we are off to a good start."

Zoe

CHAPTER THIRTY-NINE

"ZOE, we're really alive, aren't we? I was scared to death that something had happened to you. I woke up terrified. Thank Mr. Lykaios for appointing an exclusive nurse for me. When I woke up, she gave me all the information I needed to calm my heart."

I can't believe it when I hear her voice. "I didn't know he'd done that."

Christos is unbelievable. He told me he's not a saint, but I don't believe in saints or people who are always good.

Everyone has a dark side.

After the years I spent in the orphanage, I know that life is not a bed of roses. What matters, though, is that he's good where it counts.

He's dedicated to all those he . . . loves? Is love what he feels for me? He didn't tell me back when I confessed it the other day, but he still shows he cares for me with every action.

I feel closer to him after our short time together than I did during my marriage to Mike.

Maybe because, deep down, Christos never really left my head. He was always in my heart, no matter how hard I fought against it.

The night I gave myself to him again, he confessed that, since we'd parted ways, he hadn't slept with another woman. If he was someone else, I wouldn't take that seriously, but I believe him. Christos isn't the type to sugarcoat just to please whoever is receiving the message.

Two years without touching another woman because I was the only one he wanted has to mean something. So I've decided that I don't need him to tell me the exact words. Saying *I love you* is not as important as actions. I think, sometimes, actions mean more than declarations of love.

Mike said he loved me before we were married, and being the needy fool I was back then, I believed him. If I could take anything good away from our toxic relationship, it was that it helped me grow.

"You have no idea how relieved I am to hear from you. I prayed day and night. How are you feeling?"

"Like I've been run over by a truck. My whole body hurts, but the doctor thinks it's because of the time I've been lying here. An evil bonus for being over forty. By the time I'm well enough to work out again, I will have lost all my muscles."

Bia, unlike me, who thinks running is the only tolerable physical activity, absolutely loves working out and has a stunning hourglass figure.

"Does your head hurt?"

"No. And according to the doctors, everything is fine in there. What I'm afraid of right now is this virus. I want to get out of here as soon as possible, but the medical team told me that, besides waiting a few more days for observation until they confirm I'm okay to be discharged, I'll still have to get tested to see if I've been infected."

"Did they give you a date?"

"I'll be officially discharged in three days, but I won't be able to leave the hospital until the test results are in."

"When you get them, I'll ask Christos to send someone for you. I already talked to him. You can stay here with us."

"With us, eh? I'm glad to hear you've got things sorted out. You deserve to be happy, Zoe."

"I was stupid not to go after the truth sooner."

"No, you were gullible, which is a flaw in today's world. But now it's all settled, right? Nick called me and said you guys talked."

"Yes, he is a very good person. I think you should change your status to 'in a serious relationship' on social media. *Fuck buddy* is not very flattering."

"Did you say a bad word, princess?" she mocks.

"Maybe Christos is rubbing off on me. The man has such a foul mouth it makes you sound like a nun. But don't change the subject. Seriously, now. Why were you never together for real?"

"Because we don't like each other that way. We have good sex, but we don't daydream about each other out of bed, you know? I want more, Zoe. I won't settle for anything other than the whole package. I'm not even talking about getting married wearing a veil and all, but having someone to…"

"Make your body tingle?"

"That's right. I think I'm waiting for my bad guy to show up."

"There you go with that story again. Beware. I strongly believe in the saying: 'When you want something, the whole universe conspires in order for you to achieve it.' A mobster will come your way."

"Don't say that. Just the thought makes my heart race."

I laugh. "Yeah, now I know you're truly okay. Still the same crazy gal as always."

"Yes, the same one. Changing the subject, I need to say something. That Ernestine deserves a slap in the face. Not only was she a liar who got in the way of your love story, but she made her daughter live in poverty by giving all the money to some random man. How could she be so stupid? First, she got involved with a man who used to drive under the influence with a little girl in the back seat, without wearing a seat belt, then she handed over the accident compensation to a thief."

"When this is all over, I'm going to look for her. It may not help at all because I believe that a person who does what she did to her own daughter doesn't have a shred of conscience. But at least I'll tell her everything I need to say to her face."

"We talked about everything, and I didn't ask the most important thing. Did you get hurt?"

"My hand is scarred. Maybe I'll get surgery, not because it bothers me but because it might be a problem for new jobs in the future. Now, more than ever, I need the contract with Christos. My parents lost everything, Bia. There's not even a photograph of their wedding day left, nothing. The only reason I didn't lose photos of my biological mother was because, a little over a year ago, I scanned them. Otherwise, I'd have to rely only on my memories."

"If I ever find Howard, I'll kill him with my bare hands. Nick tells me he's on the run."

"Yes, he is. And as for killing him, you'll have to get in line. I hate him."

"Did he show any signs of madness before this? I'm not kidding, Zoe. The man is not normal. What he did, trying to kill us all, destroyed his career."

"It would have happened anyway."

"How so?"

"Christos had already taken action in that regard after he saw my bruised face."

"I'll tell you something. I was already rooting for you two before, but now I can say, without any doubts, that I'm a big fan of your Greek."

"He's not mine . . . yet."

"Oops. That's how you talk, girl. I'm enjoying seeing this change."

"Almost dying opened my eyes, Bia. The thread of life is very fragile. That day, when I went out to buy ice cream, I thought my world was relatively under control. I had signed a million-dollar contract, was separating from Mike, and found Christos again. And then, less than half an hour later, my universe was gone. My parents' home was gone, and my best friend was in a coma."

"I understand what you're saying. At least something good came out of a fucked-up situation. Now tell me all about your plans."

"His parents want to meet me."

"Wow, it's serious, then."

"I don't know. I'm going to visit them next week. We'll get tested first to confirm we're not contaminated. I would love to see my mother, but her doctor won't allow it because even the test can be a false negative."

"This whole situation is shit."

"You woke up from a coma with an A to Z list of swear words, didn't you?

"I'm practicing to get back on track."

"You didn't answer me about coming here when you're finally discharged."

"I appreciate it from the bottom of my heart, Zoe, but I need to be alone for a while. As soon as the borders are open, I want to go on a Caribbean vacation. But for now, I'm going to stay quiet in my apartment."

"I won't pressure you, Bia, but if you change your mind at any time, just let me know."

"Of course I will. Any news about the runway?"

"Yuri, Christos's assistant, is planning to do a virtual show. We would present the new collection, but it would be broadcasted on his brands' channels. Nothing on-site."

"I love the idea. Let me know if you need me."

"I love you, Bia. Take care. I hope we can see each other soon."

"I'm sure that as soon as the vaccine is ready, life will return to its former state."

Christos

CHAPTER FORTY

I HANG up the video call with Yuri. We spent over an hour discussing strategies for my brands during the worldwide crisis.

The only pending issue is canceling the on-site fashion shows. We've decided to broadcast them live, but until we're sure how the global health safety issue will play out, I don't want crowds gathered or mass contamination.

The lockdown did not affect my profits at all. People continue to buy, but maybe, if this goes on, the fashion sector will feel the impact, of course. Why buy clothes if you don't have to leave the house? Even I, who haven't worn jeans on weekdays in years, have turned them into a sort of home uniform, along with long-sleeved black shirts.

Bare feet, however. No socks or shoes.

I have to admit that, after spending most of my adult life in suits or blazers, it's a relief to be able to wear more casual clothes. I didn't even realize how much I missed it until I was forced to stay home.

Slowing down is not my style—I am my father's son, after all. Work always comes first. But having Zoe with me and only one maid, who lives as a housekeeper on the property and comes twice a week, has made me review my philosophy regarding various sectors of my life.

Instead of dining at fancy restaurants, we sometimes eat sandwiches or share buckets of popcorn while watching movies.

Hot tub baths, swimming naked in the pool at dawn, having sex in the middle of the day, chatting.

Things that, even with all the luxury I could afford in my adult life, I never enjoyed, or if I did, it was always with a time limit because I was always after my next million.

More contracts, more money, and inside me, emptiness.

However, I have no doubt that this peace I feel is because I am with her. I can't imagine being isolated with anyone else without this freaking me out—not even my parents. But with Zoe, I enjoy every minute of it.

It was a physical attraction that brought us together. But once we met again, there was so much more involved. I want her, not because of the past or because I want a second chance. I want her for today.

For that, however, I need to exterminate one weed: Mike Howard.

Beau still hasn't been able to find out anything about his whereabouts, which is no small feat since my friend has multiple contacts that society calls *outlaws*.

So, I only have one last card left. Someone I didn't want to involve.

My cousin, who is like a younger brother: Odin Lykaios.

Howard's reckoning will be *unconventional*, so I didn't want the family involved. After all, Odin has his own demons to fight, but I don't see any other option. As certain as the sun will rise, the bastard who tried to kill Zoe won't get away with what he did.

And who else could locate him besides the man who owns the largest technology company in the country? We're in the 21st century; there are cameras everywhere and nowhere to hide—unless you are dead or have been held prisoner in some basement. Otherwise, you'll leave a trail.

Odin and I met as adults. A mutual friend pointed out that our surnames were the same, which ended up piquing my interest because it's not even a very common name in Greece.

What are the chances of two CEOs with Lykaios as a last name? Small, I would say.

To make a long story short, we found out we are distant cousins.

Dad was delighted to be reunited with a relative. When he arrived in the United States more than thirty years ago, he lost touch with the rest of the Greek part of the family.

However, the friendship between the two of us was not easy at first. We're both distrustful and aloof men. I have no doubt that Odin ran a background check on me just as I did him.

I find his contact information on my list and touch the screen with my finger.

"Christos, did something happen?" he asks as soon as he answers.

We have in common the fact that we're direct people, no fussing around.

"Besides the seemingly doomed end of the world?"

"The vaccine will come soon. We'll have it in record time. But I'm sure it wasn't to talk about the future of the planet that you called me."

"No. I need you to find someone for me."

"The man who burned your girlfriend's house down?"

"I don't even know why I call you or Beau. We could save time and talk telepathically."

"Beau?"

"Forget it; I said too much."

"You know I won't. I never forget anything."

"Seriously, Odin. He's not someone you should know."

"You're talking like an older brother. I'm already a big boy."

"By the way, how's the negotiation going to buy that Greek island?"

"Technically, it's already mine, but I'm going to have to delay my plans a little until this shit is over."

"You talked about the vaccine. Any idea when it will be ready?"

"In a few months," he says, with reassuring confidence. I have no doubt he has access to privileged information. "When I have news about the motherfucker, I'll let you know."

"Don't you need any additional information about him?"

Odin gives one of his rare laughs. "I am the one who presents the world with information, cousin. Not the one who seeks it."

"So, we'll have to get tested before we go visit your parents?"

"Yes, and so will they. I don't know if it's necessary because none of us is leaving the house, but the doctors said it's a safety protocol. Is it okay for you?"

"Of course. I'm not afraid. I just wish I could see my family, too."

"My cousin told me today that the vaccine won't take long."

"I hope not. Today I called the insurance company to ask what will be done about my parents' house, not about mortgages, of course. There is nothing to be done on that front. They don't owe us anything, but the bank does—the house was taken by the institution. Twice."

"Why did they need to mortgage a second time?"

"Mom got sick again before I started making money from modeling. Even though my career took off very fast, it wasn't enough."

"I can take care of it."

"No. You're already doing too much. I'll pay with . . ." She stops, and her eyes widen. "Is the contract still standing? I'm asking because we won't be doing that shoot you wanted in Greece anytime soon."

"Yes, it's off for now. We'll find a way around it." He looks at me strangely.

"What?"

"I do not know what you're talking about."

"It looked like you were going to say something, then cut yourself off."

"You once accused me of being too straightforward, so here you go: Greece was an excuse. I wanted time alone with you. Isolated, where you couldn't run away."

"Even though I was still married?"

"My assistant said there were rumors that you were splitting up."

She nods, but the corner of her mouth is turned up, hiding a smile.

"Why do I get the feeling you're smiling *because* of me and not *for* me?"

She sits on my lap. "Let's say it's both."

"May I know why?"

"It's nothing. I was just thinking. A CEO, king of the world, making excuses to take me to a deserted island . . ."

"It's not deserted; we have over a hundred employees there."

"Don't ruin my dream. As I was saying, a powerful CEO..."

I roll my eyes. "Jump to the conclusion, woman. My ego doesn't need to be massaged."

"Maybe you're not ready for what I'm about to say, Lykaios."

"I'm tough. Say it."

"You were crazy about me. You just wouldn't admit it."

I pull her by her ass, settling her on my cock. "Fifty percent correct."

"Where did I go wrong?"

"The tense of the verb. I'm *still* crazy about you, Zoe."

Christos

CHAPTER FORTY-ONE

Washington, DC's Trip Day

SECURITY IS STOWING Zoe's luggage in the car when my phone vibrates with an incoming message.

> Beau: "I have news. Call me. It's urgent."

The call doesn't even have time to connect before my phone rings with another incoming call.

Odin.

What the hell? The two at the same time can only mean one thing: they have located Mike Howard.

"I found him," my cousin says as soon as I pick up.

"Really? And where's the motherfucker?"

"Dead. Car accident. Poetic justice or not, the car caught fire."

"Are you sure about that?"

"I'm not a coroner, Christos, but the forensics says so, so why doubt it?"

"Where did it happen?"

"Mexico. He crossed the border. Probably trying to get away. It's a road accident, it seems. Lost control and fell off a cliff. End of the line."

"Too quick for what he deserved."

"Yeah, I know."

I'm sure the crime Howard committed, burning down Zoe's parents' house, is a sore point for my cousin—as he lost his entire family in a fire: parents and baby sister.

"I can keep checking. I'll try by other means to find out if it was really him."

"What other means?" I find his suggestion odd.

"Again with the playing the big brother."

"I can't help it. Don't get in trouble because of me. I can check if it was Howard without you exposing yourself to danger."

"You know I would never expose myself. Erasing tracks is my specialty, but I don't want to interfere. If you really want to solve everything yourself . . ."

"You've already done a lot, bringing me this."

"It's okay. Take care, Christos."

He hangs up, and when I'm ready to complete the call to Beau, as I'm now sure it's Mike he wants to talk about, Zoe shows up. I think she notices something in my expression because a little wrinkle in the middle of her forehead replaces her smile.

"What happened? Is it my parents?" She looks terrified.

"No. They're fine, but we have to talk. Your ex-husband is dead."

"What?"

"A car accident in Mexico. The car caught fire."

"Are you sure it was him?"

No, I'm not, but I won't tell her that. If Howard is still on this planet, it won't be for long, anyway.

Before I answer, she continues. "I'm not sorry. I hope he suffered," she says, surprising me. "Because of what he did, my parents' lives were destroyed. Their history, their memories. He hurt Bia thinking it was me."

"He almost killed you too," I growl, feeling the same hate for the bastard as when I saw her in that hospital room.

My phone rings; I know it's Beau. Maybe wanting to break the same news as Odin.

"I have to answer it," I say and walk away because I have no idea how the conversation will go.

"What part of 'urgent' don't you understand?"

"I was talking to my cousin, then Zoe. He told me Mike Howard is dead."

"What?"

"Wait, isn't that what you were going to tell me?"

"No, but it seems your news is better than mine. Was it him?"

"I don't know. What do you think?"

"Well, I don't believe it, perhaps because, like you, I'm skeptical by nature. But by tomorrow morning, I'll know. Now, let's get down to business. Whether he's dead or alive, your girl will be rid of the bastard sooner than you think."

"I don't understand."

"When he married your Zoe, the professor had already been married to someone for over ten years. He's a bigamist, Christos, which means his second marriage, which turns out to be to your girl, is invalid."

"I thought nothing else we'd find about him would surprise me, but the bastard managed to outdo himself."

"It's a win-win. Any good lawyer will be able to resolve the annulment . . . I don't even know if that's the correct term because how can you annul what never existed? Anyway, any good lawyer will be able to resolve that quickly."

"I'll contact my lawyers later today."

"I'll give you some advice for free. You said you're not sure if he really died. Let your Zoe think so. If Howard is still walking this vale of tears, it won't be for long."

"I had already considered that. I don't want to involve her in my plans."

"Exactly. When we find him burned to death in a car, it will sound like heaven."

"You've got that look again, like you want to say something but are holding back. Did you regret the trip?"

"What? No."

"Look, if you've changed your mind about me meeting your family . . ."

"You should know by now that no one forces me to do what I don't want to do, Zoe."

"Okay, so what's wrong, Christos? This guessing game makes me anxious. I'm already nervous about meeting your parents, and your expression doesn't help."

I take her hand, which was resting on her thigh, and bring it to my lips, giving it a light kiss. "It has nothing to do with the trip. I still want you to meet my family."

"So, what's the problem?"

"I'm thinking of how to tell you something."

"Is it about Mike? If you're worried about how I'm feeling about his death, don't worry. I won't lose five minutes of sleep over this. I'm not sure what happened, Christos, but I've already decided that I'm going to save my tears for those who deserve them. Dead or alive, I will never forgive him for what he did to my family. How could he have the gall, knowing my mother has cancer, how hard she's been fighting to survive, to burn down the house with both of them inside? I mean, I understand that, in his crazy head, he wanted revenge. But my parents? No, you won't see me mourn his death."

"It has nothing to do with the jerk's death." I take a detour off the road. I see in the rearview mirror that the two cars with our bodyguards do the same. I turn off the engine and look at her. "Your marriage to Mike was invalid."

"What?"

I'll never win an award for diplomacy, so I dump it all at once. "It's not in me to sit idly waiting for the police to discover his whereabouts. I asked a friend to go after him."

"Wasn't he the one who broke the news of Mike's death?"

"No, that was my cousin. Anyway, my friend found out that Mike had a wife already, which makes your marriage invalid. And there's more," I continue, because it doesn't make any sense to keep the rest of the information. "You wouldn't have thought of checking your bank account with all this shit going on lately, but he cleaned it out, as well as the stocks you had invested."

Christos

CHAPTER FORTY-TWO

SHE UNBUCKLES her seat belt and opens the car door. I see her walking away, both hands on her head.

I go after her. I knew she would be pissed when she found out Howard stole from her, but I didn't anticipate such a desperate reaction.

"My good God!"

"Zoe."

"It's too much information, Christos. What did I do with my life? I'm relieved that our marriage was a sham. Not only the relationship itself but also legally. What else should I have expected from a liar who waited to put a ring on my finger before telling me about his lifestyle? His sexual deviations? That's not what I'm nervous about right now, but rather the fact that he sold the shares. They were my only investment. My mother's illness . . . The treatment requires a lot of money."

"I can afford it."

"I know you can, but it's not your responsibility. That's not why I'm with you. I always pay the bills myself."

"Zoe, we signed a million-dollar deal, which is still standing. You will be able to get your finances in order."

"It doesn't feel right to get the money. We don't even know when I'll be able to go back to work..."

"But you will. Don't worry about that. Now, let's get back to the car, or my mom will pull our ears when we arrive. She doesn't like to be late for dinner."

She comes close and hugs me. "I'm not being dramatic. I've gotten used to being alone and paying my family's bills. I don't share these concerns."

"I'm not good at sharing either, but I'm the best at dealing with problems," I joke because she still looks tense.

She lifts her head from my chest. "Your self-confidence has always turned me on. You're very arrogant but in a sexy way."

"Everything about you turns me on."

She stands on her tiptoes and wraps her arms around my neck for a kiss. I don't usually give public displays of affection, mainly because I know my bodyguards are likely watching us, but nothing with Zoe plays by the rules. I've already made peace with the fact that she's the only one in my life.

It doesn't take long until we're both breathless, our skin boiling with desire.

She takes the initiative to walk away, perhaps finally aware that we are not alone. Still, she can't hide her arousal. Her mouth is swollen from the kiss, and her porcelain skin is flushed. Beautiful as fuck.

"How do I cut ties with him, Christos? I don't want anything else from that man."

"It makes it a lot easier that you didn't change your name when you got *married*." Even though it's what I now know is a fake marriage, I still feel the word running like acid down my throat. Imagining her tied to someone for the rest of her life drives me insane with jealousy.

Imagining her bonded for the rest of her life to someone other than you drives you insane with jealousy. A voice inside my head says what I haven't had the courage to admit until now.

I look at her and realize she's staring back at me. It's as if we're both trying to unravel what the other represents in their world.

Yes, she said she loves me, but I don't think Zoe can understand what we have any more than I can. The odds were against us, and there is still a lot that could go wrong. However, life brought us together again. I'm not willing to waste this second chance.

I take her hand, and after opening the car door for her to get in, I get behind the wheel. "I'll call my lawyers as soon as we get to DC. It will be quick, and soon you'll be free."

"I didn't even feel married."

"Does the idea appeal to you?"

"What?" She feigns ignorance.

"Marriage. Building a family."

Her face turns a darker shade of red. "I've been abandoned for longer than I've had a home. In therapy, I learned that living in search of what I don't have will always be a weakness of mine. So yes, getting married and having my own family is a goal I have."

I haven't started the engine yet; my mind is overloaded with a certainty that has just unraveled. I want Zoe for myself—not for a while until we explore what we feel or what we are. I want Zoe as mine *forever*.

"And the farm," I say.

"What?"

"You want a farm too and, I suppose, lots of kids."

"Yes, as many as God wants to give me," she says, looking out the car window.

I know it's uncomfortable, but I need to know more. "What about your career?"

"As you said, I closed a million-dollar contract with a Greek who is obsessed with me," she says, trying to be jovial but failing. "I won't be able to end this commitment anytime soon."

I know that's a sore spot for her. Zoe feels uncomfortable about our relationship involving money.

"This has nothing to do with the two of us. Yes, I chose you mainly because I wanted you back, but you are beautiful, and it will be a huge win for my brands. You'll represent *Vanity*."

"What? But the contract was for a smaller brand. Vanity is a synonym for luxury worldwide. I waited more than a year and then stood in an enormous line just to buy the bag of my dreams."

"You are the face I want to epitomize *Vanity*: beautiful, sophisticated, and young. I've been wanting to rekindle this brand for a long time and show that all ages can relate to it."

"I don't know what to say. Or rather, I do know. Thanks. Modeling for a brand that is synonymous with luxury is every model's dream."

I don't take long to understand what she doesn't reveal. "But not yours."

"I don't mean to sound ungrateful, but as I've told you before, I started my career because of Pauline, and I continued because of necessity. Dieting for the rest of my life is not my idea of fun."

I had never analyzed the models' lifestyles from that perspective. For me, it was just how they made a living. "And what's your idea of fun, pretty girl?"

She looks at her hands. "I will fulfill all my dreams, Christos. I was wrong the first time, but when I get married again, it will be to someone who values me. Someone who wants to give back to the world instead of just taking. Someone I'm not ashamed to be myself with. Not always strong or brave, not always tidy or wearing makeup, but the real Zoe."

"You're beautiful no matter what you wear."

She looks out the window again. "Is that all you see in me? Beauty?"

"No," I say without a second of hesitation. "When I first saw you, perhaps, but now there's more."

"What, then?"

"I see the woman I want."

She doesn't look at me like I expected. "You already have me. But I think this relationship is only working because we're stuck at home. Soon, your life will return to normal."

"And what's my normal, Zoe?"

"Travel, parties, glamor. And none of this is part of my world, Christos, except for work obligations. I've been thinking a lot these last few days. With the money from the contract we signed, I'm going to pay off all my parents' debts and buy them another house. Then I'll go after what I want for myself, after my real dream. I will no longer sign contracts with any other brands. You will be my last."

In more ways than you can imagine, Zoe. You will be mine forever.

Zoe

CHAPTER FORTY-THREE

WASHINGTON D.C.

"I CAN'T BELIEVE I'm hugging you, my baby," Christos's mother says, and I find myself smiling because the woman has no restraint when it comes to showing affection.

I watch his reaction. I thought he would be embarrassed by his mother's over-the-top ways, how she even pinched his cheek as if he were still a little boy. But no. He hugs her, and the kiss he gives in return is long.

I feel my eyes fill with tears, thinking about my two mothers, the biological one and the adoptive one. I would love to get a hug like that too.

"Mom, this is Zoe."

As soon as Christos parked in front of the mansion, she came running out to greet us.

She is petite, a little chubby, and has gray hair in a shoulder-length cut. She is not beautiful—yes, I have that flaw. Working so much among models who border on physical perfection, I end up analyzing everyone's appearance, but she's so full of life that she's stunning. You can almost touch her life force.

Finally, she lets go of her son and comes closer to me. "My dear, what a pleasure to meet you. I'm so sorry for the tragedy you went through. How are your parents?"

Contrary to what usually happens when I'm confronted with very direct people, I don't feel uncomfortable. She doesn't sound like she wants to be nosy, but rather she's really sorry, concerned for my family.

"Nice to meet you, Mrs. Danae."

"Just Danae. I'm not that old."

"Right." I smile. "Nice to meet you, Danae. They are as well as they can be."

"I can't even imagine the nightmare you went through, Zoe, but they're all alive and that's what matters. Now let's go inside; Alekos is already complaining he's famished," she says, referring to her husband.

As if he knew we were talking about him, Christos's father appears. It's like seeing an older version of my boyfriend. The man must also have been drop-dead gorgeous when he was younger. Does Danae know how to shoot? If I had to be with her son for the rest of my life, I would definitely enroll in a shooting training course.

The thought spreads a good feeling through my chest, but I push it away. I wish I had more time with him, and I don't intend to walk away from his life, but I also don't want to delude myself into thinking we'll be together forever.

"Alekos, come meet your son's girlfriend."

He comes but first stops and gives his wife a kiss on the forehead. Then I realize that, regardless of the man's beauty, he is in love with this woman. There is no physical difference that outweighs that.

I look over at Christos and catch him watching me as his father hugs me and gives me a kiss on the cheek.

I smile awkwardly, but I am very happy with the warm greeting. Mike only had his mother, and the woman looked at me strangely the only time we saw each other.

I have serious issues with rejection and may never be able to fully get over them. Christos's parents' greeting makes my heart calm down, as I now have the courage to admit I was scared to death that they would treat me coldly.

We eat like horses, and I learn what a real Greek-style lunch is. I try *moussaka, dolmadakia,* and for dessert, *portokalopita,* an orange cake with cinnamon. It's tender and very tasty.

By the end, I feel like I'm about to explode, but the three Greeks talk as if this is a common meal for them.

Christos is a chameleon. I've been with him in public, both in Barcelona and in his New York office, and I know how powerful and imposing he is in his daily life. But here, with his parents, he seems completely relaxed. I think it's because he's among those he truly considers his own.

When she called me, Mom asked to talk to him, and they talked for about five minutes. In the end, my boyfriend wanted to talk to my dad, too, and that touched my heart.

Mike never made any effort to be nice to my parents. Even before the wedding, I never saw him giving them the time of day.

"Zoe, we need to plan a trip to Greece when this is all over. My son's island is beautiful."

"She's doing a photo shoot there, so it'll be sooner than you think."

"Excellent. Let's all go together," Alekos says, inviting himself, and I feel like laughing. "God knows we need a little break from this chaos the world has become. We can go on your plane, son."

"I would love to, but first I want to see my parents. I talk to my mom every day on the phone, but I want to *see* her. I don't know if that makes sense."

"Of course it does, sweetheart," Danae says, taking my hand. "Nothing replaces being face-to-face."

"I was going to surprise you, but I don't want to make you anxious," Christos says.

"*Surprise me?*"

"Yes. When we get back to Boston, we'll stop by to see your parents. I've already arranged everything with Macy. You just won't be able to have a hug because the doctor is still firm on the isolation, but your father will set up some chairs in the garden and we'll be able to talk."

"I thought they were still at the clinic. I mean, they were until yesterday."

"Yes, but when I arranged the clinic, I also asked Yuri to rent a house in case they wanted to get away from the hospital environment for a bit if your mother was well enough to do so."

I open and close my mouth, amazed. "Is there anything you didn't organize?"

For the first time since we met, I have the impression that he blushes. "It wasn't a big deal. I . . ."

Before he finishes, I get up and walk over to where he is, and without stopping to think about what I'm doing, I kiss him on the cheek. "Thanks."

I get ready to go back to my seat, but he pushes back his chair, pulls me onto his lap, and kisses me on the mouth in front of his parents. "Now, I consider that a thank you."

I hear Alekos laugh, and I turn away, red as a pepper.

I avoid facing any of them, but I feel the Lykaios family's eyes on me all the time.

※

Totally taking me by surprise, Alekos and his son say they are going to clean up the lunch table. Like us in Boston, Christos's parents only have a maid to clean twice a week to avoid people circulating inside the house, which lowers the risk of getting infected.

Christos has washed dishes at our house, and I have always admired that, as it has to do with how he was raised. I can't stand people sitting around waiting to be served, but my boyfriend is a man of action in any area of his life.

However, I didn't imagine that it would be like that in his parents' house, nor that the oldest Lykaios would take the initiative to send us out for a walk while they took care of everything.

"Do you feel better now that you know you're going to see your mother?" asks Danae.

"Yes, I do. Life is a very strange thing, isn't it? I've spent the last few years worrying about her cancer, and then this goddamn virus comes along and trips us up. My anxiety right now is about Mom taking a turn for the worse and needing to be admitted to a real hospital if the clinic Christos has provided isn't enough."

"Let's have faith, child. I know we are all uncertain about the future, but we need to stay positive. Getting sick mentally can be just as dangerous for the body."

"I know, but when I talk about anxiety, it's not like people usually have it, but something that paralyzes me. That's why I keep doing therapy twice a week, online."

I look at her as I speak. I'm not going to pretend to be someone I'm not to win her over. I had depression when I came back from Barcelona, and I thought it was a one-time thing because of everything I've been through, but my therapist told me it could happen again.

"There's nothing wrong with seeking help. I don't know everything about your life, Zoe, but I'm sure you're a special girl."

She takes me to her flower greenhouse, and as we walk around, I decide that I want one like this for myself in the future. I've never paid attention to flowers, but Christos's mother tells me that she considers caring for her orchids a kind of therapy.

"Why?" I ask, referring to her calling me special.

"You'll hardly find anyone more indifferent to relationships than Christos, and yet here you are."

"It's not like your son has much of a choice, is it? I'm staying at his house."

"You're a smart girl, so answer me: why is my Christos in Boston and not in New York, where his main residence is?"

I stay silent, understanding what she means. With his fortune, Christos could go anywhere in the world during this crisis, and yet he's chosen to stay with me.

A twinge of hope begins to grow in my heart.

"Our history is complicated."

"I have time, and I consider myself a good listener."

Their property is huge. We walk, now in the sun, and I explain everything to her, from the moment he caught me in Barcelona taking a picture on a forbidden floor of the ship to my return to the United States without saying goodbye and my meeting with him again.

"The accident you're talking about, in addition to physically hurting him, messed with my son's head a lot. Even if he had no reason for that, he blamed himself for the little girl. The man driving the car was drugged. Not only a little, but close to having overdosed. It could have killed them all."

"I only believed Ernestine's story because I didn't know Christos well. Anyone who spends ten minutes with him knows he's not the type to shy away from responsibilities."

"You're in love with him, Zoe."

"I think I always have been. I didn't have a choice. From our first exchange, he charmed me."

She looks at me like she knows a secret, so I continue.

"I'm afraid of getting hurt, though. My fake marriage couldn't hurt me because I never loved Mike, but Christos could destroy me."

"I'm not a spokesman for other people's feelings, kid. Every couple has its own rhythm and story, but my boy feels the same way about you. Although he hasn't put it into words, I carried him for nine months, and I know Christos. Like his father, he only loves once, and you, my beautiful child, are the chosen one."

Christos

CHAPTER FORTY-FOUR

BACK TO BOSTON

"**HOW ARE YOU FEELING?**" I ask. We're almost at the house I've rented for her parents.

"Excited. I know it's nonsense because I talk to them on the phone, but my mom and dad are all I have in the world. My real family—what's left of the biological one in Boston—other than the cousin I told you about, Madeline, I don't give a damn about them."

She said she was related to the Boston Turners. I had the misfortune of meeting the aunt she mentioned, Adley, at a gala dinner for charity a few years ago. She's insufferable and arrogant and acts as if the universe should be grateful that she breathes the same air as the rest of humanity.

"They are well," I say, referring to her parents.

"I know, and I'm very grateful for that."

"Don't you understand, after all we've been through, that there's nothing I wouldn't do to make you happy, Zoe?"

I'm not kidding, and I think she notices, but after a quick glance at me, she changes the subject. "The streets look like the ones on a TV show. The apocalypse, as if we were the only survivors."

"Anyone who has the privilege of being able to work from home is being conscientious."

We drive around in the car, and my attention, which was entirely on her, shifts to checking what she said. Rarely does a car pass us by.

"Many have lost their jobs," she says.

Everywhere we look, the few people on the streets are wearing masks.

The news that the first vaccine will start to be manufactured within a month surprised even my mother, who is an optimist by nature. Odin, once again, was right.

However, even if people start getting vaccinated, the world will never be the same.

I believe it will take a long time for them to feel safe. Maybe it will never happen again. Only from the next generation onwards. My kids will probably only talk about it as a bad time in history, but it's a new reality for us.

Kids? Where did that come from?

Despite being something I wish to have in the future, I've never found myself thinking about my descendants as I do now.

"Have you noticed that even if they keep their distance, people still stop to greet each other?" she asks as we enter the family neighborhood where her parents are living.

"I think most people miss talking to other people, especially those living alone. Not everyone is lucky enough to be locked up with a supermodel." I look at her, hiding a smile just in time to see her rolling her eyes.

"And me, with a Greek CEO. Lucky for me; other people's loss."

"What other people?"

She looks at me quickly but turns away again. "It's none of my business. I spoke without thinking."

"I haven't slept with anyone else since we met in Barcelona. I'm not guided by my dick. When I want a woman, it's just her I want, but it usually doesn't last."

"I don't want to hear about it," she says, sounding pissed at me.

"But you do because I know you feel insecure. I'm with you, Zoe, not because we have to be locked up in the house but because I want to be. If I was just after sex, a phone call would solve my problem. I want *more*."

"Can you stop the car for a moment? It makes me nervous to fight while you're driving."

"Are we fighting?"

She doesn't respond, but as soon as I find a place to pull over, she gets rid of her seat belt and gets into my lap. "I've never been good at interpreting subtext."

"What?"

"Are we together for real? Like diving headfirst into the possibility of a future?"

Her hands cup my face so I don't look away.

There is no need. I don't want to stop staring at her when I answer. "Yes, we are together for real. Are you ready for this?"

My heart beats almost painfully in my chest. Even though she's told me she loves me, a thought takes over.

What if the opposite is true, and she's only with me because she has nowhere else to go?

"Ready for what? Words, Christos. Give me literally what you want from me. From both of us."

"I want everything. A future. No more running away, physical, or mentally, Zoe. I want it all."

She looks at me like she's trying to know my every thought. Her expression turns smug, then she pulls me into a kiss that makes me forget where we are, and I want to bury myself in her body.

"As much as I like the idea of seeing your parents again, I'm dying to get home."

The corner of her mouth turns up. "Do you have to work, Mr. Lykaios?"

"A lot. Inside you, getting deep inside. You're fully healed from the bruises on your feet and hands, so we can fuck with less care."

She turns red. I've noticed that whenever I act like I really am, without using nice words to say what I want, she blushes, but she also gets aroused.

"Does that mean that, so far, what we've done has been careful?" She looks breathless.

"You'll find out later."

"If there is one good thing in the midst of so much death and fear, it's people paying attention to their loved ones again," her mother says.

We've been talking outside the house for almost two hours, and unlike most people I live with, I don't feel like leaving.

Socializing for me is usually unnatural. I do it in moderation. Zoe and I have that in common, but in my case, it's not because I'm shy; it's just a lack of desire to talk. Her parents, however, are very interesting, and Scott raised a debate that I had already considered: even when the vaccine starts to be manufactured, it won't eradicate the disease due to the mutations of the virus. We are more likely to take it for the rest of our lives, like the flu shot.

"I was like that too," I say, a little embarrassed. "I barely had time to eat. I rarely ate lunch and was always involved in a thousand commitments."

"And what has changed?" Zoe asks.

"I used to watch you from a distance; now I'm obsessed with doing it up close," I say, much more seriously than joking.

I don't know how much she's told her parents about the two of us, but they both start laughing while Zoe blushes.

"My private stalker." She recovers and faces me.

"You can bet on it." I kiss her hand. "But now, I see things differently."

"Like what?" Scott asks.

"I want to help people. I've always donated generously to various causes, but I want something more effective, like building good hospitals that are more accessible to those who can't afford good insurance."

"Yes, unfortunately, that is one of the illnesses in our country, son. Access to healthcare for all citizens, including the less privileged ones, is still a dream. Even before this situation we are experiencing, some people got sick and refused to seek care for fear of getting into huge debt."

"I have some ideas," Zoe says.

"About helping people?"

"Yes. I have always been concerned about humanity's future, but my attention is mainly focused on children and elderly people."

"Both ends of the spectrum," I say.

"Exactly. The elderly deserve a dignified end of life and often don't have any family members close by. I've been researching in my spare time for the last few weeks, and I've imagined recreation centers. A sort of free club where they can get together to play games, chat, have a meal if they're hungry." She pauses to breathe for a moment. She's beautiful at any moment, but watching her defend her ideas so passionately makes me horny. "I thought that, when everything went back to normal, we could look for volunteers willing to give an hour of their day to just listen to them in this center. Sometimes, all a person needs is a friendly ear. Loneliness can be as lethal as a physical disease."

I offer my hand, inviting her to my lap. "Each time I think you can't fascinate me any more, you prove me wrong."

She smiles, embarrassed, perhaps because we are in front of her parents, even though she has no reason to be. Scott and Macy received the news that her marriage is invalid with relief, and my lawyers are already making sure that Zoe is never associated with that jerk again.

"I'm glad to hear you have plans to help humanity, Christos. I hope other entrepreneurs like you are aware. Maybe the world needed that break."

I silently agree.

We lived so fast, thinking we were immortal—or at least that we had a lot of time to live—and suddenly, God came and proved to us that maybe our time on this planet is shorter than we thought.

"When are you planning to go to Greece for Zoe's photo shoot?" Scott asks.

"We need to organize everything to make sure that as few people as possible are needed, but I think that within a month, tops, we will go there."

"Enjoy it for me," Macy says.

"Soon, you will be able to come with us."

Zoe turns to look at me, and I see a thousand questions on her face. She is so transparent.

"Yes, *with us*," I reiterate.

Christos

CHAPTER FORTY-FIVE

A Month and a Half Later

GREECE

"WITH ALL DUE RESPECT, she is perfect," Yuri says beside me as we watch my woman posing for the last photos of the shoot. After that, we will be officially on vacation.

I'm not jealous of men looking at her. How could I be when making people look at her is her profession? As long as they don't get close, I'm fine with that.

Besides, I know Yuri isn't being malicious. He, like me, is used to seeing beautiful women. Some are beautiful in photographs after a lot of editing, but I've seen Zoe in all kinds of ways: wet hair, sweaty, in a sweatshirt, and dolled-up, like now. I can say, without fear, that for me, there isn't a more beautiful woman in the world.

"What fascinates me is not just her physical appearance but her as a whole." She is shy but also naughty during sex. She doesn't ask or say much but goes along with me, allowing herself to experience everything.

I feel my dick grow as I remember how we had sex on the beach yesterday in the middle of the night.

Zoe riding me in the moonlight is a memory I will carry forever.

And then there's her other side, something I've never found in a woman—maybe because I didn't want it either. The mixture of sweetness and determination. The courage to step in when she thinks I'm working too hard and needing a break. Without the slightest embarrassment, she comes to my lap and kisses me, not worried about whether I'm closing a deal.

As if that weren't enough, there are still the little things, like calling my mom every day, just like she does with hers, to see if they're okay or need anything.

My parents arrive tomorrow morning, but we've been here for a week. Bringing them in earlier didn't make sense when we couldn't give them any attention.

I have never watched a photo session for a catalog before, mainly because I was not interested, but I knew how much work it involved. She must be exhausted from standing around all day in high heels and a bikini—which, by the way, is driving me crazy.

"Hey, boss, I didn't mean it." Yuri catches my eye, misinterpreting my silence.

"What?" I look back at him in time to see a barely concealed smile.

"Never mind, Christos. I got it. Your problem is not jealousy of me but being mesmerized by your woman."

Half an hour later, Zoe finally comes over to us.

I can see the exhaustion in the eyes of the team and the two other models who participated in the shoot with us—they arrived three days ago.

I ignore everyone.

Yuri defined it well: I am completely mesmerized by my mermaid.

"Do you want to swim? I'm dying of heat," she says, hugging me.

"Yes, but not on the beach. Let's go home."

"They're all going to leave today, aren't they?"

"Yes. And the island will be ours."

"For twenty-four hours until your parents arrive. Oh, and let's not forget about the dozen employees."

"I told them they didn't have to come and take care of the house, but they didn't listen."

"Ah, poor little Greek tycoon. Here, he's not the all-powerful CEO; he's just a little boy."

I slap her ass to punish her for mocking me.

I told her that I was born on this island, where my whole family always lived. My parents were employees, and when my grandmother died, that was the cue for us to leave. I came back as soon as I made enough money and bought it because I knew my father had an emotional connection to the place. What I didn't count on was that I would also fall in love with my motherland again.

"They still see me as a boy. There's no way I can convince them that I'm God now," I joke, although I'm only half-joking.

She laughs. The brazen woman laughs at me.

"You should massage my ego by saying something cliché like 'you're my Greek god, Christos'."

"No ego massage needed, mister. I'm sure there's been a large contingent of females doing that before me. Besides, I have plans that involve massage, but not an ego massage, and I guarantee you'll prefer them to that."

Her sly smile makes me pretty sure these plans involve both of us naked.

I lower myself to the ground and free her feet from the high heels. Then I pick her up and start walking home without looking back.

"I don't think I'll be seeing you anymore," Yuri says as we pass.

"Goodbye, Yuri. Don't show your ugly face for the next two weeks."

"He's not ugly."

"Careful, woman, I might punish you for flirting with my assistant."

"Me, flirting with your assistant? How could I, when I have my own Greek god to give me all the pleasure I want?" she says and then gives me a wink. "Cliché enough, my king?"

"Oh, Zoe, I'm going to enjoy putting you on all fours and fucking you hard."

She swallows hard. "I hope so," she says, with an enigmatic look in her eyes.

I go straight to the room. By then, the employees are gone, so it's just the two of us in the house.

"Put me down and get naked."

I raise an eyebrow, surprised.

"Don't make me repeat that, Lykaios. I promise it will be worth it, but I'm not brave enough to give you a second order. Take off your clothes and lie face down on the bed.

"Why?"

Her cheeks turn red. "I want to try out something I read about."

"Are you going to be naked, too?"

A nod is my answer.

"Take off the bikini for me, Zoe."

She doesn't hesitate. She reaches behind her back and unclips her strapless top. Her nipples are hard, and so is my cock.

I run my tongue over my lower lip. "The panties. Now."

She lowers them down her slender thighs.

"Jesus, Zoe, there's not a damn time I see you naked that doesn't make me crazy."

I threaten to step forward, but she stops me with a raised hand.

"No way you're going to spoil my plans. Naked, now, Lykaios."

Christos

CHAPTER FORTY-SIX

STILL STARING AT HER, I take off my white T-shirt and then pull down my jeans and boxers. My cock bounces, hard, thick, pointing up, and she gasps.

"I asked you to lie on your front, but I'll have to adapt."

I can't hold back a smile. "Do you have any idea how crazy you drive me with this mixture of innocence and daring?"

"Get on the bed, or I'll forget the whole script, Christos."

I obey, curious about that statement.

She goes to the suite's bathroom, and when she comes back, she has a bottle in her hand that looks like perfume. "Scented oil," she says as if she can read my mind.

"You're really committed to the massage idea," I say, trying to keep my tone neutral when, in fact, I'm already crazy with lust, imagining those tiny hands on me.

"I do everything with commitment, Greek, and my goal today is . . . to drive you crazy." She gets onto the bed and kneels by my ankles. "I'm going to try a tantric massage," she says, not touching me yet.

"Really?" I can barely focus on what she says. Zoe has me out of control just by breathing, and seeing her so close and naked is robbing me of all concentration.

"Yes. Do you know what it's for?"

"I'm not sure."

"I read that it's a good way to connect with your partner." Her hand finally touches my foot, and it's like a shock of lust. The oil is warm.

She uses both hands now, and they're smeared with oil. When she starts running them up my legs, my heart races.

"Do what you want, Zoe, but then I'll get you so good. You will scream my name every time I thrust into that tight little pussy."

She bites her lip, and I'm sure if I touch her now, she'll be soaked.

Zoe didn't joke when she said she was committed to the massage, though, because she presses deeply against my skin. She's touching my thighs, very close to my cock, and I swear to God I feel physical pain from desire.

Surprising me, she opens the bottle again and smears oil on her breasts. She tugs at the hard nipples, pulling them, and I growl because I can't stop myself.

"Fuck!"

She smiles with her head down and leans forward.

I almost go crazy when I'm holding both of her breasts; she takes my cock between them and starts jerking me off. I stop her and jump out of bed.

"Don't move, or I'll start a sex strike today."

I lie down again, and it's really worth it because her soft mouth opens, and she starts to combine sucking on the head of my cock with masturbation.

I grip the sheets on the side of the bed, forcing myself to lie still.

She sucks me hungrily, her tongue sliding along my length, and I have to think of everything I loathe most to delay my release.

I think she's playing some kind of game, too, because when she realizes I'm on the edge, she stops.

Again, she kneels on the bed and rubs her oiled hands over her body. Abdomen, thighs, and butt. She lies on top of me and starts rubbing and sliding. I lift her up a little to bring her tits up to my mouth.

She looks like she's going to protest, but I don't let her, biting her nipple, sucking hard.

She screams and starts rubbing her clit down my length.

"So naughty. This hot pussy is dying to come, isn't she?"

"Yes, but like I said, Lykaios, I have plans." She turns in my arms, lying on her back against my body. Then, she looks back. "Why don't you massage me too?"

"Only if it's my way."

Before she knows what's happening, I part her thighs with my feet. I finger her pussy, thumb attacking the pleasure point as my middle finger enters her entirely, and she moans and squirms. My shaft fits between her ass cheeks, and my breathing gets louder.

"Play with your tits," I command.

I squeeze her belly, continuing to masturbate myself with her ass, while another finger follows the first one, dilating her sex.

Moving too, she rises, making my head fit perfectly into her pristine opening. She pushes against me, and my cock thickens further.

Am I understanding this correctly?

I test, withdrawing my fingers from inside her and sliding them between her legs until I reach her from behind. I press one, and she wiggles.

Fuck!

My fingers are wet from her sex. "Look at me. If you want this, look at me, Zoe." I'm crazy with lust.

I turn her around, and now we're face-to-face.

"Spread your legs wide."

Her breathing has quickened. When I press her from behind again, she bites and licks me.

"Want me to fuck you here?"

I insert my fingertip into it, and she wriggles anxiously.

"I don't wanna hurt you."

"I'm dreaming about it. To belong to you completely."

Shit. This woman will be the death of me.

I move her body off of mine, leaving her on the bed on her stomach. I put a pillow under her.

"Open that pretty ass for me. I want to see you."

She hesitates but obeys.

Beautiful as fuck, horny, offering herself.

I bend down and suck on her, my tongue playing where she's never been touched. I use that to lubricate her, but I don't think it will be enough, so I open the bottle of oil and coat a finger with it.

I play with her opening, pressing a little more before pushing in. Letting her get used to it while I bite into the hard flesh of her buttocks and thighs.

She moans, and I can see the fluids oozing from her thirsty sex. I lean forward and fit my cock into her pussy. I'm not delicate. I put myself inside fully, down to the base.

We scream in excitement.

I push the hair away from her neck and bite hard. I want to mark her so she'll remember she's mine.

"More."

"More what?"

"Harder. Don't hold back; show me I'm your woman."

I get on my knees and lift her, fucking her on all fours. I knock against her without pity, the thrusts of my hips pushing her face down on the bed.

She starts squeezing my cock. Her inner muscles drive me crazy.

I touch her clit, pinching it lightly, the way I know makes her come, and as I expected, half a minute doesn't go by before she's moaning, coming all the way back, taking me right down to my balls.

I fall into bed exhausted, but I'm nowhere near finished.

I withdraw from her, and with the head of my cock soaked with her liquids, I play in her virgin place.

"Ask me to stop," I command, completely crazy. Hallucinating with the desire to know that we are going to break down the last barrier between us.

"No. I want you inside me. I want you to possess me in every way. I am your woman."

She's still smeared with oil and me, oozing with her cum. I fit into her, leaning forward but not letting go of my weight. When she feels me touch her, she wiggles.

"Shhh . . . don't push yet. I don't want you to feel pain."

She stills and waits. I thought I'd already experienced all forms of crazy desires with Zoe, but this new experience is taking me out of orbit.

I push a little; feeling her stretching makes me grit my teeth. It's hot and tight as fuck.

I move my hand down to her pussy, massaging her clit, and slowly but with determination, I make my way into her body.

She whimpers in pain and pleasure but doesn't pull away. She gets her ass up instead, and I thrust in farther.

"So good, Zoe." I wrap my arm around her neck and shoulder and give a thrust that takes me halfway inside of her.

She bites me.

"I'm going to fuck you so good. Fill you with my cum. I'll make it run down your thighs and pussy."

"Oh!"

I slide two fingers into her sex, and she sucks me inside. "Do you like it? To be taken by me in every way at the same time?"

"I am yours, and you are mine. I love everything we do."

And with that, she knocks away my last shred of consciousness, and I slam into her.

She screams. Cries. Bites. Stiffens beneath me.

"Mine. You are mine."

I think she needed to hear that, because a moment later, without my asking, she starts to move.

I kneel, and I start a slow back and forth, crazy in equal parts, as much for the pleasure of having her muscles squeezing me as for seeing her whimper to fuck her harder.

My hands are like claws on her hips. I hold her still, lost in the feel of her heat.

I fuck her at a steady pace, but I lose what little control I have left when her hand starts to pleasure herself.

"Wanna come, baby?"

"Please."

"Put two fingers inside your pussy."

I finger her clit when she obeys me. Before long, she's pushing back.

I give up any attempt to take it easy and take her hard.

The howls, screams, orders, and requests we make at the same time are probably heard all over the island.

There is no shame. Just a delicious fuck between a couple crazy about each other.

"I'm going to come," she warns, and I grab a handful of her blonde hair.

"I want it hard. Can you stand it?"

"Yes," she says between horny groans.

"Do you like it? I know you're loving it. You're soaking my hand."

"Ahhhhh..."

We lose ourselves for long minutes, greedy for the prize, for the little death. The road is as delicious as what we know will come at the finish line.

She rears up one last time and comes all over me, making me a prisoner.

That's the end of me.

I go in and out. When I come back, I fill her with my cum.

As promised, it runs down her thighs, oozing.

The Neanderthal inside of me wants to beat his chest.

My woman.

"I love you, Zoe. Since always, and forever."

Zoe

CHAPTER FORTY-SEVEN

"DID you say that in the heat of the moment?" I ask.

"No. I love you."

I open my eyes, finally awake. I'm still not recovered from everything that happened. A little discomfort in my body is nothing to the feeling of being possessed by the man I love.

I shudder as I remember his words and actions as he took me.

"I'm crazy for you. Love is too simple a concept to explain, but I'll borrow it until they come up with a better one."

I lift my head from his shoulder and look back.

Christos has run me a bath and has been holding me in the lukewarm water for nearly an hour.

We didn't talk because there was nothing that could explain what had happened.

Surrender, desire.

I am his. I was always his. How could I think there could be another?

"I'm fine with love," I say, turning around and straddling him but staying on his thighs so I don't tease him.

"It's more, Zoe. I fought it because my pride demanded that I couldn't seek you out, but I knew."

"Knew what?"

"That no matter how much time passed, we belonged together."

"If we didn't see each other again, you would eventually find someone."

He shakes his head, saying no. "I never loved anyone before you, and I will never love anyone after you," he says, tucking a strand of my hair behind my ear. "I think I'm like my father. I can't imagine him getting married again if something happens to Mom. I knew no one would ever replace you since we met."

"I'm going to say goodbye to Yuri," I say, pulling up my shorts but still not wearing a top. He walks into the closet, and from the way he's looking at me, it's like we didn't just make love again after our bath.

"Yuri must be gone by now," he replies, frowning.

We both know it's a lie. The yacht is still moored in the marina.

I turn my face to the side, trying to understand why he looks so angry all of a sudden. "Are you jealous of your assistant?"

"Of course not."

I hide a smile. "Don't be silly." I approach, still without a shirt or bra. "I'm yours, Greek."

He holds my breast and massages the nipple with his thumb.

I groan.

"And yes. All mine now."

I cling to him, my legs wobbly. It's unbelievable the power he has over my body.

"Are you sure you want to go?"

The self-confidence in his tone makes me, even against my will, push him away.

"Cocky."

He shrugs his shoulders but doesn't deny it.

I put on a T-shirt. "I just want to thank him for what he did for my parents. With all the fuss of commercial filming and photo shoots, I didn't have time. He's a good friend, and I value people like him."

"He is. Just don't say it too much."

"Jesus!" I laugh out loud, shaking my head. I just finish getting dressed and untangle my hair with my fingers. I don't even wear sandals.

I run down the stairs and head straight for the marina.

"Yuri!"

He's stepping onto Christos's yacht, which will take the team, including the photographers, cameramen, makeup artists, and the two models, back to the shore. He turns back when I call him. "Zoe, has something happened?"

"No," I say, breathless. "I just wanted to say thank you. You were very good to my parents, organizing both the clinic for Mom and the house for them to live in during the lockdown. I owe you an eternal debt of gratitude."

"It wasn't a big deal. I just did my job," he says, seeming uncomfortable.

"That's *my* job. Take care of them, I mean. But you were wonderful. Thank you."

I wave goodbye and turn my back to return to the mansion, but first, I hear the captain shouting that someone is missing aboard and that they have to leave before the storm hits.

I go inside two steps at a time, and after wiping my feet on the mat, I head upstairs to the second floor, where I hear Christo's voice.

"Get dressed." His tone is harsh and relentless.

Having no idea what's going on, I walk to where I think he is—the kitchen.

"You don't know what you're missing." I recognize that the person he's arguing with is one of the models who participated in the shoot. My blood boils.

Get dressed?

What the hell is going on?

Before I reach them, she speaks. "If it's a woman you want to vacation with, why not me? I'm younger and prettier."

"Get out."

"She's crippled. Those scars on her feet, especially the one on the hand, are disgusting."

For a moment, I'm shaken. I look at my feet. Yes, I still have burn scars because my skin is too thin, but the makeup artist managed to cover it all up. The hand one is a little worse, but not gross.

"Get out, for fucks' sake! Didn't you understand what I just said? You are fired!" Christos yells.

I go into the kitchen, and, at the same time, the girl puts on the top she had taken off, showing her breasts to my man.

"What do you think you're doing?" I ask.

I see her bottom lip trembling.

"Get out!" My boyfriend orders again.

"Wait a moment. Let her answer me. What do you think you're doing, Hanna? You said you're younger than me, but you must be at least eighteen, or you wouldn't be here. I'll be twenty-one soon, but that's not the point. I've lived a lifetime longer than you."

"Zoe, I—" she starts, but I cut her off.

"Do you think offering to have sex, getting naked in front of a man, will make him appreciate you? In ten years, if not sooner, your ass and boobs will start to sag. Gravity, love. No one escapes that. At this rate, you will be known not for being photogenic but for having sex with your bosses. An easy fuck, as it's called in our country."

"I'm sorry," the phony says.

"I'm not done." I take two steps closer to her. "The one who spoke to you just now was the old Zoe. There's still a little bit of her in me. She is kind and compassionate. She forgives easily, too. But unfortunately, that silly girl stayed behind. The one in charge now is the angry Zoe. You are disgusting, someone who uses the fact that I have scars to try to make me smaller."

"You're jealous because you know I'm right. He'll get sick of you," she growls, her face transfigured with hate.

"Don't get me wrong, I'm angry, yes, because he's *mine*, but Christos is a big boy and knows how to shoo women like you. The main reason I despise you is for talking about my scars."

Yuri comes in, out of breath. "Hanna, what the hell are you doing here?

"Offering herself to my boyfriend, but she missed a trick. Bye, Yuri." I turn around and run up the stairs. I'm really angry, maybe more at myself than her, for letting her make me lose control.

I barely reach the room, however, when Christos grabs my arm.

"Zoe."

"I'm not upset with you. I've been modeling for almost two years now. I know how it goes in the industry. It's not the first time I've seen a girl show her boobs to a guy as some sort of business card, but it's the first time I've seen one do it for *my* man. I lied. I wanted to smack the living shit out of her."

He approaches, like when someone does a wild animal; I don't think he knows what my reaction will be.

"Are you jealous?"

"No. Jealousy doesn't begin to define it. I want to kill her."

"It wasn't what it looked like," he says, wrapping me around the waist. "I was worried when she talked about your hand. I don't care. I—"

I place my fingers over his lips. "I know. And neither do I. I could have lost my parents and my best friend, Christos. These scars are nothing. It wasn't my self-esteem she hurt. It was jealousy at its worst, but I didn't want to give in."

He laughs, which makes me relax despite all the stress from a few moments ago. Seconds later, however, he gets serious, pressing our foreheads together. "I have a gift. I was going to wait until your twenty-first birthday, but I don't want to leave anything else on hold when it comes to the two of us." He gives me a light kiss on the lips and walks away.

"Don't leave."

"Yes, sir."

I hear him going down the stairs. A minute later, he comes back with a paper in his hands.

"What is it?"

"Open it."

I read, my mouth getting huge. "A *farm*?"

"Yes. In North Carolina. Your dream of being a farmer will now come true."

"It was a distant plan. I don't know what to do with a farm."

"We will have many employees, but we can also learn together."

I look at him in disbelief, and I think he sees the question on my face because he nods in agreement.

"Yes, that's right. I'm asking you to be mine."

"I thought we were past that part. I *am* yours."

"Let me try to do better, then." He goes to the bedside table and takes out a jewelry box.

Then he kneels at my feet, and my heart races into a mad rush.

"I planned to do this with our parents present, but nothing between us follows a script, Zoe." He opens the Tiffany's box, which contains a princess-shaped diamond ring. "I had to find you and then lose you to be sure you're the one I've been waiting for my whole life. I was your silent pursuer. I loved you, even when I still didn't know it was love and—"

I don't wait for him to finish talking; I pull him by the hand, and he gets up.

"I love you," I say, "and I want to live by your side for as long as I have left in this world."

"You still didn't answer."

"Yes. Yes. Yes! There's nothing I want more than to be your wife."

Zoe

CHAPTER FORTY-EIGHT

"**CONGRATULATIONS**, baby. Would I sound too smug if I said I knew this was going to happen?"

"How?" I ask my mom, smiling.

"I'm old, but I can recognize a couple in love when I see one."

"Oh, that's true," Danae interjects. "I also noticed when they were at our house. I think we know our kids pretty well, don't you, Macy?"

I smile when she refers to her son as a child. When I look at him, he's shaking his head, too, probably for the same reason.

We're all gathered in the main house on the island, telling my parents over video call that we're getting married.

Danae and Alekos arrived earlier today, and my mother-in-law—yeah, I guess I can call her that now—was overjoyed when she heard the news.

I still can't believe it. I feel so happy, but I'm afraid it was all just a dream.

Earlier today, Christos met with his legal team. They said that the false marriage issue would be resolved within two months. My fiancé didn't like this and demanded a month as a deadline. Then he told me that he wanted us to get married as soon as a judge ruled that my relationship with Mike was invalid.

"So, where are you planning to get married?" my mom asks.

"On our farm," I answer quickly, looking at Christos.

"You have your answer, my dear mother-in-law. Zoe decides, I say yes."

I roll my eyes. "As if."

"Said like that, even a stranger would believe him!" his mother says, laughing. "You and your father are the same. If I let him, Alekos would even choose the color of my underwear."

"Too much information, Mrs. Danae," Christos says.

My mother laughs.

There's a light mood all around, and I wish for a future with a house full of children, family Christmases, and lots of love.

Those last two are already guaranteed. I feel loved and welcomed by both Christos and his parents. That, in my book, qualifies as a jackpot.

"I'm going to talk to Yuri and see if he can help me with the wedding arrangements, and I'm sure Bia will want in as well."

"Speaking of whom, how is she?" Mom asks.

"Well, after what happened, she said she wants to make changes in her life. She no longer wants to be an agent. She'll leave everything in Miguel's hands and take a year's sabbatical. She's already a hundred percent recovered from . . . our accident."

I look at Christos and see his jaw clenching.

"I'm glad divine justice was done," his mother says. "That cruel man got what he deserved," she finishes, referring to Mike.

"Well, we have to go now, sweetie. We loved the news. I hope I'm well enough to attend your wedding."

"You will be, Mom. I'm sure."

We spend a couple more minutes talking in the living room, but then I excuse myself and leave. I have something to do.

I go up to my room, and with my phone and *little Pauline* in hand, I leave the house and head for the beach.

Half an hour and many photos later, I sit on the sand, looking out at the sea.

"Hey, friend, I hope you can see from heaven how happy I am. I'm going to marry my Greek, I mean, my *Greek god*, according to his ego," I joke. "I didn't come to talk to you before because, right after the fire, my head was a mess. I don't know how to deal with difficult news, and I received it in bulk. My parents' house was destroyed, Bia was in a coma, and in the midst of it all, I moved in with Christos."

I smile thinking about what he said the other day, that life took a turn and we ended up in the same place—in each other's arms.

"Needless to say, I'm beyond relieved that my marriage to Mike, which never really worked, even in the eyes of the law, was a lie. He's such a bad person; I can't even list which parts I hated the most. No, that is not true. With everything he did to me, the one thing I won't ever forgive him for was trying to kill my family. God may one day think he deserves a second chance and get him out of hell, which is where I'm sure he is, but I reserve the right to hate him for now. Anyway, I just wanted to say 'hi' and reassure you that I haven't forgotten about our project. The photo shoots will go on, but the modeling career will not last much longer, I hope. I will always carry you in my heart wherever I go, but the time has come to live my life a little too, Pauline."

"Want some company?"

I look back and see Christos coming my way. I pat the sand beside me. "Yours? Always."

"Taking pictures with your friend?" He positions himself behind me, hugging me with his arms and legs. I feel surrounded by a wall, and the feeling is delicious.

"Yes. I haven't done it in a while because I like to send good vibes when I talk to Pauline, and at first, right after the fire, I was really upset."

"Fucking pissed off."

"What?"

"You don't have to temper your feelings, Zoe. You are human, and you have the right to go crazy sometimes. You weren't upset; you were fucking pissed off because that bastard had nearly destroyed your entire world. He lied about marrying you when he was already married. Then he stole you and, in the end, tried to kill you. You have the right to express how you really feel. Scream, allow yourself to curse, and feel angry."

"I internalize my feelings."

"Most of the time, so do I. I'm not good with words. But I don't think it's healthy for you to hold back when you're angry."

"Even if it's with you?"

"Especially with me. We are *forever*. I don't want a TV commercial kind of relationship but a real one. I'm Greek, and I have a hellish temperament. I'm controlling and arrogant, and I have no doubt that we will fight many times."

"You can bet on it. After all, I love making up with you afterward."

I feel his chest flutter behind me, and I know he's laughing.

"Am I going to have to take you to sex addiction therapy, future lady Lykaios?"

"No, thank you. I'm fine with my addiction. In fact," I say, getting up, taking off my shorts and shirt, leaving only my bikini on, "I want more."

NEW YORK

One Month Later

"Are you telling me I'm single now?" I ask the lawyer who is talking to Christos and me on a video call.

"Yes. In fact, Miss Turner, you have always been. All that was needed was for the authorities to register that."

Ignoring that we're not actually alone, I jump into Christos's lap and hug him.

I was working on a painting when he sent the maid to let me know he wanted to see me. I've enrolled in an online painting course to de-stress. I'm not *Picasso*, but I like my creations. The course has helped me manage my anxiety.

We arrived in New York three days ago. We went back to Boston from Greece because I wanted to see my parents, but Christos had to come here to deal with some business issues.

"Did you hear that? Let's get married," I say to my fiancé, happy as a fool.

"Thanks, Steve," Christos says, ending the call with the lawyer. "Tomorrow?" he asks me with one of his rare smiles.

"Not so quickly. I have yet to give my final approval for the dress. And there are some party details to figure out."

"Leave it in Yuri's hands. I'm sure he'll sort it out quickly."

"Also, Bia. She already told me that she wants to be the one to arrange the reception."

"Okay, Miss Turner. As long as it means I won't wait long until I see you walking towards me in a white dress."

"And I can't wait to have you naked on our wedding night."

"Sassy girl."

"*Your* sassy girl."

I am finishing the last few strokes on a painting I want to give as a gift to my mother when my phone rings. I don't answer right away because I don't recognize the number, but the caller is insistent, and huffing, I give up on trying to ignore it.

"Hello?" I answer, in a bad mood.

"Zoe?"

"Who is it?"

"Nelly Howard. Is this a bad time?"

Mike's mother? What the hell does she want?

"Huh . . . no. I'm sorry, I didn't recognize the number." *Nor your voice because you never wanted to interact with me.* But I keep that second part to myself.

"You wouldn't have. We only met once."

Something in her tone pisses me off, so I decide I'm not going to prolong the suffering. "I don't mean to be rude, but is there a particular reason you're calling me? When my parents lost everything, I understand you said you didn't want to talk to any of us."

"Yes, I was very angry."

"With me? Forgive my bluntness, but it was your son who tried to kill me and my family. So if anyone should be mad, it would be me."

"Yes, I know. I was depressed. The police notified me sometime after the fire at your parents' house that my Mike had died in a car accident."

"If you're expecting me to apologize for not calling to offer my condolences, that's not going to happen. I have some faults, but falsehood is not one of them."

"I didn't expect to hear you were sorry, and I didn't call to cause a fight, just to have an honest chat. I went back to church, and the priest advised me to try to make amends with the past. Fix my mistakes."

"I don't get it."

"When Mike married you, I knew he was already married. That's why I didn't show up at the registry office that day. I didn't want to be a part of that scam."

"What? Are you telling me that you knew your son was committing a crime, knew he was deceiving me and my family, and you kept quiet?"

"Yes. I know what I did wasn't right."

"Wasn't right? You let your son drag me into an illegal relationship!"

"I'm not asking you to understand my reasons. I just wanted to apologize. When you become a mother, you'll see that there are no limits to what you would do for your child."

"I will never become that kind of mother. Loving a child means raising them with good principles, and that includes teaching them right from wrong. When you failed to tell me the truth, Mrs. Howard, you gave Mike your blessing. I wish you luck in asking God for forgiveness, but you won't get it from me. Have a good afternoon."

I hang up the phone, feeling my chest lighten. Maybe that's what Christos meant about externalizing when I'm angry. I could have offered her my forgiveness, but it wouldn't have been truthful. I don't intend to harbor resentment, but I don't want anything to do with Mike, and that includes his mother.

Christos

CHAPTER FORTY-NINE

Weeks Later

NEW YORK

"I HAVE A GIFT FOR YOU. I think I'll even give it to you in advance as a wedding gift."

"Cleaning day, Beau*?" I ask hurriedly. I know he's telling me he found Howard.

I never had any doubts that he would. I didn't believe the car accident story for a second. It sounded very convenient to die that way when the police were after the damn bastard.

"Yep. You know how good I am at creating rodent traps—and, in fact, at exterminating as well."

"That's not what we agreed."

"Shall we agree on something, then? The cleaning company is mine, buddy. I don't need a partner. Besides, in the current scenario, it would be impossible to do it any other way. The cleanup was not done in the United States but in Nicaragua."

---

* This character will have a book in the future.

"What?"

"Enjoy your life, Christos. You have a beautiful woman at home. Your business is making money, not dealing with rodents. Let people like me handle the ugly side of life. I will always be vigilant."

I disagree with what he's said. I can kill without remorse for those I love; Zoe is my world.

I wish I had made Howard suffer.

What settles me is knowing that, whether his death was at the hands of Beau or his men, it would have taken hours and been painful.

To make things better, the phone rings, displaying Odin's number.

"Your wife finally has the book of her past closed. Ready to start writing a new story?"

"Feeling poetic, cousin?" I assume he's talking about the false marriage annulment because I don't think he'd have any way of knowing that Beau hunted and exterminated Mike. Or would he?

"Excited, I would say. Getting the shot will allow me to follow through with my plans."

We learned today that vaccination will start soon.

Odin doesn't elaborate on his plans. We have never talked about it, but I know what it's about to start. I don't try to dissuade him, though, because if I were in his shoes, I would do the same.

"So, as soon as you get the shot, you're going to Greece?"

"Yes. To my island."

"Is it yours now?'

"It is, and all those who occupy it. Mainly Leandros Argyros."

"What about the rest of his family?"

"I don't take revenge on women."

"Is revenge what you seek?"

"Why name it? But I would call it a reckoning."

Who am I to judge him if I'm satisfied with Mike Howard's death right now?

"How did you know Zoe's past was finally tied up?"

"Just because you asked me not to intervene doesn't mean I stopped investigating. You are my cousin. Your life is mine, too. Anyone who threatens you is my enemy."

I feel touched by what he says. Odin has managed to be even more skittish than I am, and he is basically alone in the world. I know how much our friendship means to him.

"That goes both ways, so keep in mind I'll be on the lookout when you travel to Greece."

"I had no doubt about it, but don't worry, I have it under control."

"Are you coming to our wedding?"

"I wouldn't miss it for anything."

WEEKS LATER

"What else is missing?"

"Something came up, but other than that, there's the pastry tasting. With social distancing, scheduling appointments has been chaotic."

"Could have been worse. I didn't imagine that the vaccine would be ready this year. Our parents will be the first to take it. As for us, I think we're only in group four."

"Maybe not," she says enigmatically.

"Why do I think you're keeping a secret?"

"Because I am, unfortunately, a terrible liar."

I was working in my apartment's library when she came in mysteriously. I thought it was related to the ceremony, but now I realize there's more to that sly, beautiful smile.

"I can't disagree," I say, leaning back in my chair and patting my thigh.

She straddles my lap, facing me. "That I'm a terrible liar?"

"Yup. The worst in the world. You would starve if your means of living was playing poker."

"That's not good for my self-esteem."

"Being a liar is not a good quality, so I'm not trying to destroy your ego; keep in mind that your eyes give you away. They shine like gemstones when you're happy."

"In that case, a pair of sunglasses would solve my problem."

She's getting off-topic, and I'm more curious than ever.

"You said that in addition to the pastry tasting, there's been an unforeseen event. What happened?"

"God, you don't miss a thing."

"No. So what?"

"There's an issue with the dress."

"I thought you had already decided on one. Didn't the *Vanity* stylist promise to design it?"

"Yes, and he did. It's beautiful, but it won't fit my body."

"What?"

She smiles. "We're going to have to adjust it. Extend it a little."

I stare at her without understanding at first, but then I notice the barely concealed happiness. "Have you gained weight?" I ask to be sure, but my heart is already beating hard against my rib cage.

"Yes. I'm almost five pounds, and I'm pretty sure I'll get even bigger soon."

"Words, Zoe. I want to hear it. I need to hear this," I plead, cupping her face.

My hand shakes a little. It's not easy to get me emotional, but she seems to know all the right buttons to push.

"I'm pregnant," she says, and a tear falls down her cheek. "We're going to have a baby. I know it wasn't what we agreed on, but . . ."

I kiss her because there's nothing I can say that will convey what I'm feeling.

We created a life.

My love for her is now going to be materialized in a tiny piece of both of us.

When we break the kiss, she's smiling.

"I was afraid to tell you because we hadn't talked about it yet, but I'm so happy! I feel like I've been levitating since the moment I found out earlier today."

"You thought I wouldn't be happy?"

"I know you love me. I feel it in every cell of my body, but a child is a never-ending responsibility."

"I deal well with responsibilities, but this," I say, placing my hand on her belly, "is not a responsibility; it's our love and our future. My whole world."

She snuggles into my arms and lays her head on my chest. I hold her tight.

I believe that everything happens for a reason. It was no coincidence but fate intervening when Beau found and eliminated Mike Howard a few weeks ago. It happened at the right moment, as if the pieces on the board of life were finally falling into place.

Zoe

CHAPTER FIFTY

Two Months Later

"YOU MIGHT FEEL a bit sore in your arm, miss," the nurse who had just given the first shot of the vaccine tells me.

Contrary to our initial thoughts, there were already enough shots for everyone, even though they prioritized senior citizens. I decided to get mine before the wedding because, even at the risk of being bigger on the day of the party, I knew I'd feel more relaxed knowing that everybody is immunized.

Bia came along. This is the first time we've met after all the tragedy, even though we've spoken on the phone almost every day. Lately, mainly in relation to the wedding.

"I don't like being in pain," she tells the nurse, pulling up her sleeve to get her dose.

"The other option is much worse," I point out.

"Don't tell me that. Thank God life will finally get back to normal. Once you're married, I'm finally going on vacation to the Caribbean, starting my long-awaited sabbatical year."

"A cruise?" I ask as we walk back to the car.

"No. My friend married a millionaire." She stops and smiles.

"*Another* friend of mine besides you," she corrects herself, "married a millionaire. Although, in Christos's case, the right thing to say is *billionaire*."

"And will they lend you an island?" If she wants to travel, she could go to Christos's island in Greece.

"Are you jealous?"

"Yes, I am."

"Perhaps during my wanderings next year, I might pass by yours."

"Just let me know if you really want to go."

"Speaking of Greece, the commercial and catalog you made on Christos's island are scattered all over the world. Do you have any idea how many phone calls and emails Miguel has received every day from brands wanting you to represent them?"

"Let's get rich," I joke.

"You're already rich. The contract you closed with Christos got you to such a level you're envied among the catwalk elite. But according to Miguel, you got a proposal from *Vanity's* rival. They are willing to double Christos's offer for an exclusive contract and still pay his fine if you decide to change boats."

"Does this company know that my Greek is not only my employer but also my future husband?"

"Probably, even if you haven't announced your marriage in public yet."

"Because Christos decided to do that when we go to the opera, in an exclusive introduction to high society, a little more than a month from now. My belly will already be visible, and the gossip websites present will have two topics to talk about at once. It will be good, even, because when they find out I'm pregnant, they'll quickly give up offering me a fortune to model."

"I don't know. This new *Vanity* commercial is so popular now, I believe they would be willing to wait for you to have the baby."

"I doubt very much that they don't know that Christos and I are together. Gossip runs wild in our industry. Do they really think I would break a contract with my future husband in exchange for more money?"

"Love, you don't know what some people are capable of for a few extra bucks in their account."

"Some people are, but not me. Even if I wasn't in love with Christos, no amount of money would make me break a contract. I will stay exclusively with *Vanity* for the agreed five years; then, I'll stop modeling altogether."

OPERA NIGHT

A Month and a Half Later

"I'm a little nervous," I say before he opens the limo door. "No, let me rephrase that. I'm *very* nervous."

"I know. I already know you, Zoe. You are emanating electricity."

"They'll eat me alive when I get out of the car. Mainly because of the dress I chose."

He looks at my rounded belly. Because I'm thin, if I wore a loose dress, I could still hide it, but with this tight and strapless dress, there's no doubt.

"Did you do it on purpose?"

"Yes. I'm not ashamed of our boys."

We found out we are having twins. It was a surprise and a joy, too. Two babies at the same time are a blessing. I just didn't understand how it was possible until talking to Madeline on the phone—my cousin and, I think, the only blood relative who likes me. She told me that her mother had a miscarriage of twins once. Then she told me about cases of twins in the family, saying that's probably why I was blessed.

She's a sweetheart, and she's going to be here tonight. Unfortunately, so is her mother, but life isn't perfect, is it?

"Fuck gossip, Zoe. What matters is the two of us. Or rather, the four of us. No one will make us ashamed of our family."

"Never. I think the nerves are more because I don't like to be in the spotlight."

"Not drawing attention in your case is impossible. You are beautiful. Go inside with your head held high. I will be by your side every step of the way."

The car door opens, and I see the bodyguards already in place. Christos gets out and offers me his hand, and as I step out, I'm blinded by flashes. It's scary because even with the security guards' human barrier, they look like flies on honey.

It's as if now that they're all vaccinated, they've given themselves the right to forget about good manners. I'm used to the harassment, especially at the end of a fashion show, but what's happening today is surreal.

It can only be because of *Vanity,* or possibly for being on Christos's arm, or perhaps for both things together.

I keep a frozen, impersonal smile, and my face is stiff with tension. The only thing that reassures me a little is Christos's arm around my waist while his other hand cups my abdomen.

I ignore the questions that seem to come from all sides, concentrating on not tripping.

My heart beats too fast, and my hands are cold. It's more difficult than I imagined, and I can only breathe a sigh of relief when we finally enter the theatre.

"Everything ok?" Christos asks.

"Yes," I lie and then correct myself. "Anxious."

He kisses my lips. "I don't want to be here either, but we need this public appearance. Otherwise, the world would turn upside down when they found out about the marriage and the pregnancy. It will be better this way. Tomorrow, Yuri will make an official statement in the newspapers."

I nod, praying that the night will go by quickly.

"Zoe?" a hesitant voice calls out to me, and I turn around to see who it is.

It's my cousin, Madeline Turner.

"I can't believe we're finally meeting again," she says.

We don't kiss or hold hands. It's horrible, but people have avoided doing it even after taking the shot. I think this will be another scar in the collective memory: the fear of hugging and kissing.

"Madeline, I'm so glad to see you. You're beautiful."

"Thanks," she says shyly. She really is beautiful. Fair skin, huge blue eyes, and delicate as a fairy. She wears a long, red, flashy dress that doesn't match her personality at all. I'm sure she wasn't the one who chose it.

"Madeline, this is my fiancé, Christos. Christos, this is the cousin I told you about, Madeline."

They exchange pleasantries, and a man approaches, catching my fiancé's attention. I turn to talk to Madeline but freeze when I hear someone say, "Zoe, how wonderful to see you again, darling!"

Oh, Jesus. Hypocrisy has a first and last name: Adley Turner, my aunt. Or rather, Madeline's mother, since she was never an aunt to me.

And "darling"? She offered me a maid's uniform the last time we saw each other!

I turn towards the voice begrudgingly.

The woman has a smile so wide—and fake—it looks like she's got a tattoo on her face. "You never visited me again, but I'm not one to hold grudges, so I'll disregard your ingratitude."

I can't hold back an eye roll.

"I'm very happy with the campaign's success," she says, looking at my pregnant belly, clearly marked by the dress.

Maybe I'm too sensitive, but I feel like she's insinuating I got the job because of the belly bump since *Vanity* is Christos's.

"Thanks," I reply dryly.

"But I see you won't be able to shoot for a long time." She takes a step forward with her hand outstretched as if to stroke my belly.

I walk backward, but before I can move any farther, Christos's voice booms. "No."

It's an undeniable 'no'—the kind that leaves no doubt and is brimming with subtext:

Don't come any closer.
Don't bother my wife.
Don't touch my children.

She freezes, her smile fading a little. "Christos Lykaios. I heard some talk that my niece was"— she pauses dramatically, and I want to hit her —"*working* with you."

I hear a disgusted sigh from Madeline, and I feel sorry for her. She's probably ashamed of her mother's behavior.

My fiancé puts his arm around me. "She is not just working," he says at a volume anyone inside the VIP can hear. "She is mine in every way. Zoe will be my wife and the mother of my children."

An "ohhhhh" is heard, and then silence reigns for almost half a minute.

Adley is the first to recover. "Oh, what a joy!" She completely changes her tone. "Congratulations, Zoe. I am very happy with the news. When is the wedding?"

I hit my limit of masochism for the day.

Ignoring the viper's question, I turn to Madeline. "Can you join me in the toilet?"

"Of course."

I take Christos's hand and give it a kiss. "I'll be back."

He looks at me like he wants to say something but holds himself back. As we walk away, I notice a bodyguard following us.

Zoe

CHAPTER FIFTY-ONE

"I'M SORRY ABOUT EVERYTHING, ZOE."

"It's not your fault, Maddie," I say, calling her by her nickname. "No one chooses the mother they have."

She lets out a huff of laughter. "I know that better than anyone."

"You're coming to my wedding, right?"

"Yes, I am. I've never been to North Carolina. I'm really excited, but I wanted to ask you a favor."

I stop walking. "Of course."

"Please help me choose a dress. My mother always criticizes all my clothes, and when she helps me, they look like this," she says, pointing to her current outfit.

"It's beautiful, but it doesn't suit you."

"I know. I'm not that fancy; I don't like to show a lot. With all due respect," she says, looking at my dress, where there's a large slit that leaves my left thigh exposed.

"I'm used to dressing and undressing. I'm not ashamed to show my body anymore. But at the beginning of my career, I was much shyer. Therapy helped with the process."

"And speaking of not being ashamed, I'm thinking about doing something crazy," she says.

"What kind of something?"

"I'm running away to London. I'll get a job. Live life."

"What?"

"Do you think I'm not capable?"

"If you're asking me about mental strength, I think anyone is capable of anything. I just don't understand the reason for the sudden change."

"I've been planning this for a long time. I want to get out from under my mother's wing and go to Europe. I can't take the pressure she's putting on me to get married anymore. I finished college, but I can't work because it would 'embarrass the Turners' good name,'" she says, mimicking her mother.

I laugh because she sounds just like her. "What do you need to carry out this plan?"

"Moral support, mostly."

"Well, that you already have. Count on me for whatever you need. Actually, I just had an idea. There is a friend of Christos, Kamal. He is a *sheikh* and a businessman. CEO, actually. My fiancé mentioned he was looking for an assistant in London."

"My goodness! Do you think I could do that?"

"Well, you have some qualifications. As I understand it, he wants someone to travel with him and teach him Western culture and social etiquette."

"Tips on social etiquette? Is he rude?"

"I have no idea. But if you want, I can talk to Christos about it."

"Of course! Do you think this man would consider me for the job?"

I decide to be honest. "I don't know. I've never met a *sheikh* in my life. Unfortunately, he won't be coming to my wedding because he has a commitment for the same week; otherwise, Christos could introduce the two of you. But I promise I'll talk to my fiancé about it."

The bathroom is empty, and after we've used the stalls, we touch up our makeup and talk about a new lipstick brand that's just been released and doesn't test on animals.

Suddenly, the door opens, and in the mirror, I see the last person I would ever imagine seeing tonight.

Ernestine Lambert, Pauline's mother.

She is still a beautiful woman, although she's a shadow of her former beauty. She's well-dressed in a long black gown, completely comfortable as a high-society lady.

She looks surprised to see me. I think we're both in shock, actually, but I recover first.

"Hello, you liar. What are you doing here?" I ask.

Yeah, I think the pregnancy hormones are working on me in a really crazy way. I'm in a phase where if someone pisses me off, I feel like ripping the person's head off.

"Zoe, it's a pleasure to see you again! Regarding your question, you weren't the only one who got a billionaire, sweetheart."

"I can't say the same. I take no pleasure in seeing you again." I turn to my cousin. "Madeline, can you go outside and make sure no one comes in?"

She leaves without arguing.

"We don't have anything to talk about, Zoe. Or do you want to apologize for being that murderer's lover?"

"If you open your mouth to talk about my fiancé again, I'm going to hit you. In fact, you won't say a thing. I will. How can you look in the mirror after what you've done? You're rotten, Ernestine. She was your little girl. Your girl to love and to protect. You knew who put her in that condition and yet lied to all of us. You took advantage of the fact that Pauline was too young to remember the real culprit. Why? To earn people's pity? So that no one would know what an irresponsible bitch you are? Not satisfied, you handed the compensation over to another boyfriend while your daughter was in need!"

"You don't know anything."

"Maybe not, but what I know makes me sick. I never thought I'd say something like this, but Pauline was lucky to go to heaven. God took her because you didn't deserve her. Liar, gold-digger. You are a waste of a human being, as rotten and vile as that rat that caused the accident. I hope that when you die, the two of you meet in hell. Live a shitty life, thinking about what your daughter has suffered because of you. Or at least the consequences of your actions."

I leave before I do something stupid, like shoving my hand in her face. Don't get me wrong; it's not being at a fancy party that's holding me back; it's a concern for my babies. I don't want to harm them, so even though I feel mad, I decide to leave.

When I get to the hallway, Maddie is still in position, like a soldier.

Christos is talking to a bodyguard, and a few steps away from him, there's an old man with white hair.

My intuition tells me this man is with Ernestine, and when I see her come out of the bathroom in my peripheral vision and walk towards him, I follow.

"Nice to meet you. I'm Zoe Turner. I don't know what your relationship is with Ernestine, but if you want advice, run while you can. What is someone who doesn't have an ounce of love within them to protect their own daughter capable of doing to a stranger? If you want to look for me, I'll tell you the whole story."

I take a business card out of my purse and hand it to him. Then I turn my back on them and walk over to my man.

He puts his arm around my shoulders and starts walking me back to the hall. We are followed by Maddie and the bodyguard.

"What just happened?" he asks, not seeming to understand anything.

"Do you know who she is?"

"I'm not sure I know her. The face is familiar to me, but—"

"The liar responsible for our breakup. Pauline's mother."

His face gets angry, and he stops walking. He tries to go back, but I grab his arm.

"No, love. It's over. It's finally over."

Beau Carmouche–LeBlanc
CHAPTER FIFTY-TWO

\\\\\\\\\\\\

The Day Before Christos's Wedding

SOMEWHERE IN CENTRAL AMERICA

"WHY DON'T you just fucking kill me?" he shouts.

There is no longer any dignity in what is left of him. There is not a single vestige of the arrogant, wife-beater professor.

"So rude, doctor. Your former students would be shocked by that language. Not all, of course. Those you fucked are probably used to it."

"What the fuck did I ever do to you?"

"To me? Nothing. But last time, you got the victim wrong, Mike. Unfortunately for you, you messed with the girl of a good friend of mine."

"Who? Why don't you at least tell me what I'm being accused of?"

"Because it wouldn't be as much fun," I reply indifferently.

Howard doesn't know it yet, but today is his last day on this planet. I let my men take care of him for months, but I came personally to finish the job.

"Ahhhhhhhh!" he screams in desperation, and I fold my arms, leaning against a wall.

"What? Not so cool when you're the victim and not a helpless old couple, is it? Or your ex-wife . . . oops, wait. She was never your wife. I just remembered. Neither on paper nor biblically."

"Am I here because of that bitch? I never wanted her; I was only interested in her money," he lies because I doubt any man alive could be indifferent to the beauty of Lykaios's bride.

"I don't believe you. However, that doesn't matter anymore, my friend. She's fine. Her parents, too. Macy recovered from cancer. Scott is healthy as a bull, and you, you are here, stuck in a basement in the middle of nowhere, being tortured for months. Was it worth it?"

A glimmer of hope appears in his eyes. "No. I'm sorry."

I take the blade I like to work with, and in a single blow, I end his life.

"It was a rhetorical question, Mike. By the time you got in my friend's way, you were already dead. You just didn't know it yet."

Christos

CHAPTER FIFTY-THREE

Christos and Zoe's Wedding Day

NORTH CAROLINA
SHE'S COMING FOR ME.

Beautiful, smiling.

Mine.

We've gone through a lifetime to get here, but from today onwards, only death can part us. Maybe not even death.

Zoe has blossomed. At the same time, her appearance remains caught between girl and woman.

She's been laughing and joking a lot lately, and I believe Macy's recovery was a big factor in that equation.

Oh, and our boys, of course. She loves being pregnant and is happy to see her belly grow.

She's also more confident. She's bold enough to occasionally displease one person or another.

My mom, my mother-in-law, Zoe, and Bia planned the entire wedding, using Yuri as a last resort. I suspect he thanked his lucky stars because when the four of them started talking at the same time, only a translator could understand.

When I asked why she didn't hire a professional wedding planner, she replied that this would be her one and only wedding, so she wanted to do everything she had always dreamed of.

A few days ago, we made the farm in North Carolina our permanent home. The move was discussed with the entire family, and when my parents said they would move to Chapel Hill to be closer to us, she cried.

However, I knew her happiness would never be complete without Scott and Macy around. So, after talking to my in-laws, I bought them a house next door to my parents. Thus, the four will be able to participate in their grandchildren's lives—not only the twins to come but also many others, as we plan to contribute generously to the planet's population.

Zoe walks arm in arm with her father, and Scott looks very proud of his little girl. He whispers something to her, and she smiles.

God, the woman is so beautiful. I am completely in love with her, with everything about her.

We have our disagreements like any couple—usually because of my overprotectiveness and the fear of something happening to her—but the fights don't last. Zoe has the power to calm my reactive nature.

She's still in therapy, and her anxiety disorder has subsided, although sometimes it rears its head. The other day, she woke up in the middle of the night and asked me what would become of the babies if we died.

I know it's her mind playing tricks. It's not something you can avoid. I have read about it. Anxiety disorder is not *drama*, as most people think; it's a real diagnosis.

I even took an online course to learn how to help her deal with it. I learned that an anxiety attack can be triggered by anything. We've talked about it and tried to create strategies to avoid them, but it's not always possible.

Anyway, there are almost no sad moments now, and every day spent with her is a novelty.

Zoe's kindness is a match for her beauty.

She finally stands in front of me, and Scott hugs her before pinching her cheek. Dad comes down from the pulpit, breaking protocol, to kiss her on the forehead.

I think my wife needed it—the feeling of being welcomed into a family that loves her. Together with Macy and Scott, we form a whole package, and our kids are coming to add to it.

We opted for a small ceremony with only fifty guests—mostly family members like Odin.

Beau apologized, saying weddings aren't his scene. I didn't take it the wrong way. He's already proved that he is my loyal friend. Everyone deals with what they can.

I was persuaded by my assistant to grant entry to a few handpicked journalists and photographers. Although I wasn't too happy about it, Yuri argued that if we didn't allow them to come, the press would speculate and turn the beginning of our marriage into hell, trying to find news.

After Macy and Mom hug her too, I finally come face-to-face with the woman of my life.

I kiss her, satiating some of the eternal hunger for her, rather than just accepting her hand to make our way down the aisle. I ignore what the celebrator of our faith, the orthodox church, says. For me, the ceremony is just a protocol for society, like the sheet of paper we will sign.

Zoe is mine, and I am hers.

There is nothing and no one that can change that fact.

Her small hand squeezes mine, holding me tight, and I can feel how excited she is.

She turns to face me, and I know it's time for the vows. She smiles and kisses my hand before speaking.

"I was very anxious . . ." She pauses. "No, I *still am* very anxious, but I stayed that way a little longer because, in addition to never having spoken before an audience"—she turns to the guests, smiling—"I wanted everything to be perfect. At the same time, I didn't want something rehearsed, because my story with my love has never followed a script."

Shaking her head, she points to her face, which is red. I know how hard it must be to be the center of attention.

"I love you," I say.

"Me too." She gives me a light kiss. "When I met my Greek, the one you call Christos Lykaios, I knew from the start that he was my Prince Charming. A reluctant one, aloof, but my heart already knew before we both realized that he would be mine *forever*. Unlike fairy tales, the prince and the princess parted ways for a while. She was lost and scared, but the prince was not a man to give up easily. He found me once, and then he found me again. He loved and protected me. Thank you for joining us on this very special day. In a little while, you'll witness the true beginning of our history and say: *and they lived happily ever after.*"

Zoe throws herself into my arms for a long kiss.

When we finally pull away from each other, I prepare to declare my devotion to her in public.

"I planned to recite a poem, but I've just decided on something more real that doesn't echo what perhaps thousands of couples have repeated all over the world. There are no words to express what you are to me, Zoe. You are my wife, lover, mother of my children, my home, and my soul. You are my only, the first, the eternal. My love."

Zoe

EPILOGUE ONE

Wedding Night

I THOUGHT THAT, after so much time together, the thrill of making love to Christos would subside, but I feel overwhelmed like the first time.

I like everything about him, especially the way he looks at me. His gaze is deep and full of unspoken words, but it radiates so much love and desire that it makes me dizzy.

I'm just a few steps away. I feel beautiful, regardless of having gained several pounds.

"Do you have any idea how crazy it drives me to see you exposing yourself to me with that round belly holding our babies?

I shake my head no, but it's a lie. One corner of my mouth turns up, and he knows I'm teasing him.

We undress for each other, but while my husband is naked, gorgeous, and has an inviting hard-on promising a delicious night, I keep my panties on.

I run my fingers over my sensitive nipples, and I hear a husky sound coming from his throat. "Are you going to let me play with your body?" I ask.

"I'm yours, woman."

I walk close.

"Take off your panties." But as soon as he says it, he kneels in front of me. "No, I'll do it."

He pulls down the garment slowly, and feeling his fingers on my hot skin makes me shiver in pleasure.

I'm naked now, but he doesn't spread my legs, just my lower lips. He sucks my most sensitive spot, and I have to lean back to keep myself from falling.

"You told me you were mine," I moan, desperate. My plan to seduce him is going downhill.

"Yeah, I am, but I never promised to sit still." He drapes one of my thighs over his shoulder and tastes me with his mouth open, devouring me hungrily.

Before long, trembling, I melt into his lips.

He carries me to the bed and gets in with me.

"You play dirty, Lykaios."

"I can't resist, Zoe. You're delicious," he says, running his tongue over his lower lip.

He's lying on his back, and I'm straddling his thighs, but our sexes aren't touching yet.

I close my eyes, the force of my love for him making tears well up.

"Look at me," he commands as he holds my hips, fitting us together.

He invades me slowly, as if tasting, and I moan loudly.

When he has me completely, he doesn't move; he just feels me, open to him—soul, body, and heart.

One hand caresses my rigid nipple while the other rests on my belly.

"Ride me," he commands.

He holds me by my butt cheeks, lifting me up. I release my body, taking him slowly.

The adjustment between us is difficult. My tight sex is stretched to accommodate every inch of him, making us moan as it travels inch by inch inside my walls.

"I love you," he repeats each time I descend onto his thick hardness.

My hands rest on his shoulders. I'm crazy with pleasure, but I'm also flooded with a love so intense it robs me of the ability to speak.

Perhaps sensing this, he takes control, taking us on a ride that is also an unbreakable connection. He takes a deep hold on me; all I can think about is how perfectly we are together.

"More," I beg.

He touches my clit and sits up on the bed, sucking on my nipples, his strokes speeding up wildly.

"You're so hot," he says, and when he shifts his hips, getting the perfect angle, I scream out his name and come.

I grind on him, determined to drag him along with me, and I feel victorious when I see his tense face as a warning that his own release is close.

"I'm going to come."

"Give me everything. Fill me up."

"Zoe . . ." he howls.

Our bodies create their own cadence, ceaselessly seeking each other in constant strokes for several minutes.

He thickens inside my body, and when the first spurts of his orgasm fill me, I feel complete.

He lies down, pulling me off himself and positioning me on my back. Minutes pass, and I can still feel the beating of his heart—our hearts—racing.

"How is it possible that it always get better?" I ask.

"Because it's not just physical, my Zoe, or our perfect fit in search of pleasure, but a meeting of skin, smells, mouths, tongues, and most of all, our souls."

"Who is she in Odin's life?"

We're on our way to New York. Christos has a meeting there. I want to shop for the babies and get a haircut with a Brazilian hairdresser whom Bia recommended. I'm sick of my current style.

When he found out we were coming, Odin invited us to have dinner at his house. According to Christos, a woman will be there: Elina

Argyros.

"If I could guess, I'd say she's his girlfriend. What other name can you give a couple living together?"

"Roommates?"

He smiles. "Odin with a roommate? My cousin is the most independent human being who ever lived."

"So were you, Mr. Lykaios, and yet here we are."

He looks serious for a moment, then unbuckles my seat belt, and leads me by the hand into the bedroom of his—*our*—plane.

He lies down on the bed and pulls me to his side. "Because I was missing you in my life, Zoe. Even before I met you, I knew I still hadn't found the right person."

"How could you know?"

"Souls recognize their other half, even if brains don't."

"Even when we fight?"

"Sharing life with someone is not simple, but everything in life is worth it—even your mess."

"I'm not messy. You are a neat freak."

"I don't deny it, but I don't mind picking up your panties scattered across the closet floor. They smell delicious."

I laugh so hard I lose my breath. "I don't even have words to express how perverted that sounded, husband."

"I thought that point was already established. I'm a pervert, but only when it comes to you, woman."

"Well said, Christos. I've been more jealous than usual. Preserve your life."

"I'm crazy about you, Zoe Lykaios. How can you feel insecure?"

"Because sometimes I still don't believe it."

"Believe what?"

"That we turned a fairy tale into real life."

Christos

EPILOGUE TWO

Lykaios Twins' Birth

IT'S as if all the emotions I haven't allowed myself to feel throughout my life have been accumulated on a mileage card for me to experience with Zoe.

I look at my wife in the hospital bed with a baby in each arm while the nurse photographs her as requested. I can't move, transfixed by the flood of love that washes over me at the sight of the three of them reunited.

Adonis and Demetrius came into the world like real Lykaioses, screaming at the top of their lungs, announcing their debuts, so no one could doubt there was another generation of arrogant Greeks on the way.

Zoe smiles as she looks from one to the other. Happiness radiates from her like light.

My wife shines. Complete, beautiful, motherly.

My heart hammers in my chest, and I say a silent prayer, thanking God for my family.

The nurse now asks the four of us to pose for a photo. I do it on automatic, my brain not functioning normally because, right now, I'm all heart.

After she's photographed us, she walks away, giving us privacy, and I kiss my wife and each of the babies, trapping them in a protective fortress.

"You're very quiet, Mr. Lykaios," Zoe says as the nurses get my boys to return them to the nursery.

"Because I can't find the right words."

"For what?"

"To show you what I'm feeling, so I'd rather just hold it and thank the universe, God, fate, whatever brought us together. I love you, my Zoe."

Ten Years Later

Lying on a towel, we watch our kids sit at the picnic table with their grandparents.

We have a team of five, but we still weren't satisfied, so we're expecting another little girl next Christmas.

There are four biological children—two sets of twins, boys—and one child of the heart, Elijah, the youngest.

Our parents are passionate about the children, and although Zoe's mother's health still needs care, she's rid of her cancer, and it hasn't come back. It's always hanging over our heads because we're always expecting it to return, but as Macy herself says, why live suffering in anticipation?

The second set of twins gave us a scare. Yes, I know it's lucky, but four babies with little time between them basically requires a war operation: an army of servants and a lot of love from the grandparents because Zoe and I continue with our careers.

I have adjusted my life to be closer to the children because I miss my family when I'm away.

Zoe had been off the catwalks for over five years when our contract ended, as she insisted on fulfilling it entirely. Now, she runs two non-profit organizations that aim to care for children and the elderly in need.

The current pregnancy with our Athina was a surprise, but we also very much desired a girl.

I wonder how she will deal with our five little boys. For better or worse, they all have my temper. Even Elijah, only two years old, seems to behave like his brothers. They are always trying to mark their territory and are somewhat controlling.

"Athina wants to join in the fun with her brothers," Zoe says, probably because our little girl is moving in her belly.

"Really?" I snuggle her closer in my arms.

She nods in agreement. "I think we're in for a surprise with this one."

"God, don't say that. I was hoping she'd be born with your temper."

She laughs. "Your genes are stronger, but I'm fine with that. I enjoy getting all the Lykaioses in line."

"I don't care. You can keep trying."

She looks back, lost in an expression of outrage and laughter.

"You're so arrogant," she says, pulling me in for a kiss, "but in a way that drives me crazy."

"All yours, woman. Use me at will."

"That is exactly what I intend, Greek. Our parents will stay with the children today. Get ready to have a sleepless night."

"Was that supposed to be a threat? Because it sounds like paradise to me. Take everything you want from me, Zoe. I'm yours."

The end!

Bonus

In the following pages, you will find bonuses from the upcoming book in this series as well as from another book that will be published soon.

Odin Lykaios

BONUS

GREECE

HE'S DYING.

The only person who knows what I've become is dying.

I don't know if I love him.

I don't think I can really love anyone anymore, but he saved me.

Not only took care of me until I was healed, but also helped me be reborn.

My savior paid for my studies and taught me four more languages besides the ones I already knew from my parents. In addition to Norwegian and Greek, I'm now fluent in English, German, French, and Italian.

I underwent two regenerative plastic surgeries, but incredibly, the fire didn't disfigure my face. The hardest hit area was my back. I still have some marks.

I covered them up with a tattoo before I went to live on that bastard's island.

I don't mind being marked. The scars on my skin are nothing compared to what I have etched in my memory. I only got the tattoo so as not to arouse suspicion.

For all intents and purposes, I'm Odin Lykaios only. No one knows my middle name is Hagebak, except my savior and Aristeu, my father's cousin, whom I moved in with about a year ago after I fully recovered.

Living on the island of Leandros Argyros was a decision my savior and I made. I needed to study the enemy closely, and my father's cousin is his head gardener.

Even though his closeness poisons my blood every day, I've learned a lot since I arrived.

"How is everything going?"

I look at the man who is more bone than skin, and I know he won't live long. Yet, on his deathbed, he seems as focused as ever on helping me get my revenge.

"I'm leaving in two weeks."

I got a scholarship to study at a university in the United States, which was also part of our plan. To the letter, I need to follow the script to destroy Leandros.

I completed high school in Athens and only moved in with Aristeu when I was in my senior year.

I don't know how he managed it, but my savior not only got all my documents, but he also legally adopted me.

He's not Greek. When I asked where his last name came from, he only said that he came from somewhere in Scandinavia.

Was that why he kept helping me? Did the fact that I was born to a Norwegian mother make him think there was a bond between us? I don't know for sure, but I don't care either, to be honest. There's nothing I really care about other than making Leandros Argyros pay.

Our plan started when I moved to Athens. There, I started playing basketball, and given my height, it wasn't difficult to stand out.

My grades have always been excellent, too.

I had nothing else to do but study, play basketball, and hate.

However, I returned to the island every weekend. Always watchful. Always with both eyes on that damn bastard.

"All I have will be yours."

I don't thank him or say I don't need it. I always knew I would be his heir. It's not the first time we've talked about it. As he told me, he has no living relatives, and receiving this initial sponsorship will ease my plans.

"But you must promise me that you will never back down. Don't feel sorry for anyone, Odin. They didn't feel sorry for you."

I stare at the gaunt-skinned man. "Why are you like this?" There is no accusation in my question; I am just curious. I know why I'm empty and why there's so much hate inside me, but now I can see that he also has a story behind his desire to help me.

"It doesn't matter. I don't have much time left. Just promise me you won't give up."

"I couldn't give up, even if I wanted to. I want to be able to go back to sleep, and that will only happen when it's all over."

"You must be merciless."

"There is no room for pity inside me."

"Great, now I can die in peace."

"But I want answers. So far, I've followed your lead, but there's a reason you hate him, too. Why?"

"How do you know I hate him?"

I don't bother to answer. I stare at him, and he finally gives in after a while.

"At the right time, you will know everything. Along with the will, there is a letter. Give me your word that you won't read it until your revenge is complete."

"Why?"

"You've trusted me until now. I ask you to have a little more faith. Don't try to find out my motives beforehand. When it's all over, I promise you'll have the answers."

"You have my word."

I don't usually walk around the island.

I can't draw attention, even though I'm sure he doesn't know who I am.

Lucky for me, despite being half Scandinavian, I look like a Greek. There's nothing that betrays my Nordic ancestry other than the name.

Still, I don't trust myself not to kill him right away, so I try to stay behind the scenes.

Death is not enough for him.

There has to be public humiliation, the loss of everything he has built, his honor, and in the end, his life.

Today, however, I had to walk.

It's the anniversary of my rebirth.

The date I lost my family and was rescued to avenge them.

My savior died the same night I went to visit him, but not before we went over our entire plan. Soon, I will leave Greece and be away for a long time, so I decided to take a stroll to say goodbye to my land.

I'm sitting on the beach when I see a thoroughbred Arabian horse trotting across the sand right next to the waterline.

I love to ride. It was one of the many things my savior taught me, but I can't expose myself because of my secret.

I observe the elegance of the Amazon on the horse with fascination. She rides it without a saddle, and even before she's close enough, I know who she is.

Elina.

The eldest daughter of my enemy. Her blonde beauty always mesmerizes me.

The girl doesn't look Greek.

Every time I get the chance, I watch her from afar.

I reckon she can't be more than thirteen, so our age difference is five years. She looks like her mother, but her skin has nuances of mixed races.

Like me, Elina is not one hundred percent Greek. Cinthya, her mother, is English. Unlike her sisters, she's tall.

I don't speak to any of the Argyroses—not even Theodoro, my cousin Orien's best friend—but I've studied them and their parents.

Elina's sisters have matriarchal personalities with submissive postures. The blonde is different, though. She demonstrates independence, a desire for freedom that shines through even when riding.

I follow her with my eyes, knowing that the moment she passes me, she will turn her head to look.

She always does.

As for me, even though I really want to continue admiring her, I pretend not to pay attention. There would be only one reason I would approach an Argyros: to destroy her father.

I have no room for feelings other than hate—at least until my revenge is carried out.

I have no intention of involving the bastard's children in my plans unless absolutely necessary. It's not their fault they were born to that monster. I too will have children one day, and I don't want them to be held responsible for my sins.

Despite planning a family, I don't think I'll ever be able to love a woman like my father loved my mother.

When it's all over, I'll find a wife to carry on my last name. It will not be an arrangement involving feelings but a deal we both profit from.

As soon as I believe she won't be able to see me anymore, I turn in the direction she's gone, but to my surprise, I notice that she's dismounted from her horse and is walking towards me.

I'm so shocked I can't move, but I know I must act when I see her smiling.

I get up and start walking in the opposite direction, but she doesn't seem willing to give up.

"Is your name Odin?"

I stop walking and wait.

It's funny how she talks very slowly as if she is testing every word. I've never heard anyone talking like that.

"Theo said you came to live here only a year ago. Where are you from?"

I turn around, and for the first time, I can get a good look at her face. She's at that intermediate stage between being a teenager and a woman, but you can already tell she will be stunning.

Blonde hair in an almost golden tone, flawless skin, and the most beautiful green eyes I've ever seen.

She is smiling and has a disarming expression.

I find myself almost smiling back.

The girl is charming.

Then my savior's voice appears in my mind and I remember who she is.

Who we are.

"Why would that be any of your business?"

Her face instantly reddens, but she doesn't flinch, which I'm in awe of.

"Why are you talking to me like that? I didn't mean to offend. I was trying to make friends."

I stare for a moment, in silence, at the innocent girl. I'm confused about what to do for the first time, but in the end, I know which way to go.

"And who says I want to be your friend? Find a child your own age to play with. I'm not interested in stupid little girls."

She takes two steps back like she's been physically assaulted, and I'm ashamed of myself, but I don't want any ties to the Argyros.

"I'm sorry," she says and lowers her head, but then she lifts it again, and when she does, her whole posture changes. "I'm not stupid. I was trying to be nice, but I shouldn't expect anything different from an employee. Your social class has no idea how people should behave in society."

I'm not offended by what she says—I don't expect anything different from an Argyros—but I'm amazed that she's so young and already has a defensive demeanor.

Any other girl her age who heard what I said would have burst into tears. So, while I don't want to approach her because she was born under the Argyros surname, a small part of me admires her.

"One day, I'll make you swallow every single one of those words," I promise.

Her chin rises even higher. "I'll be waiting."

"Are you sure about this, son? I don't feel good knowing you'll be on the other side of the world."

I face the simple man who, along with my two cousins, is the only family I have left in Greece.

As far as I know, the part of my maternal family that lives in Scandinavia doesn't give a damn whether I'm alive or dead.

"I can't stay. I need to study."

"And that's the only reason you're leaving, Odin?"

He's never asked me directly about my plans for the future, but I suspect he knows.

When I came to live here a year ago, Aristeu told me that he had searched for me for a long time when he heard about the fire that killed my family and that he had already lost hope that I had survived. We lived on another island, and even when they were alive, my parents and Aristeu were never close. As far as I know, Mom and Dad visited him only once, and I wasn't with them.

My savior said that Leandros doesn't even know I exist. He didn't see me on the day of the fire, so he had no idea there was a survivor.

Keeping myself isolated while I recovered was a major concern of my savior; we couldn't risk anyone getting suspicious.

When I came here, I asked Aristeu to say that I was a distant nephew, explaining to my uncle that we didn't know whether whoever killed my parents would come after me.

I was supposed to stay under the radar until I was ready so I could work on my revenge.

I don't know if Aristeu believed that, but maybe he did. He's a man with a generous heart and, like all good people, gullible.

"Tell me the truth: are you going to look for whoever set your house on fire? Do you know who he is? Does this person live in the United States?"

He's never asked me so many questions directly, and while a part of me feels guilty for leaving him in the dark, keeping him ignorant of the facts surrounding my relatives' deaths is also a way of protecting him.

"I don't want to lie to you. Don't ask me something I can't answer right now."

"Revenge leads nowhere, son."

"I don't care what name you call it, but I made a promise and nothing will change my mind."

"Promise? To whom?"

I don't answer.

"You don't know anyone there. This idea of living in America is crazy. You're just a boy," he insists.

"I will survive. You don't need to worry about me."

"How can you be sure you'll find what you're looking for?"

Before I can control myself—because until now, I've never shown any feelings in front of anyone other than my savior—I say, "Because hate moves me. Every day I get out of bed, every time I walk this earth, I don't allow myself to forget."

He looks genuinely scared, but he recovers quickly. "That's not healthy, Odin. Cultivating pain, feeding anger. This feeling is only poisoning you, son."

"Aristeu, there's no cure for me. Take care of Orien and Milena. I'll be fine. When I finally get what I want, I will get you and the boys out of here."

"I'm not going anywhere. This is where the love of my life is buried. I can't go far."

"I won't argue with you. Take care of yourself and take care of my cousins. Especially Milena. Don't let her near the Argyroses. If you want my advice, send her away. You mentioned once that her mother has family on Kea Island. Send her there until she has completed her studies. She's not safe here."

"What do you mean, she's not safe? She was born here. Besides, Milena doesn't want to study. All she wants is to find a good husband to take care of her." He looks at me. "You found out something about your parents' deaths, didn't you? I know you didn't tell me everything. Who's responsible, Odin?"

"You don't need to know that."

"I can't stop you from leaving, but I want you to leave with the certainty that you are like a son to me, and I will miss you."

"I'll be back. I can't give a time frame right now, but I'll return to Greece one day."

He shakes his head from side to side but finally looks resigned. "God bless you, son."

"It would be a novelty."

"Don't say such a thing."

"Why? It's the truth. It would be unheard of if he started blessing me now."

"I will pray for you. I will ask for a little light to come into your heart. I know what you went through was horrible, but maybe those responsible are already dead."

Again, I keep silent because it's not my place to shatter his illusions. He hugs me, and I allow it. However, I don't feel like hugging him back. After looking at him one last time, I turn my back without saying goodbye.

From now on, I'm on my own.

This is the day I've been waiting so long for.

From plans to action.

At this exact moment, the life of Leandros Argyros begins its countdown.

Madeline Turner

BONUS

Three Months After Zoe and Christos's Wedding

LONDON

AS THE ELEVATOR ASCENDS, I vow not to check my reflection for the fifth time, but my resolve crumbles.

What if I have lipstick on my teeth?

I'm really here. I couldn't believe it when Zoe told me that this man, *Sheikh* Kamal, was going to interview me in person. Unless I have unrealistic expectations, I think his wanting to see me is a good thing, right?

I take another look in the mirror.

Jesus, it's like a compulsion. But it's just that I'm feeling so beautiful.

I'm the very image of an executive, with a dark gray, knee-length pencil skirt and the white silk shirt Zoe chose for me.

Elegant and professional. Mildly sexy, she told me.

I blow a lock of hair out of my eyes. This Chanel haircut that Mom always insisted I wear is pissing me off, and I decide I'm going to let it grow out.

The elevator arrives at its destination, but I don't move. My insecurity is coming back in full force.

The door opens, and a woman, whom I believe is one of the secretaries, waits for me to leave. As I'm still catatonic, she looks at me like I'm crazy.

"Good morning, Miss Turner."

"Good morning," I say carefully. I've been honest about my very mild dyslexia but speaking slowly is a habit I picked up to escape my mother's criticism. "I'm here for the interview with Mr. Kamal."

"*Sheikh* Kamal," she corrects me.

Ouch!

She looks me up and down, and I dislike the woman straight away. Then I remember what Zoe told me.

Don't let them intimidate you.

Okay, come on, world, I tell myself. *I'm ready.*

Nervously, I step out of the elevator, not paying attention to what I'm doing, and apparently turn the wrong way because I bump into someone.

I let out a high-pitched squeal, and it has nothing to do with the fright but everything to do with the hot coffee splattered down the front of my shirt.

With my skin burning, I don't think and rip off my shirt. My breasts ache from the boiling liquid, and it's only when I hear laughter that I realize they've all stopped to pay attention to my involuntary *striptease*.

There is someone, however, who looks at me angrily.

I know who he is.

Kamal Hafeez.

My employer. Or ex-employer now, it would be better to say.

Also by D.A. Lemoyne

The Tycoon's Obsession (Book One of Lykaios Family)

About Love and Revenge (Book Two of Lykaios Family) – Coming soon.

Seduced by Contract (Book One of Kostanidis Family) – Coming Soon

About the Author

D.A. Lemoyne started writing in August 2019 with her first book, "Seduzida". Since then, she's written over 80 books and some popular series, keeping readers hooked along the way.

When she was only eight years old, her grandmother, a literature teacher, introduced her to the world of books. She had a personal "library" in a room at the back of her apartment and Lemoyne was immediately drawn to the books, and her grandmother was so touched by her interest that she decided to gift her the entire collection.

She lives in North Carolina with her husband and their dog, Cookie. She loves to write, cook, and always has friends over at her place.

Lemoyne's stories are famous for their awesome plots that really grab readers' attention. People love the passion of her male main characters and the strength of her heroines.

She's a strong believer in the power of love. Her greatest passions include reading and writing, allowing her to dive into human emotions and craft heartwarming stories that deeply connect with readers.

Contact: dalemoynewriter@gmail.com

Made in the USA
Monee, IL
07 October 2024